FRANCES CLASPED HER HANDS, AMAZED AT THE VIEW

"There's the orchard, and Rainbow Lake, and Preacher Eli's smithy, and Christine's dairy cows—and Rosetta's goats are grazing along the fence behind the Kuhns' cheese factory!" she whispered, pointing as she noticed each detail. "And look at the way our homes shine in the afternoon sunlight!"

Frances shaded her eyes with her hand, enthralled with what she saw. "I had no idea how much land Mattie's planted for her produce stand," she remarked, gazing at the evenly spaced rows of vegetables emerging from the dark soil. "It doesn't seem you and I have walked such a long distance, yet from here, the lodge and the entryway sign at the road look like part of a toy village."

"We've come a long way," Marlin remarked softly. "I'm glad you've walked with me, Frances. Our community has taken on even more of a glow because I'm seeing it through your eyes."

Frances focused on Ruby's stacked white beehives in the orchard, not daring to look at Marlin. The tone of his voice made her pulse thrum with an unusual sense of energy, as though the preacher had something on his mind besides the view.

We've come a long way.

New Beginnings
at PROMISE
LODGE

Charlotte Hubbard

ZEBRA BOOKS
KENSINGTON PUBLISHING CORP.
www.kensingtonbooks.com

ZEBRA BOOKS are published by

Kensington Publishing Corp.
119 West 40th Street
New York, NY 10018

All Kensington titles, imprints, and distributed lines are available at special quantity discounts for bulk purchases for sales promotion, premiums, fund-raising, educational, or institutional use.

Special book excerpts or customized printings can also be created to fit specific needs. For details, write or phone the office of the Kensington Sales Manager: Attn.: Sales Department. Kensington Publishing Corp., 119 West 40th Street, New York, NY 10018. Phone: 1-800-221-2647.

First Printing: October 2019
ISBN-13: 978-1-4201-4510-6
ISBN-10: 1-4201-4510-X

ISBN-13: 978-1-4201-4513-7 (eBook)
ISBN-10: 1-4201-4513-4 (eBook)

10 9 8 7 6 5 4 3 2 1

Printed in the United States of America

For Paula and Kevin,
inspiring second-timers at this love and marriage thing

ACKNOWLEDGMENTS

Thanks, Lord, for bringing me back to Promise Lodge with characters and story ideas that make so many of us wish we lived there for real!

Many thanks to my editor, Alicia Condon, for your ideas and enthusiasm, and to my agent, Evan Marshall, for your continuing friendship and publishing savvy. My books benefit so much from your insights and guidance!

Special thanks to Vicki Harding, innkeeper of Poosey's Edge B&B in Jamesport, Missouri, and to all the Amish neighbors you consult for me. What a gift, that your research assistance is only an email away! Thanks and blessings, as well, to Joe Burkholder and his family, proprietors of Oak Ridge Furniture and Sherwood's Christian Books in Jamesport.

1 John 4:7–8 (KJV)

7 Beloved, let us love one another: for love is of God; and every one that loveth is born of God, and knoweth God.

8 He that loveth not knoweth not God; for God is love.

Chapter One

Dressed in her Sunday-best black dress, Frances Lehman strode along the road to the lodge building. It was a picture-perfect April day, complete with sunshine that shimmered on Rainbow Lake, a sky the color of morning glories, and the sweet scent of lilacs filling the air—exactly the kind of day Rosetta Bender and Truman Wickey deserved for their long-awaited wedding. Every marriage ceremony was a joyful event, but this wedding marked a turning point: because Bishop Monroe Burkholder and the preachers had agreed that Amish and Mennonites could intermarry, Promise Lodge would be considered far more progressive than most Old Order church districts.

Frances was pleased to belong to this community. It had been settled only a year ago when Rosetta and her two older sisters had purchased an abandoned church camp and transformed it into a new Plain settlement. Even though she'd lost her husband, Floyd, a month ago, Frances felt hopeful and at peace in this place, where spousal abuse wasn't tolerated and women had unusual freedom to run businesses—to determine how they'd live their lives. Maybe it was the warmth in the springtime air, but Frances couldn't help walking with more spring in her step. Living among women who had such positive, can-do attitudes was a balm to her lonely soul.

"Frances, wait up!" a familiar voice called out behind her. "I thought we were attending the wedding together."

Suppressing a sigh, Frances slowed her pace—but only a little. Her brother-in-law, Lester Lehman, had lost his wife and son the week before Floyd had passed, so he deserved her patience and sympathy. But he was such a wet blanket. His presence—and his constant hangdog expression—never failed to bring her down.

"I've been thinking about this a lot lately," Lester was saying as he caught up to her. "As the male of the Lehman family, it's only right that I take care of you and Gloria. It's just plain silly for you and me to roll around like BBs in boxcars, living in two separate houses—"

Frances closed her eyes, half afraid of what he'd say next.

"—so why don't I move into that back bedroom at your place?" Lester continued earnestly. "The siding and window business Floyd and I started here is going great guns, so you'll want for nothing, Frances."

Her eyes flew open in dismay. What was Lester thinking, suggesting that they live together without being married? It was one thing for him to come over for meals with her and her daughter, Gloria, several times a week—and she'd washed his clothes and cleaned his house a couple of times, too. Any decent woman would do such basic housekeeping tasks for a brother-in-law who'd lost his wife.

No matter how progressive we've become at Promise Lodge, however, I can't believe our leaders will allow unmarried men and women to live together—thank goodness, Frances mused. *What chance would I ever have at happiness with Lester living in my home, casting a constant shadow over me?*

An uneasy silence stretched between them as Frances

tried desperately to come up with a *no* that didn't sound harsh and heartless. As they passed Preacher Amos and Mattie Troyer's house, the lodge came into view ahead of them. Several folks were entering the rustic, timbered building, talking excitedly as they anticipated a day of celebration, but none of them could rescue her from this difficult situation. The men would encourage Lester to marry her—a man needed a wife to run his household, after all. The women would probably sympathize with her, but their opinions wouldn't dissuade Lester from trying to court her and tie the knot.

"I thought you'd show a little more enthusiasm, Frances," Lester muttered. "It's time to talk about being practical by—"

"*You're* doing the talking, Lester," she blurted out.

Lester frowned. He was a handsome man with a full head of dark hair, and for most of the years she'd known him, he'd been pleasant and cheerful. But his wife's passing had beaten him down. He needed time to grieve, because he'd also lost his son—not to mention Floyd, his brother and business partner—which had taken a huge emotional toll, as well. The downward lines on Lester's face were etched so deeply that Frances wondered if he'd completely lost his ability to smile.

"I'm only doing what Floyd would've wanted," he protested. "You can't tell me you enjoy being alone, now that he's gone."

"With Gloria around, I never lack for company or entertainment," Frances pointed out, hoping to change the subject. "If she's not baking something to impress Allen Troyer—and probably burning it, bless her heart—she's dreaming up other ways to get his attention. Are you sure you want to deal with her romantic fantasies, and her fear of ending up a *maidel*?" she teased.

"I raised a couple of girls, you know," Lester reminded her gruffly. "Gloria needs a father figure to tell her what a husband is *really* interested in—and to see that she spends her time preparing to be a wife instead of flitting around and flirting."

Frances looked away, her heart sinking further. At twenty-three, with a mind of her own, Gloria wouldn't take kindly to Lester's advice. In January Frances's younger daughter, Mary Kate, had married Roman Schwartz, whom Gloria had already set her heart upon, so Gloria was determined to marry Allen despite his protests that he wasn't interested in her. Life with her older daughter was an emotional roller-coaster ride, and Frances doubted that Lester's presence would improve that situation.

"I know you mean well, Lester," she began, "but maybe it would be best to reconsider—or to wait awhile before you—"

"Wait for *what*?" Lester cut in. "You need a man to tend your stable chores and pay your bills and fix things around the house. It doesn't make sense for both of us to maintain homes—"

"*Gut* morning, folks!" a cheerful voice called out behind them. "Can't stop to visit—sorry! I'm running late for the preachers' meeting before church."

Frances turned to see Preacher Marlin Kurtz approaching at a jog. As he caught up to them, he waved and kept going. "*Gut* morning, Marlin," she said. "It's a beautiful day for a wedding!"

"It's a blessed day for all of us!" he called back over his shoulder.

Frances smiled at the preacher's enthusiastic response. When Marlin had arrived at Promise Lodge with his family for a fresh start after losing his wife, he'd agreed to serve as the deacon—and to preach occasionally—because their church district already had two preachers, Amos Troyer and Eli Peterscheim. Marlin manufactured barrels in a small factory he'd built beside the home he shared with his son and daughter-in-law. The Kurtz family had been a welcome addition to the Promise Lodge community.

"Well, we might be blessed but that doesn't mean we're happy," Lester remarked sourly as he followed Marlin's progress toward the lodge. "You and I aren't finished discussing my idea, Frances. It's my earnest prayer that you'll come to see reason sooner rather than later, so we can both get on with our lives."

With that, Lester strode off toward a group of men who'd gathered on the lodge's front porch, leaving Frances to gape after him.

I'm getting on with my life pretty well, all things considered, she thought. *The last thing Gloria and I need is a storm cloud taking up residence in our home, spoiling our springtime.*

Marlin smiled at the congregation, gathering the thoughts that would conclude his sermon and the church service that preceded the wedding ceremony. Several families from the Mennonite church the Wickeys attended in Cloverdale had joined them, along with folks from Coldstream, where Rosetta and her sisters had lived previously, so the twelve new pew benches he and Preacher Amos had built for the occasion had come in handy.

"It's a joy to see so many of you here to celebrate Rosetta and Truman's marriage—and it's a momentous occasion for Promise Lodge," Marlin said as folks nodded their agreement. "Because Bishop Monroe has been willing to consider that God's love for us is bigger than any rules established by our forefathers in the Old Order, we're progressing into a new era—a new understanding of what it means to be people of faith in today's world, even as we honor our traditional beliefs."

Marlin gazed at the bride, who beamed at him from the front row of the women's side, gripping the hands of her sisters, Christine and Mattie. "Rosetta, one of the first things I admired about you when I came here was your way of planning for happiness," he continued. "You understand that happiness doesn't just happen—it's a conscious choice we make dozens of times each day. Your marriage to Truman is a shining example of what's possible when we plan for the best rather than accepting the limitations of the past or shying away from a future that rocks the boat."

Rosetta's smile rivaled the sun as she nodded—and then gazed at Truman, who sat directly across from her on the men's side. He appeared so happy and so deeply in love that Marlin envied him. He'd felt the same way when he'd married his Essie nearly twenty-five years ago.

"I wish you two all the best as you become one," Marlin concluded. "May God's grace bless you all the days of your life together."

As Marlin returned to the preachers' bench, Bishop Monroe rose to address the congregation. "It's my special pleasure to welcome Zachary Miller from the Mennonite Fellowship in Cloverdale to share his message before Truman and Rosetta exchange their vows," he said, gesturing toward the guest preacher. "We're pleased to welcome all of you folks to our celebration today."

Marlin settled on the wooden bench beside Amos Troyer and Eli Peterscheim, who nodded at him to acknowledge his sermon. He was always pleased to take a turn at preaching, because the two men beside him—as well as Monroe— could have insisted that he stick to minding the district's money and reading the Scriptures. Weddings were a special treat, a time when people came together for an entire day to celebrate a couple's love as a reflection of God's love. This was the first wedding sermon he'd given since Essie's passing, and the flow of God's inspiration as he spoke had lifted him above missing her so badly, like the wings of a snow-white dove.

In the past few months, Noah Schwartz had married Deborah Peterscheim, and Mary Kate Lehman had married Roman Schwartz—a positive sign for the future because these young couples had new homes and were starting families at Promise Lodge. In addition, Preacher Amos had married Mattie Schwartz—his childhood sweetheart—and Bishop Monroe had married her sister Christine after falling in love at first sight. Marlin saw these second marriages as an indication that midlife could bring a chance for new happiness these folks hadn't foreseen when they'd come to the tiny town of Promise, Missouri, to start fresh.

As Zachary delivered his message about the ups and downs of marriage with occasional twists of humor, Marlin noted the happy expressions on the faces in the congregation. Despite how hard they'd worked to turn an abandoned church camp into a new Plain community and reestablish their businesses, the people of Promise Lodge exuded such a positive energy—

But Frances Lehman looked like she'd cut into an onion. Was she on the verge of tears because the wedding was making her miss her deceased husband, Floyd?

Or is she upset because Lester was lecturing her about how she needs a man—presumably him—in her life?

Marlin considered this. Overall, Frances had been handling her grief quite well during the past month. She'd helped prepare the food for Rosetta and Truman's wedding dinner. She crocheted with other ladies at the lodge, and she hadn't missed any church services—even though she'd sometimes appeared subdued and caught up in her own thoughts. That was only natural as she became the head of the household and took on tasks Floyd had always handled.

Marlin thought some more. What had Lester been saying as he'd jogged past, on his way to the preachers' meeting? Something about doing the stable chores and fixing things around Frances's house.

What would need fixing in a house that's only a few months old? Marlin wondered. *And Frances only has a couple of buggy horses, which her son-in-law, Roman, has been tending.*

Trying not to be obvious about it, Marlin looked at Frances. He suspected that Lester's tone of voice had seemed heavy-handed to her, and that she probably wasn't ready to consider taking another husband. Although it was customary for Amish men to look after the single and widowed women in their families—and it wasn't unusual for in-laws to marry after they'd lost their spouses—he could understand why Frances wasn't responding well to Lester's remarks.

When Lester enters a room, he sucks the joy right out of it. Marlin blinked at this unexpectedly harsh thought. He liked Lester—a lot—but it was a sad fact that Bishop Floyd's brother wasn't handling the loss of his wife nearly as well as Frances was bearing up after her husband had passed. Delores Lehman and their son had died in a nasty traffic accident only a month ago, so Lester had a lot of grieving to do yet. A lot of memories to deal with.

Marlin had often seen this situation when the wife died first. Most men weren't prepared to cook, wash clothes, or manage other household functions, and as the business of daily living overwhelmed them, they became crankier and more depressed.

There but for the grace of God—and sharing a home

with Harley and Minerva—I would have gone, Marlin acknowledged, thinking fondly of his son and daughter-in-law. *Lowell and Fannie are blessings, too, because they make me laugh.* His younger son and daughter certainly kept him on his toes as a parent.

Lester's two daughters, on the other hand, had recently married and remained in Sugarcreek, Ohio. Despite his girls insisting that he should live near them, Lester had returned to the new house he'd built for Delores at Promise Lodge. It had to be hard, waking up each day to see the furnishings from their house in Ohio—bleak reminders of his loss. Lester had no one to talk to at home, no one to love. If it hadn't been for Truman's finding him long-term siding and window work at the housing project he was landscaping, Lester would be even more emotionally adrift.

Marlin glanced at Frances again. As sorry as he felt for Lester, he could certainly understand why Frances didn't want to take up with her brother-in-law. Lester's gloomy presence was enough to depress anybody.

So talk to her about it. Be the light, like you're always preaching. If anyone needs a friend, it's Frances—and Lester, of course, he added quickly.

He shifted on the wooden bench, suddenly enthusiastic about spending time with Frances. His barrel-making business had kept him indoors a lot recently, fulfilling orders for rain barrels, and the half barrels folks used for planting flowers, and decorative barrels with checkerboards on top, so he was due for some time outside. It was a beautiful spring day, with the lilac bushes in bloom and a cloudless blue sky that shimmered with sunshine. Surely he and Frances would both benefit from walking in the fresh air— nothing romantic, because he wasn't looking for another wife, and he didn't want Frances to think he was.

If she's out for a walk, she won't spend the rest of the day washing dishes!

Marlin nearly laughed out loud, anticipating the smile he'd bring to Frances's face when he rescued her from yet another afternoon of kitchen duty. She helped the other women willingly, of course, but the ladies had cooked and cleaned up for several recent weddings—and everyone benefited from a break in routine now and then.

He focused on the sermon Zachary Miller was bringing to its conclusion. If he planned for some happiness, who knew what might happen? Joy was like skimming pebbles across a pond: once a pebble splashed happily on the surface before it sank, the ripples would spread deeper and wider than the eye could see.

But you have to pick up the pebbles. You have to be the initiator, with a positive, joyful intention, or you'll just be throwing rocks.

Chapter Two

Frances sat up straighter, determined to share Rosetta and Truman's joy as they repeated their vows—because it was a waste of her time to brood about her overbearing brother-in-law. Rosetta looked radiant in her beautiful blue dress and the special white apron Truman's *mamm*, Irene, had sewn for her. What with milking her goats, making soap to sell, and managing the apartments in the lodge and the cabins behind it, Rosetta was usually up to her elbows in work. It was wonderful to see her beaming at Truman as though he was the only other person in the room—or in the world.

To Frances, it seemed like only yesterday that she'd been standing in front of a bishop with a young, vibrant Floyd Lehman. Even before he'd become a preacher and then a bishop at a younger age than most men were called to serve, he'd been decisive and outspoken—a man who knew what he believed, and who could persuade others to follow the light of Christ, as well.

The years had flown by and their lives had been filled with two daughters who'd brought much love and many challenges into their marriage. Even after the unthinkable had happened to Mary Kate, leaving her pregnant by the English stranger who'd attacked her in a ditch by the road,

Floyd had prevailed over their tragedy: he'd moved them to Promise Lodge so Mary Kate could escape the gossip and stigma that would've come with raising a child out of wedlock in their very conservative Ohio church district.

You took better care of us than you did of yourself, dear man, Frances mused as she glanced at Amos Troyer on the preachers' bench. When Amos had been fetching a Frisbee from the roof of the barn beside Rainbow Lake, the corner of the building had collapsed—and Floyd had rushed over to break Amos's fall. Both men had been hospitalized and wheelchair-bound . . . but Amos had taken physical therapy while Floyd had insisted that God was the only doctor he needed. A stroke had weakened him further, and from there, he'd simply faded away.

But you followed God's plan as He revealed it to you, Floyd. You stayed true to your convictions—and to your family.

Frances smiled. Floyd's convictions had sometimes rubbed her—and the other women here—the wrong way, but now that he was gone, she chose not to dwell on his stubbornness or his insistence that women were to be subservient to their men. When she thought of Floyd, she sensed his presence—as though his arms were wrapped around her, supporting and encouraging her—so she didn't feel so alone. His spirit had helped her through a lot of desperate moments and sleepless nights as she'd thought about how she and Gloria would handle their finances without any income in their foreseeable future.

Lord, I hope you'll grant Rosetta and Truman as much love and joy as you gave to Floyd and me, she prayed, dismissing her thoughts about money. *You obviously created them to be together, and we're so blessed that Bishop Monroe has allowed interfaith marriages at Promise Lodge.*

Her heart thrummed as Rosetta's voice rang confidently,

repeating the age-old vows after Bishop Monroe. Truman's handsome face was alight with love as he, too, spoke the words that would bind them in holy matrimony.

Moments later, the bishop beamed out over the congregation. "Truman and Rosetta, I pronounce you husband and wife," he proclaimed. "Every one of us in this room wishes you all the best of the love and grace God can grant you, for all the days of your life together."

Frances rose to her feet with the women around her, beaming at the newlyweds. Beside her, Beulah Kuhn and her sister, Ruby, let out contented sighs.

"They're married, at last!" Beulah said. "I was a little worried when that misunderstanding about Maria came between them."

"*Jah*, but Truman's a *gut* man and he worked it out," Ruby put in with a nod. "The way I hear it, Maria's new bakery in Cloverdale is going like gangbusters—and we'd best get into the kitchen like gangbusters and put out the food for this huge crowd!"

"I'm right behind you," Frances said as she sidled out of the pew row with them. As Mennonites, the Kuhn sisters were wearing colorful floral-print dresses—and as *maidels*, they rented lodge apartments from Rosetta. Frances suspected that the outspoken sisters had pointed out to blond, blue-eyed Maria that her flirtatious ways with Truman were inappropriate—and that Rosetta had called off the wedding earlier in the spring because of her. Ruby and Beulah were good-hearted ladies and wonderful cooks, beloved by all at Promise Lodge.

As Frances passed through the lodge's large dining room, she noted the pretty white tablecloths on the long tables. Mason jars with stalks of celery sat in the center of each table, a traditional Amish wedding centerpiece—except the Kuhns had added sprigs of fresh lilac blossoms as a way to celebrate this wedding that broke with Old Order tradition. The dessert table was spread with cut pies and cookie trays. Two tall chocolate wedding cakes with mocha frosting sat on stands behind the raised *eck* table in the corner, where the wedding party would eat. Ruby had made them double layered and triple tiered so they would provide enough cake for everyone. To the Kuhns, the ultimate sin was running short of food.

Frances inhaled deeply as she entered the kitchen along with Christine's daughters, Laura and Phoebe Hershberger. "Oh my, but the turkey smells *gut*," she said to the younger women. "It's nice that your *mamm* and your aunt Mattie get the day off from kitchen duty to be in the wedding party."

"*Jah*, but look at all of us next-generation helpers," Laura said, gesturing at the others who were streaming into the kitchen. "What with your Gloria and Mary Kate, and Lily Peterscheim and her sister Deborah, and Minerva and Fannie Kurtz, and the Helmuth twins, we'll get this job done!"

"Ruby and Beulah have this meal so well organized, all we have to do is set the pans in the steam table and keep them replenished," Phoebe pointed out. "Our wedding meals run a lot more smoothly because we can serve them in the lodge building, too."

"You've got that right," Beulah said. She opened an oven and began taking out large stainless-steel pans of food. "Working in a kitchen that was designed to feed a couple hundred campers—and serving the food buffet-style in a big dining room—is a lot easier than fixing a wedding meal in a family home."

"You sisters could start up a business, catering Plain weddings," Minerva teased as she removed lids from the big pans. "You've got it down to a fine art."

Ruby waved her off. "The last thing we need is another

business to run. My bees are in full buzz now that the flowers and apple trees are blooming, which eventually means more honey to bottle and sell—"

"And we can barely keep up with orders at our cheese factory," Beulah put in. "The Helmuths' new nursery has made a lot more customers aware that we have fresh cheese made from Christine's cows' milk and Rosetta's goats' milk."

Frances nodded, along with the other ladies who were bustling around the kitchen. She was pleased to see that Gloria and Mary Kate were filling water pitchers, and that the meal seemed to be coming together with a minimum of fuss despite the fact that they were feeding twice as many people as they usually did at a wedding.

"I'm glad Rosetta and Truman wanted turkey rather than the chicken and stuffing 'roast' most couples have," Frances remarked. She placed serving forks in the metal pans of meat, and stuck large spoons in the pans of mashed potatoes, green beans, and creamed celery. "Baking and boning the turkeys ahead of time made this meal a lot simpler."

"I'll say it did," Beulah agreed as she and the Hershberger girls placed the big metal pans on rolling carts. "My favorite recipe for mashed potatoes can be made ahead, too, because you add cream cheese and sour cream to keep them firm and moist before you reheat them. When you've cooked for a crowd as long as Ruby and I have, you learn all sorts of tricks to simplify the process!"

Frances pushed a loaded cart into the dining room, and Minerva followed with a second cart. Phoebe and Laura came along to lift the full metal pans between them, deftly slipping the hot, heavy containers into the openings of the steam tables. As wedding guests came into the dining room to be seated, Frances noticed Preachers Amos and Marlin at the dessert table with Truman's mother, Irene—discussing the many options they had for sweets after the main meal.

"What would you recommend, Irene? We don't have a *thing* to choose from," Amos teased as he gestured at the slices of pie and the cookie trays.

Irene's laughter rang above the guests' conversations. "It's not my place to say, because I made several of those pies," she replied. "I don't see how you can go wrong with choosing your favorite kind."

"But what if they're *all* my favorite kind?" Marlin joked. He approached Laura and Phoebe as they placed the last pan of hot food in the steam table. "Maybe you ladies can help me decide on pie. You appear to know a lot about putting on these meals."

Laura chuckled modestly. "Practice makes perfect."

"Maybe you should close your eyes and point," Phoebe suggested. "The pie you choose is bound to be yummy. It's the only kind we know how to make."

Frances laughed at their banter. "You might have to take whatever's left, if you wait much longer," she teased. "Folks are already taking their desserts to their places while they wait for the wedding party to go through the buffet line."

Frances smiled at Preacher Marlin and pushed the cart toward the kitchen—but when applause broke out, she turned to watch the newlyweds enter the dining room. It warmed her heart to see Truman grasping Rosetta's hand and the way both of their faces radiated such happiness.

"Takes you back a few years, ain't so?"

Frances's eyes widened when she realized Preacher Marlin was standing close behind her. His wistful voice had thrummed beneath the congratulatory chatter that filled the room. "*Jah*, it does," she replied, determined not to let the moment make her teary-eyed. "Who knew that *forever* wouldn't last nearly as long as we figured on when we took our marriage vows as young adults?"

Marlin's brown eyes softened. "You said that exactly right, Frances," he murmured. He glanced around the noisy crowd and leaned closer. "Would you like to go for a walk after dinner? It's a beautiful day—and if I sit around too long after eating this big meal, I'll nod off," he added with a boyish smile. "And if you'd like to talk about what Lester was saying when I passed you this morning, I'm a *gut* listener."

Frances's mind began spinning like a whirligig. Was Marlin inviting her for a walk because he wanted to spend time with her? Or did he intend to point out the wisdom of pairing up with Lester? "I—well, if you—"

"I'd like to congratulate the newlyweds—and to make an announcement," Irene Wickey called out above the crowd's noise.

Grateful that Truman's *mamm* had everyone's attention, Frances focused on the slender blonde who was standing between her son and Rosetta with her arms around their waists. The more she thought about Marlin's invitation, the more she wondered why he'd sought her out. Had Lester put him up to it? Had Marlin joked about nodding off to make his mission on Lester's behalf appear more like a—

A date?

Frances sucked in her breath. Floyd had died only six weeks ago, so it was too soon to think about socializing with a man.

Preacher Marlin's sensitive enough to realize that, said the voice in her head.

"After much thought and prayer," Irene continued confidently, "I've decided to move into an apartment here in the lodge as my gift to Truman and Rosetta. That way, they can enjoy their marriage without a buttinsky mother and mother-in-law hanging around all the time."

A moment of surprised silence rang in the large room. The expressions on Rosetta's and Truman's faces were priceless as they considered what Irene had said.

"But Mamm," Truman protested, "it was never our intention to squeeze you out—"

"The house on the hill has been your home for years!" Rosetta exclaimed. "Please don't feel you have to leave on our account."

Irene smiled as though she'd expected her son and new daughter-in-law to say such things. "Truth be told, I'm looking forward to keeping up a smaller place," she admitted. "I've seen the way these Promise Lodge gals get along so well together, and I want to join them! *Gut*ness knows I can move all the furniture I'll need out of the house and you'll never miss it!"

"We'll be happy to have you, Irene!" Beulah called out from the kitchen door. "What with Mattie and Christine marrying and moving into their new homes—and Maria going back to Cloverdale—we've got a lot of apartments for you to choose from."

"Oh, but it'll be *gut* to have somebody besides Beulah to talk to!" Ruby teased.

Everyone laughed, and some of the folks applauded Irene's decision. Rosetta and Truman appeared overjoyed as they hugged his *mamm* between them. Mattie and Christine were quick to reassure her about apartment living at Promise Lodge.

"There's something to be said for a bunch of friendly hens living in the same house without any roosters bossing them around," Mattie put in—even as she grabbed Amos's hand.

"*Jah*, it's like a nonstop hen party," Christine agreed, beaming at Monroe with obvious adoration. "You can cluck about what's on your mind and nobody gets her feathers ruffled!"

Frances nodded. She'd sometimes envied the independence that *maidel* Rosetta and her widowed sisters had enjoyed while they'd lived in their apartments and were establishing the Promise Lodge settlement. What with the money Rosetta collected as rent, and Mattie made from her produce stand, and Christine earned from selling her dairy herd's milk, the three of them had done very well—especially considering that they had no men in their family to look after them.

Maybe you and Gloria should move into the lodge, the voice in Frances's head suggested. *Lester's not allowed to live here—and you wouldn't have to worry about the upkeep of the house. You could sell the property when new folks came to Promise Lodge, and live on that money for quite a long time.*

Where had that idea come from? After a lifetime of living in a house with her parents and then with Floyd and the girls, Frances had never considered moving into a smaller, rented space—

But it's something to think about. Gloria would be in favor of an apartment because she wouldn't have to cook or clean an entire house. The days—and evenings—wouldn't feel nearly so long if we had Ruby, Beulah, and Irene to talk to. . . .

When Marlin cleared his throat, Frances realized he was still waiting for her answer to the invitation he'd made before Irene's announcement interrupted their conversation. It also occurred to her that even if the preacher did speak to her on Lester's behalf during their walk, she had *options*. If she wanted to move into a lodge apartment, who could stop her?

Now you sound like Rosetta—independent and determined to do things your own way. Floyd would never approve.

Frances inhaled deeply to settle her nerves. She suddenly had a lot of things on her mind, not the least of which involved the nice-looking man who was patiently awaiting her response. "A walk sounds like a wonderful idea," she heard herself saying. "We have a lot of *gut*—younger—helpers in the kitchen today, so they'll never miss me if I slip away instead of washing dishes, *jah*?"

Marlin's face lit up as though she'd said something unexpectedly wonderful. "I was hoping you'd see it that way," he said. "With such a crowd here, nobody'll even realize we've left the party. I'll wait for you out back, by the cabins, after we've eaten dinner with our families."

Chapter Three

The dining room was so full of guests—and Frances was so busy refilling pans on the steam table—that sitting down for dinner seemed out of the question. She occasionally glanced toward the table where Preacher Marlin sat with his married son, Harley, and his younger son, Lowell, because his daughter, Fannie, and Minerva, his daughter-in-law, were helping with the meal. From what she could see of the preacher's plate, he would soon cut into his raspberry pie. It was just a matter of time before he'd go outside to wait for her.

A smile tickled Frances's lips. Her day had taken an exciting turn: even though she had no romantic inclinations toward Marlin, she was about to secretly slip away from the humdrum of washing hundreds of plates and pans and utensils—hopefully without attracting anyone's attention. After she wiped some spillage from the steam table, she pushed the cart into the kitchen to make a quick turkey sandwich. Pans of food were arranged on the center kitchen counter, alongside a stack of clean plates and silverware.

"Better fix a plate and take a load off, Frances," Beulah called from the worktable. She and Ruby were sitting with Irene and Alma Peterscheim, while some of the younger helpers stood or sat on tall stools at the kitchen counter with their meals. "The guests and the wedding party are having a fine time, so we're having a quick bite before we get back to work."

Frances hoped her face didn't hint at the secret she was keeping. Even though it was too soon for these ladies to be matching her up, they would make a big deal out of it if they saw her walking with Preacher Marlin—who, except for Lester, was the only unmarried man at Promise Lodge. "A turkey sandwich will hit the spot," she said as she forked a slice of turkey breast onto a piece of soft homemade bread.

"Oh, but you don't want to miss this cranberry salad!" Irene remarked as she took a forkful from her plate.

"*Jah*, put some of *that* on your sandwich!" Ruby teased. "It'll tickle your taste buds!"

Frances spooned some of the deep red salad onto her turkey and folded her bread around it. At least her stomach wouldn't growl while she was talking with Marlin—but how would she escape this clutch of hens without them clucking over her?

Oldest trick in the book. Use the bathroom—the one that's just off the lobby, near the front door.

Closing her eyes, Frances savored the contrast of the salted turkey and the cranberry salad, which was sweet and tangy with chunks of fresh apple and oranges. She loved wedding meals, because brides often requested side dishes Frances didn't prepare at home. When she'd polished off her sandwich, she plucked a dense chocolate brownie from their container and bit into it.

"You're entitled to use a plate, you know," Alma remarked. "The servers deserve a meal every bit as nice as the one the wedding guests are eating, even if we're not sitting with them."

Frances nodded. Preacher Eli's wife had five children, and three of the four who still lived at home were boys, so she knew about finding time to nourish her own body and soul while she cooked for them.

"I suspect Frances and Gloria don't cook as much or dirty as many dishes now that Floyd's passed," Minerva observed gently. "I could easily get into the habit of eating a sandwich on a paper towel, if I weren't fixing meals for Harley and Marlin."

"Me too!" Fannie agreed from her stool at the counter. "I'd be all for using paper plates, except Dat and Harley would fuss at us."

Frances laughed along with the rest of the women. At fourteen, Fannie was on the brink of young womanhood, even though she still had the endearing, coltish look of adolescence about her. She had her *dat*'s dark brown hair and expressive eyebrows, but otherwise her facial features probably resembled her deceased *mamm*'s.

"Oh, *jah*," Lily Peterscheim chimed in from beside Fannie. "Dat would tally up the price of the paper plates our family would go through in a day, and remind us that using real dishes doesn't cost us anything except the water to wash them. *Home economics,* he'd call it."

Frances nodded, letting the conversation continue around her. As though she were headed for a bathroom break—which she was—she walked into the hallway, but instead of using the half bath tucked under the back stairway, she continued through the meeting room filled with pew benches. She walked toward the front lobby, her heart pounding as she hurried past the doorway to the noisy dining room, hoping to remain unnoticed. Frances grabbed the knob of the bathroom door—

But it was locked!

With so many people here, of course someone would be in the bathroom, she reminded herself impatiently. She heard the faucet running, so she stepped back toward the meeting room—

"Seems we had the same escape plan," said a low male voice.

Frances's cheeks burned even as she had to laugh. Marlin was coming out of the bathroom, smiling like the cat that ate the canary as he dried his hands on a paper towel. "*Jah*, well—you've caught me," she blurted quietly.

A slow smile spread over the preacher's face as he considered her words. He wadded his paper towel into a ball and tossed it expertly through the bathroom's open door and into the wastebasket. "See you by the cabins," he murmured. "If we go that direction, we won't have as many eyes following us—not that we have anything to hide," he added quickly.

As he headed for the lodge's front porch, Frances ducked into the bathroom and shut the door. The face she saw in the mirror startled her. Although her dark hair was as neatly tucked up under her *kapp* as it always was, showing a bit of silver at the temples, those rosy cheeks and sparkling eyes belonged to a much younger woman.

You haven't looked this excited in a long time.

And that made no sense. It had been a game, slipping away from the kitchen undetected, but this walk with Marlin was a chance to discuss her situation with Lester—certainly not a romantic topic, nor a reason to feel like a single woman meeting her beau.

Frances quickly used the toilet, befuddled by her mixed emotions. She reminded herself that she'd been recently widowed, and that some decorum was called for while she grieved her late husband—and that Marlin was an honorable man, a preacher whose job it was to counsel members of his congregation. Had Preachers Amos or Eli—or Bishop Monroe—overheard her agitated conversation with her brother-in-law, any of those men might have invited her to talk about her troubles.

And that's exactly what you'll tell anyone who asks why you were walking with Marlin, she told herself firmly. *Everyone knows how depressed Lester is—and maybe, from talking to you, Marlin will get some ideas about how to help the poor man.*

Frances left the bathroom determined to focus on Lester's problems rather than on any other reasons she might take a walk with an attractive, unattached man on a beautiful spring day. She had to convince Marlin that she didn't want Lester to become a permanent fixture in her life—perhaps framing her words so that Lester's welfare seemed a bigger concern than her own.

Once outside, she paused at the porch railing. The black buggies from Coldstream were parked along the fence near Christine's cow pasture, where the guests' horses were grazing. It was unusual to see so many cars along the side of the road—a sign that several Mennonites had joined them today. Frances peered around the thick trumpet vines at the end of the porch to see where Marlin had gone.

At the sound of her footsteps, he turned. Marlin cut a trim, striking figure in his black vest and trousers as he stood beside the nearest cabin. His white shirt made the shaven skin above his dark beard look tanned, as though it was June instead of April. Although the broad brim of his black hat was angled against the sun, hiding his eyes, Frances sensed that he was studying her closely.

It was no time for standing like a deer in the headlights. At any moment, wedding guests might come outside for some fresh air, after all. Frances descended the porch stairs, again reminding herself of her mission. No one could question her intentions if she was seeking advice on how to help Lester.

"I'm glad you're walking with me, Frances," Marlin said as she joined him. "It's wonderful to have so many folks here celebrating Truman and Rosetta's wedding, but the noise level in the dining room was giving me a headache. Much nicer out here, with the sunshine and the scent of lilacs and the birds singing."

Frances matched her steps to his as they walked in front of the cabins. Several Promise Lodge residents had stayed in these little brown buildings while their homes were being built—and Allen Troyer and the Helmuths' unmarried cousins, Cyrus and Jonathan, were living in a couple of them now. It *was* a lovely day, with so many bushes and trees in bloom—much more pleasant than being cooped up in the kitchen over a sink full of steaming dishwater.

"I appreciate your concern about the conversation you overheard this morning," she began, choosing her words carefully. "Lester's depression is becoming more of an issue, I fear. I feel bad for him, what with losing his wife and his son—as well as his brother and business partner," she added with a shake of her head. "I understand why he feels he should look after Gloria and me, but . . . well—"

"He'll drag you down into the depths of his sorrow, and it'll take you both longer to recover from your losses."

Frances smiled gratefully at Marlin. "*Denki* for understanding that," she said. "I suspect that many of the men here would side with Lester, saying he was doing his duty by Floyd."

Marlin clasped his hands behind his back as they kept walking. "Not a one of us can deny that Lester's a fine fellow—that his heart's in the right place," he remarked. "When he lived amongst us before returning to Ohio to fetch his family, helping us build our homes, you couldn't have asked for a more congenial neighbor. But Monroe and I have both noticed Lester's drastic change in personality."

Pausing as they reached the final cabin in the row, Marlin held Frances's gaze. "Now it's not a matter of his glass being half full or half empty," he continued solemnly. "Lester seems to believe he has no glass at all."

Swallowing hard, Frances nodded. "What do you think I should do? He's not asking me, he's *insisting* that he should move in—as though my opinion, my doubts, don't stack up against his intention to support me," she said in a rush. "But he hasn't mentioned marriage. He's thinking to move into the back bedroom."

Marlin's eyes widened. "Lester knows we don't allow unmarried men and women to live together," he said with a frown. "Are you sure he wasn't working his way up to a proposal?"

Frances suddenly felt odd discussing this subject with an attractive, compassionate widower. But Marlin was a preacher—a counselor—and he'd asked her a legitimate question. "Truth be told, I was so shocked when he insisted on moving in that I—I changed the subject a time or two, hoping he wouldn't mention marriage," she admitted. "It's too *soon* for me to keep company with another man—although I suppose someday it'll come to that. It's no secret that with Floyd gone, I don't have any income."

As Marlin ambled around the side of the cabin into the shade, thinking, Frances followed him. He pushed his hat back enough that his eyes were clearly visible, as brown—and warm—as dark chocolate. "What if Lester's financial support wasn't part of the picture? What if he returned to Sugarcreek to be near his daughters, for instance?"

Frances blinked. She'd become so caught up in Marlin's gaze that his question caught her off guard. "Roman already looks after my horses, and he's told me that Gloria and I are welcome to move in with him and Mary Kate and little

David," she replied softly. "I thanked him, but I'd do that only as a last resort."

The preacher nodded. "Roman's a solid young man, and he does pretty well on his income from selling the milk Christine's herd produces," he said. "But I can tell you that it's an adjustment to live with your kids after years of maintaining your own home as the parent. It's a possibility for you, however."

She wasn't surprised to hear Marlin's observation, and it had occurred to her that living in a home where the man of the family was so much younger than she might feel awkward. Frances wondered if she should mention the other idea she'd had. If nothing else, Marlin could point out any disadvantages she hadn't thought of—and he'd be nice about it.

"I—I've also considered moving into an apartment at the lodge, and selling my property to folks who come here looking for a new home," she said softly. "I have no idea what Floyd paid for our land, or what the house might be worth, but—but surely the money would cover my expenses for a long time."

Marlin nodded. "Rosetta's apartments are a unique opportunity for single Plain women—something you won't find anywhere else." He laughed softly. "I can recall Bishop Floyd insisting that our women shouldn't be running businesses—much less giving ladies a place to live independently, without men ordering their lives."

Frances caught a hint of humor in his observation, a gentleness that showed his respect for her late husband—and for her situation, as well. "*Jah*, it's occurred to me that Floyd wouldn't have approved of my idea," she agreed. "On the other hand, he brought us to Promise Lodge because he wanted a more welcoming place for Mary Kate to have her baby. He was a stickler for following the Old Order's ways, but he was a devoted *dat*—a cream puff when it came to his girls' happiness."

"He was," Marlin agreed reverently. "And I believe he's resting easier now because he knows that whether Lester stays at Promise Lodge—or if he goes back to Ohio—your neighbors will see that you and Gloria are taken care of. That's the beauty of living in a faith-based community, amongst folks of like mind. It provides us all a safety net when we suffer tough times."

Frances turned so Marlin wouldn't see her blinking back tears—even though she sensed he would understand why she was crying. It felt good to talk with a man who listened to her concerns and saw her side of the situation Lester had put her in.

"What if I tell Monroe and the other preachers that we should meet with Lester, sooner rather than later?" Marlin suggested. "What with the four of us discussing his plan to move in with you, we ought to be able to ascertain whether his depression has affected his thinking—and we can gently set him straight if we need to. I'm sure Mattie and the other wives would be willing to share Lester's household chores, too, so you wouldn't have to shoulder that load alone."

Frances let out the breath she'd been holding. "That sounds like a fine idea," she said gratefully. "I really am concerned about Lester—but I'm concerned about my own well-being, too. Maybe that sounds selfish and un-charitable—"

"Why should you—or any other woman—be made to feel as if you had to marry? Especially so soon after your loss," Marlin added solemnly. "If Lester's not aware that he's rushing you, we preachers could help him see that. Frankly, it's too soon for Lester to remarry, too, because he's acting out of desperation—not thinking straight because of his deep grief."

Frances felt so relieved, she couldn't find words. For a few moments she stood silently, her head bowed and her eyes closed, trying to sort out her emotions. "*Denki* for your wisdom and your kindness, Marlin," she finally murmured. "God chose well when He saw that the lot fell to you on the day you became a preacher."

He briefly grasped her shoulder. "I'll remember your words on days when being a preacher tries my patience and makes me doubt my qualifications."

Frances raised her head, smiling. "I suspect you'll have one of those days when you talk to Lester about this."

When Marlin burst out laughing, the air around them rang with his merriment. Was it her imagination, or was the sunshine brighter and the sky a deeper blue than it had been moments before?

"*Jah*, from the snippets I overheard when I jogged past you this morning, Lester sounded like he'd be doing you a big favor by becoming the man in your life," the preacher remarked. His dark eyes sparkled when he held her gaze. "We men tend to see ourselves as the be-all and end-all—at least until somebody sets us straight. I'll ask Monroe to set up a visit with Lester soon, all right?"

Frances felt her shoulders relax. Talking with Marlin had released a lot of anxiety. "I'll appreciate any help you fellows can give me—and any other alternatives you might think of, far as an income goes," she added. "It's a real blessing to be surrounded by such *gut* friends as I wait for God to direct me down the next path He'd have me follow."

Marlin gazed around them, taking in the lush greenery and blooming mock orange bushes that formed a boundary between the last cabin and the property the Helmuths had purchased for their nursery. "I'm glad we've got that settled, so we're free to stroll around and admire all the finery Mother

Nature's adorned herself with," he said in an awe-filled voice. "When our family moved here late last summer, I knew Promise Lodge was a beautiful place, but I had no idea how this land would burst into bloom come spring. Shall we enjoy some of the scenery, Frances?"

She fell into step beside him, looking between some of the bushes toward the Helmuths' nursery. "It's *gut* to see those rows of sapling trees and bushes Sam and Simon have planted since they arrived. Makes me want to get some spirea or snowball bushes to plant around the house, to cover the foundation."

"Our place could use a little landscaping help, too," Marlin remarked as he started across the yard behind the lodge. "Most of us have been so busy getting our businesses and homes established, we're just now thinking about flowers and shrubs. Even so, it's a wonderful thing to step out onto the porch and see so many of these lilac bushes and forsythias that have surely been here for decades, judging from their size."

"Credit goes to Truman and his crew for trimming these bushes, as well as the underbrush that had taken over the orchard," Frances said. She pointed toward the fenced pasture ahead of them, laughing when a black-and-white border collie jumped to its feet. "There goes Queenie, keeping Harley's sheep away from the fence. I hope your son doesn't mind that Noah's dog thinks she's in charge of his flock."

Laugh lines crinkled around Marlin's eyes as he followed the dog's progress. "Harley considers Queenie a full-time shepherd he doesn't have to pay—and she's *gut* insurance against coyotes."

Frances chuckled as the woolly sheep turned as a group to trot toward a different section of the pasture in response to Queenie's herding. "Is there anything as lovely and peaceful as sheep in a springtime pasture?" she mused aloud. "Every time I see those ewes with their lambs, I think of the twenty-third psalm."

"It's a sight that centers me—makes me right with the world again—whenever I feel myself getting unduly anxious about a problem, or about Lowell and Fannie," the preacher put in reverently. "It's different, raising my two youngest without Essie. Minerva's patient with them, but she's not their *mamm*."

"And she's only six or seven years older than they are," Frances observed. "She's with them in the classroom, though, so she spends a lot of time with them."

As they passed alongside the pasture, the grassy ground gradually rose up the hill that led to the Kurtz place, and to Bishop Monroe's new home. Frances had only been to this section of Promise Lodge once, when she and Floyd had been deciding which acreage they wanted for their own. The property looked different with a two-story cream-colored house on it, as well as a single-level building with a green metal roof that housed Marlin's barrel factory. He seemed to have set aside his thoughts about his younger children, so she let the subject rest.

It was a pleasure to walk in the sunshine and fresh air without having to hash out any more details about family members. She and Marlin topped the hill, walking at an easy pace while covering a lot of territory. They stopped at the top of the next rise.

"Here's a sight I never tire of," Marlin said, gesturing toward a spacious pasture surrounded by a white plank fence. "Church leaders in the Iowa district we came from would consider Bishop Monroe unduly extravagant, when it comes to those huge red barns he's built for his Clydesdales—not to mention the pretty penny he paid for that fence. But you can't argue with the way he did his property up *right*, so the clients who buy his horses and have them trained here believe he runs a top-notch business. Which he does."

Frances nodded, gazing at the massive brown horses with the white hooves that grazed serenely beneath the trees. "I suspect your Lowell and Lavern Peterscheim love every minute they spend working for the bishop, too—even when they're mucking out the stalls in those big barns. It's nice that those two boys have become such fast friends since you moved your family here. Before you came, Lavern was the only young fellow that age at Promise Lodge."

"Lowell and Lavern are in horse heaven when they're around the bishop's Clydesdales," Marlin agreed. "Monroe allows the boys to handle and ride the horses some, too, after he's gotten a day's work out of them. It's *gut* for both of them to have a boss that's not their *dat*, and it's giving them a taste of trades besides the barrel making and black-smithing they've been around all their lives."

Marlin gestured for Frances to turn around. "And *this* is the panoramic view you have if you're the bishop," he said lightly. "Promise Lodge property spreads as far as the eye can see. If he took a notion to, Monroe could stand here and watch the comings and goings of just about every family in his district."

Frances clasped her hands, amazed at the view. "There's the orchard, and Rainbow Lake, and Preacher Eli's smithy, and Christine's dairy cows—and Rosetta's goats are grazing along the fence behind the Kuhns' cheese factory!" she exclaimed, pointing as she noticed each detail. "And look at the way our homes shine in the afternoon sunlight!"

Frances shaded her eyes with her hand, enthralled with what she saw. "I had no idea how much land Mattie's planted for her produce stand," she remarked, gazing at the evenly spaced rows of vegetables emerging from the dark soil. "It doesn't seem you and I have walked such a long distance, yet from here, the lodge and the entryway sign at the road look like part of a toy village."

"We've come a long way," Marlin remarked softly. "I'm glad you've walked with me, Frances. Our community has taken on even more of a glow because I'm seeing it through your eyes."

Frances focused on Ruby's stacked white beehives in the orchard, not daring to look at Marlin. The tone of his voice made her pulse thrum with an unusual sense of energy, as though the preacher had something on his mind besides the view.

We've come a long way.

Determined not to imagine any romantic undertones Marlin hadn't intended, she reminded herself that she'd agreed to this walk so she could air her concerns about Lester. It was too soon to be enjoying the company of an attractive, unattached man—

But you'd be hard-pressed to find a nicer fellow than Marlin, the voice in her head countered.

Frances blinked. She was suddenly aware that a lot of time had passed since she'd slipped away from the kitchen. "You know, I should probably head back," she said in a rush. "By now, the other ladies will be wondering where I've made off to—"

"*Jah*, you're probably right," Marlin said with a sigh.

"—and there'll be no end of explaining to do when they realize you've left the party, too," she continued. "And if *Lester* figures out that we've gone for a walk—"

"Then maybe he'll come to realize that you have your own life, and you have *options*," he interrupted gently. Marlin briefly squeezed her shoulder before heading toward the road that led back to the lodge. "If anyone asks, you were expressing your concerns about him and I was giving you some preacherly counsel. Not that it's anyone else's business, unless you make it their business."

Frances slowed her stride, letting his words sink in. Anyone who might be out looking for her could see that she and Marlin were walking two or three feet apart, so why had she become anxious about what people would think? "You're right," she murmured. "I—I didn't mean to turn into a nervous Nellie."

Marlin chuckled. "You're right, too, Frances. People will talk—and we'd better be ready for that."

Chapter Four

Later that afternoon, as Truman and Rosetta's guests from Coldstream and Cloverdale began heading home, Phoebe paused in the kitchen doorway with her empty plastic dishpan. Clusters of folks still sat at a few of the tables farthest from the kitchen, but it wouldn't be rude to clear the dishes and utensils the crowd had used after the newlyweds had cut their wedding cake. On the dessert table, one center tier of a chocolate cake remained. A large wedge had been cut from it and a few plated slices of cake sat nearby—and its rich, mocha buttercream frosting was calling Phoebe's name.

"All right, girls, you can do as you please," she said to her sister Laura and Deborah Schwartz, who were going to help her clear the dining room. "I see a chance for a second slice of that fabulous cake and I'm going for it— before anybody else gets the same idea!"

Deborah's eyes lit up. "We *have* been on our feet and working all day—"

"And my first slice of cake was a lot smaller than I'd hoped for," Laura put in as she set her dishpan on the nearest table. "Let's do it. We can sit at the *eck* and pretend we're in a wedding party."

Phoebe laughed, quickly clearing the frosting-smeared

plates, forks, and crumpled napkins from the raised table in the corner. Within moments the three of them were perched on chairs that overlooked the roomful of long, white-draped tables, with plates of cake in front of them. She closed her eyes over her first mouthful of sinfully delicious cake, allowing the mocha frosting to melt over her tongue.

"I'm going to have Ruby bake this cake at *my* wedding," Laura announced with a wistful sigh.

"Why wait until you get married?" Deborah asked. "We'll have birthdays and other special occasions, after all. Like maybe . . . a baby shower."

"*Jah*! Bernice and Barbara will be having their wee ones in June," Laura put in excitedly. "We'll have to start planning their party soon."

Phoebe cut into her cake again, wondering how to express the question that had been tickling her imagination lately. She and Deborah had grown up together in Coldstream, and she'd noticed a certain glow about her best friend lately—after suspecting Noah Schwartz's bride had been sticking close to home because she didn't feel well. "Something you're trying to tell us, Deborah?"

The blonde beside her giggled. "Matter of fact, there is! You can plan for a party early this fall, if Minerva has predicted my September due date accurately." Minerva Kurtz acted as the community's midwife as well as the children's teacher.

A rush of joy made Phoebe drop her fork to embrace Deborah. "I guessed right! Congratulations!"

"Oh, but this is exciting news!" Laura chimed in as she hugged Deborah from the other side. "Are we allowed to share this, or is it your little secret for a while longer?"

Deborah wrapped her arms around them. "Noah and I told our parents last night, so it's official. Mamm and Mattie had already figured it out, of course, but they were nice enough to let us have our moment and announce our happy news to them."

"You're eating for two, so you need another piece of cake," Laura said as she rose from her chair. "And I'm getting myself another piece to celebrate. Phoebe?"

"Sure—since you're already up." Phoebe laughed at their overindulgence. "Deborah deserves an announcement party, ain't so? We should get the ladies together and start crocheting for you and the Helmuth sisters soon," she added.

Male voices made her glance toward the lobby, where Allen Troyer was standing with Cyrus and Jonathan Helmuth, who'd come to Promise Lodge to help Sam and Simon run their nursery. The three of them entered the dining room, and after exchanging greetings with the older folks who were still chatting, they headed for an empty table.

Allen watched Laura carry three plates of cake, a smile lighting his handsome face. "Looks like we got here just in time to nab the girls' leftovers—if we hurry," he said to his friends. He focused on Phoebe, pointing to the table nearest him. "Will it be okay if we sit here? I'll even clear these dishes and take off the tablecloth, if you want."

"Fine by us," Phoebe replied. The three young men spent a lot of their spare time in the lodge, probably because their cabins were very small—and because the Kuhn sisters saw to most of their meals. "Consider yourself warned, though. The ladies in the kitchen—one in particular—might draft you to help wash dishes."

Allen's smile said he knew to whom she was referring. "She can try, but we three guys will be too engrossed in business to be lured away." He held up a roll of paper he'd had under his arm, and then quickly moved the dishes and the tablecloth to the far end of the table. When Cyrus and Jonathan joined him with the platter that held what was left of the chocolate cake, they all sat down.

Deborah leaned closer to whisper in Phoebe's ear. "There you go, girl. Allen's mighty fine, and those Helmuths are pretty cute, too—all of them working *gut* jobs," she pointed out. "I'm thinking you and Laura might be ringing wedding bells soon."

Phoebe waved her off, paying more attention to the cake her sister was handing her than to Deborah's suggestion. "Wouldn't surprise me if they're all going into Cloverdale to visit Maria's new bakery," she remarked with a shrug. "They thought she was the cat's pajamas—"

"Puh! Maria has nothing on you," Deborah protested. "Just saying."

"I get dibs on Cyrus," Laura murmured as she resumed her seat at the table. "But who knows? Gloria may sweep him off his feet—"

"Or knock him over with a pan of her brick-bat brownies," Phoebe teased. She slapped her face playfully. "But that was a mean thing to say—and here she comes."

Like a bee to a blossom, Gloria Lehman buzzed from the kitchen and headed straight for the table where the fellows had settled. She was balancing a glass pie plate on one hand and held a spatula in the other, smiling so brightly—so hopefully—that Phoebe felt a little sorry for her. No matter how many times Allen told Gloria he wanted nothing to do with her, she kept coming back for more.

"I bet you guys are ready for a snack, *jah*?" she asked sweetly. "I saved you back some pie! There's cherry and chocolate cream and blackberry and—oh! What's this you're looking at, Allen?"

With a resigned expression, Allen glanced at the young woman who'd come to hover over him and his friends. "We've got cake, *denki*," he pointed out.

"*Jah*, I don't have room for even a *bite* of pie," Jonathan put in.

Gloria paid no attention to their rebuffs. She was avidly studying the large piece of paper they'd unrolled on the tabletop, holding the pie plate at her shoulder. "This looks like a diagram of a house—but it's only got one room?" she asked with a confused frown. She pointed with her spatula. "What's this circle?"

"The toilet," Cyrus informed her brusquely.

Gloria let out a huff. "You don't have to get so testy about—oh!—"

Phoebe winced as the pie plate slipped from Gloria's hand and landed facedown on Allen's paper. All three young men sprang from their chairs, exasperated. Allen plucked the spatula from Gloria's shaking hand and stopped Jonathan before he could lift the pie plate.

"If you steady the plate, Cyrus and I can pick up the diagram and flip it over so the—the mess—stays in the pan," he suggested quickly. "Seems better than trying to pick up all that loose, gooey pie."

With a wail, Gloria ran for the kitchen door. Phoebe fetched the dishcloth in her plastic tub. "Why did I figure something like this would happen?" she murmured to Laura and Deborah. "If it weren't for bad luck, Gloria would have no luck at all."

"She brings it on herself," Laura remarked with a shake of her head. "Let's finish our cake and clear the tables. That little episode ruined my party mood."

Phoebe wrung out the wet dishcloth and approached the guys' table. After Cyrus had rolled both ends of the diagram, Allen deftly slipped his hand underneath the pie pan—and with one smooth move, the three of them flipped everything over. When Cyrus lifted the paper, splotches of cherry, chocolate, whipped cream, blackberry filling, and piecrust were clinging to it, but most of the pie remained in the plate. After Jonathan moved the glass pan, they spread the page on the table again.

"Well, it's colorful," Cyrus remarked with a shake of his head.

"At least the damage is all in one spot," Allen muttered as he carefully lifted loose pie fillings with the spatula and dropped them into the pie pan. "If you guys have *any* idea how I can get that girl to stop pestering me, I'm all ears."

"Will this help?" Phoebe asked, offering him the damp cloth. She glanced at the precisely drawn sketch of a rectangular structure, complete with dimensions and lines where windows and a door would be. "I'm really sorry she messed up your work, Allen. This looks like a new project you're building, *jah*?"

Allen scraped off the last of the mess and accepted the dishcloth. "Not just a new project, but the new business I'm starting," he replied. "It's a tiny home. They're all the rage amongst folks who don't want to live in regular-sized houses anymore—and if you put wheels on them, you can move them from place to place."

Phoebe's eyes widened. "A tiny home? How tiny are we talking about?"

"This one's about three hundred sixty square feet," he said as he dabbed the paper with the cloth. "It's got a main room with a small kitchen area and bathroom at one end, and the bedroom is in a loft—and above that there's a small storage area."

"Think of it as cutting a Plain family's front room in half, and arranging all your stuff in that space," Jonathan explained. "Or, it's about the same size as one of the cabins, except the space is vertical."

Cyrus glanced around them. "You could probably park three or four tiny homes in this dining room, *jah*?" he asked. "That blows my mind, but from what I've read, single folks are building these structures for a lot less money than a house would cost them. I think you're onto something *big*, Troyer."

"Or not so big," Allen quipped. "I can't see Plain families living this way, but a lot of English who want to go green with a smaller footprint are embracing this idea. So I am, too."

Phoebe could only shake her head at what she'd heard. She decided to focus on the more practical issue rather than asking what a footprint had to do with a house. "But where do you put your kitchen table and your bedroom furniture and—and your *family*?"

Allen straightened to his full height. "The whole idea behind a tiny home is to get rid of *stuff*—to live with only the possessions you really need, on a very small scale with a lot of appliances and tables built into the walls," he replied. "It's not for everybody. You'll get a better idea of it when this one's built and I'm living in it."

She nodded doubtfully—although her curiosity was piqued. "That'll be something to see."

"*Denki* for your help, Phoebe—and for asking questions that show you're interested in this new project I'm taking on." Allen flashed her a dazzling smile before he focused on the tiny home's diagram, smoothing it with his hand. "I have a feeling I'll be redrawing this diagram on clean paper before I start construction. The last thing I need is a bunch of ants crawling all over everything."

Jonathan, the older and taller of the Helmuth brothers, nodded. "That pie goop soaked through where your kitchen and bathroom go, so your dimensions and notes got saturated."

"What a waste of *gut* pie, too," Cyrus remarked glumly.

"If Gloria had left it on the table—and left us alone—I would've been on it like a duck on a bug."

Sensing the fellows were back to having their own conversation, Phoebe returned to the *eck* with her dishcloth. Her sister and Deborah had stacked the dishes and were removing the white tablecloth.

"Somebody spilled coffee, and there's chocolate frosting smeared over here," she said, pointing to the stains. "We should check all of the tablecloths and treat the stains while we're gathering them up."

"I'm on it," Laura said. "A laundry stick and an old tooth-brush, coming right up."

As Laura headed for the kitchen, Deborah smiled demurely. "I'm telling you, Phoebe," she murmured, "Allen's looking you over. You were obviously interested in his diagram, and he's building *homes* now—just the right size for newlyweds."

"You're making this up," Phoebe retorted under her breath. "He's nice to look at, but he'll probably never settle down or join the church. Now that he's gotten his plumbing and electrical licenses, who's to say he won't live English—especially if his tiny home business takes off? He certainly won't be building those for Amish folks."

Deborah laughed as she went to clear the next table. "Some days *I* could be happy in a little house that only took a few minutes to redd up."

"Where would you put the baby?" Phoebe challenged.

With a shrug, the blonde stacked glasses and cake plates in her plastic tub. "Might have to hang a basket from the ceiling and keep her in there. In a house that small, at least I'd always know where she—or he—was."

Phoebe shook her head, sensing their conversation was just whimsical wishful thinking on Deborah's part. *She loves the new house Noah and the other men built—just the way she wanted it,* she thought.

With a glance at the three young men, who had their heads together over Allen's diagram, Phoebe began clearing the table next to the window.

And besides that, Deborah was so wrapped up in Noah while we were growing up that she paid no attention to Allen. She's pegged him all wrong. He'll be gone from Promise Lodge before summer's end—probably driving his horse-drawn tiny home on wheels.

Chapter Five

Marlin inhaled the cool air, taking in the colors of a fiery-bright sunset as he walked home from the wedding festivities with his family. He and Harley and some of the other men had cleared the lodge's meeting room by stacking the pew benches along the walls, so he was warm from the exertion—ready to relax in his recliner. When Lowell and Fannie spotted Queenie running toward them, they jogged off into the grass to find sticks to throw for her.

Harley, however, seemed uncharacteristically quiet. As soon as the kids were out of earshot, he cleared his throat. "You were out walking with Frances," he said in an accusatory tone.

Marlin sensed he was about to catch an earful, so he reminded himself to remain calm. "She's been very concerned about Lester's depression," he said. "She asked my opinion about—"

"From what *I* saw, Lester was the *last* thing on your minds!" his son blurted out. "You could've stayed in the dining room for your little chat."

Resentment was rolling off Harley in waves, and Marlin thought carefully before he responded. Minerva remained focused on the road—which could either mean she was keeping her opinion to herself, or that she wanted no part of the uncomfortable conversation her husband had initiated.

"The dining room was very noisy," Marlin pointed out. "And Lester could've overheard our conversation if he'd slipped around behind—"

"Maybe it's Lester you should be talking to," Harley suggested tersely. "Why would Frances be a valid judge of anyone's depression? She's still deep in her own grief—so it's not the *least* bit appropriate for her to be out strolling with you!"

At first Harley's attitude had puzzled Marlin, but now it was making him defensive. "Who are you to say what's appropriate for a woman who's old enough to be your mother?" he asked before he could catch himself. "What's this really about, son?"

Harley pivoted so he was standing in front of Marlin, staring him down. Except for his beard, the full face and light brown hair beneath his black hat were the image of Essie's. He'd grown a few inches taller than his *dat*, which he often joked about and used to his advantage—but this time he wasn't teasing. "You have no business looking after Frances Lehman!" he muttered. "Why were you walking her up to the house? From the looks on your faces, you'd forgotten all about Lester—"

Marlin's eyebrows rose. From the lodge, his son could've seen two people walking on their property, but he doubted facial features would've been discernible from that distance, unless . . .

"—and you were discussing something much more personal—"

"Were you watching us through binoculars? Spying on us?" Marlin demanded. He crossed his arms, matching his irate son's stance as he noted the deep color Harley's face had taken on. Ordinarily his older boy was laid-back and easygoing, but an innocent stroll with Frances had obviously gotten his dander up.

"Mamm is rolling in her grave! You promised to love her forever, but you've forgotten all about her, ain't so?"

Marlin took a deep breath to compose his thoughts. Minerva had joined the kids and the three of them were playing with Queenie as they continued toward the house. Her sensitivity was usually a godsend when Harley started talking about his deceased mother, but at this point it was best that she'd left them to this conversation. He needed to address his son man-to-man.

"I promised to be faithful to your *mamm* until death parted us," he countered gently. "And I will love her forever—don't you dare think otherwise." Marlin paused, trying to keep his frustration and his deep feelings for Essie in perspective. Some of what he'd discussed with Frances— the part about Lester moving in with her—was confidential, so he continued with caution.

"I'm sorry it upset you to see me walking with Frances, but as a preacher and a counselor, it's my place—my responsibility—to listen to her concerns," Marlin insisted in a low, controlled voice. "Had Amos or Eli or Monroe overheard the way Lester was talking to her as they walked to the wedding, any of them would've taken Frances aside to hear the whole story."

"That's fine—because they're all married! I know what I saw," Harley countered in a huff. "Why would you consider pairing up with Frances—or any other woman—when you've got a home with us, and Minerva's doing your cooking and laundry? What else could you possibly need?"

Companionship. A wife who's mine and not yours.

Marlin blinked. Until Harley had confronted him, he'd skimmed over how badly he missed having someone to care for, who cared for him, as well. At twenty-three, married to

an attractive, affectionate woman, his son had no inkling of
the toll loneliness could take on a man who'd lost the love
of his life—and this wasn't the time to set him straight.
From his earliest childhood, Harley had adored his mother
to the point he'd placed her on a pedestal in his heart. His
dat had always come in at a distant second place. The way
Harley saw it, no woman his father might consider for a new
wife would ever measure up to Esther Kurtz.

Marlin approached the subject from a different angle, because it was bound to come up again—and because he
didn't want the emotional wildfire Harley had kindled to
burn the bridges of their relationship. "I know how close
you were to your *mamm*, and how badly you miss her—"

"You have no idea!" Harley spat. He turned away, probably to hide tears he considered unmanly. His hands
clenched and unclenched at his sides.

"—and I appreciate the way you and Minerva were willing to move to Promise Lodge so we could have a fresh
start—"

"*You're* the one who wanted to get away from the memories of Mamm!" Harley retorted. "*I* was perfectly content
to stay in that house with her furniture, and to eat in the
kitchen where she cooked our meals, and to imagine her
still being there with us. It was a great comfort to me—not
that you cared!"

Marlin's eyebrows rose. He'd sensed Minerva, as a new
bride, would forever feel she was living in Essie's shadow,
so he'd built the young couple a house at Promise Lodge,
where he could reside in the attached *dawdi haus* . . . so they
could all move past their grief and get on with their lives.
He'd known Harley had been somewhat reluctant to leave
Bloomfield, but he hadn't anticipated the lingering pain—
the bitter vehemence with which his son was speaking to
him nearly a year later.

"I'm sorry, Harley," he whispered. "And I'm grateful that you and Minerva have shared your home with me. If you feel so strongly about it, maybe you'd be better off seeing if you could buy back the place in Bloomfield."

Harley sucked in his breath, his eyes wide. "I've thought about that a lot, believe me. But Minerva likes her new house and the friends she's made here."

"I like it here, too. I don't want to go back—I want to keep moving forward," Marlin explained gently. "My barrel business is doing well here—"

"And you did pay for the house and the pastureland for my flock," Harley put in bluntly. "It isn't as though I have the money to repurchase the farm in Iowa, even though I'd like to—if Minerva would even consider that an option."

Silence filled the space between them. Marlin allowed his son's thoughts to go where they would, because pointing out that Harley had two strikes against moving back to Bloomfield wouldn't ease the tension between them. After several moments, he tried again. "What can I do to help you with your grief, son? We all take our own time getting over losses, but your *mamm*'s been gone nearly three years. It's not healthy to let your feelings for her keep eating away at your soul."

"I don't want to see you alone with Frances again."

Marlin exhaled slowly. He removed his hat and smoothed his hair before replacing it, giving himself time to consider his response. His son had a right to his feelings—but as a father and a widower, he had emotional rights, too. "Setting aside our personal thoughts on this matter," he began softly, "you surely realize that our Old Order neighbors will expect me to remarry one of these days, because a preacher is to model the behavior he expects from his congregation. In Genesis, God tells us that it's not *gut* for a man to be alone—"

"So you're ready to get hitched again—is that what you're

telling me? And Frances is available, so she's the one?" Harley interrupted. "I don't care about Genesis and these Old Order rules you're throwing up to me! I don't like it that you want to replace my mother!"

Marlin sighed. He saw no immediate way to settle the anger that had sprung up between him and his son—and it saddened him. "You're jumping to some serious conclusions, considering that Frances and I have only taken a walk together while talking about her brother-in-law's emotional state," he pointed out with the last iota of patience he possessed. "You're in a bit of a state yourself, son, and I hope time and the *gut* Lord will heal your troubled heart. We'll talk about this again, hopefully when you can see things more clearly."

"*Jah*, we will," Harley said without missing a beat. "But don't count on my vision improving. I saw what I saw."

When his son turned and headed up the hill, Marlin was relieved that he was walking in the direction of the sheep barn rather than the house. He prayed that tending his flock would soothe Harley's soul, even if it didn't change his opinion about his *dat* walking with a woman other than his *mamm*.

Marlin inhaled deeply, allowing his emotions to cool as the temperature dropped with the setting sun. As he continued up the road, he reminded himself that he'd expected some repercussions if anyone had seen him out with Frances. He just hadn't figured on their coming so fast or so furiously.

At least you know where Harley stands on the subject, he thought ruefully. *Hopefully, he'll keep his rancor to himself rather than upsetting Fannie and Lowell. They lost their mother at a much more difficult time in their lives than he did.*

* * *

"Were you *really* out with Preacher Marlin?" Gloria demanded incredulously. She was sitting in the porch swing as Frances arrived home from the lodge, her expression a cross between a glare and a pout. "I wondered where you'd slipped off to this afternoon while I was drying dishes. Why would you be interested in *him*?"

Frances blinked, taken aback by her daughter's point-blank questions and her negative assessment of Marlin. Before she could reply, however, Lester came out of the house to chime in.

"I saw them with my own eyes, Gloria," he said, crossing his arms as he leaned against the doorjamb. "Did you strike up such a *cozy*-looking conversation with Marlin to get my goat, Frances? Is this the thanks I get for offering to take care of you?"

Frances clamped her mouth shut to keep it from dropping open in utter amazement. How on earth had her daughter and her brother-in-law come to such outlandish conclusions about the walk she'd taken with Marlin? Had Lester been inspiring Gloria's active imagination with his speculations before she'd gotten home? Even as she searched for words that would explain the true situation—and help the two of them see reason—Frances had a feeling Gloria and Lester were going to believe what they'd already assumed. It was a tricky matter, as well, to explain to Lester that he and his idea about moving in had been Marlin's reason for asking her to walk with him.

"If you must know," Frances began, doing her best to hold Lester's gaze without bursting into tears, "when Preacher Marlin passed us this morning and overheard your offer to take care of me—"

"I'm doing the right thing and you know it!" Lester blurted.

"—it was your *tone* that made him wonder if your grief

was getting the best of you," she continued doggedly. "He—and everyone else—has noticed the drastic change in your attitude, and we're concerned about you, Lester."

One of Lester's dark eyebrows rose. "You really expect me to believe that, Frances? I saw the way you were walking toward his house—the way he touched you—"

"Is that how it was, Mamm?" Gloria asked in a tremulous voice. She rose from the porch swing to go stand beside her uncle. "That's just wrong! Dat's only been gone a month and you're already—"

"He died six weeks ago today. I've missed him every hour of every one of those forty-three days," Frances retorted miserably. She looked from her daughter to her brother-in-law, despairing of wiping away the accusation on their taut faces. "You've got this all wrong—both of you. If Floyd were here, he'd be telling you to *think* before you spoke to me this way."

"But he's not here. That's the problem," Lester said in a rising voice. "I'm trying to be the solution for you, Frances, but instead of talking to me about it like a reasonable adult, you've gone running to Marlin, making a play for his sympathy."

Frances was too stunned to respond to such a preposterous overstatement. From where she stood, it seemed Lester and Gloria were blocking the door to her home as though they weren't going to allow her inside until she admitted she'd been wrong to talk to Marlin and begged their forgiveness. It seemed there was only one direction she could go. She took a step back, grasping the porch post for support . . . wondering if she should spend the night in one of the lodge apartments.

"Truth be told, Lester," Frances said in a quavering voice, "it was your *solution* that alerted Preacher Marlin to your emotional state. You *know* it's wrong for us to live together without being married!"

"So we'll get hitched!" Lester blurted. "I was doing the decent thing, giving you some time to get over losing Floyd before I asked you—"

"Hold it just a second," a male voice behind Frances stated. "Let's take a *gut* look at what's going on here."

Relief flooded Frances's soul as Marlin approached the porch and stopped at the bottom step. It had surely been God's own timing that the preacher had been going up the road just as she'd gotten caught in the crossfire of Lester and Gloria's questions.

"Okay, so what *is* going on?" Lester demanded. "Half the population of Promise Lodge—not to mention wedding guests from out of town—saw you and Frances strolling to the top of the hill, up to your place!"

Marlin's face was a picture of placidity, a balm to Frances's soul. "So if that many folks saw us walking, out there in the open, we were hardly engaged in some secretive meeting, ain't so?" he asked calmly. "Apparently, you and everyone else witnessed every moment Frances and I spent together."

Frances wanted to cheer. Marlin wasn't rising to Lester's bait, and his cool composure was the inspiration she needed to get through this trying moment.

"Matter of fact," Marlin went on, "when I heard you declaring that you should marry Frances just now, you re-confirmed the concerns we both have about how well you're holding up after the losses you've suffered, Lester. I was troubled when I overheard the way you were speaking to Frances on the way to the wedding, suggesting you should move into her house—"

"That's none of your business!" Lester snapped.

"Ah, but it is," Marlin continued smoothly. "And to be

sure we don't mistake my opinions and actions as those of a widower speaking in his own interest, I'm asking you to come to the weekly meeting we preachers have with Bishop Monroe at ten on Saturday morning. Or will that interfere with your schedule at the townhomes where you're installing windows?"

Lester glowered but he brought his temper down a notch. "What with Truman getting married today, he told me we wouldn't be on the job again until next Monday."

Marlin looked at Frances. "Will ten o'clock on Saturday work for you? We meet at Monroe's place. I think you should be present at our meeting, so all sides of this matter are fully disclosed and understood."

She nodded. "I'll be there. *Denki* for considering my position, and for seeing to this problem so promptly."

Marlin gazed at Gloria, his facial features softening. "Would you like to come, too, Gloria?" he asked. "I'm sure this matter of your *mamm* being seen with a man other than your *dat* is upsetting to you."

Gloria sighed loudly, rolling her eyes. "Sounds like something for you *older* people to handle. I've got enough to think about without listening to you and Uncle Lester squabbling over who'll look after my mother."

As her daughter went inside, letting the door slam behind her, Frances suspected that Gloria had again felt the sting of Allen's rejection. No doubt the details would come spilling out with a waterfall of tears later on, after Lester was gone.

"Shall we talk on the way to your house, Lester?" Marlin asked purposefully. "You have a lot on your plate, dealing with the loss of your wife and your son—not to mention your brother and business partner. Nobody can blame you for wanting Frances's company and her help with your meals and laundry."

Lester looked away, spearing his fingers through his shaggy dark hair. "You folks have no idea," he rasped.

Marlin nodded sadly. "Maybe it would help if you told me about it—got some of the pain off your chest," he suggested. "My loss hasn't been as tragic as yours, but I know about the lonely days and nights—especially because I moved away from the friends I had in my previous church district, as you did."

Lester stepped away from the door. "We're not finished with this conversation," he muttered as he passed Frances to descend the porch steps.

"It's not my intention to shut you out," she said. "But it's got to be a two-way conversation. I have a say in how I'm going to live out my life, Lester."

As her brother-in-law headed for the road, she noticed how stooped his shoulders were—how old and defeated he appeared. It was sad to see what grief and pain had done to a man who'd previously been so cheerful and full of positive energy.

"*Denki* for your help, Marlin." Frances gazed at him from her spot beside the porch post. "I was between a rock and hard place until you came along."

Marlin tipped his black hat at her. "A similar conversation with my son prepared me for what I saw as I was passing your place. Like it or not, we're the talk of the town."

"Maybe we should give them something to talk about," Frances teased, but then her hand flew to her mouth. "Oh my, that was hardly an appropriate thing to—"

"Actually, it's the best idea I've heard today," Marlin said with a chuckle. "Why should we let other people's accusations get the best of us? Why can't we be friends on our terms instead of theirs?"

Frances smiled. "That's a *gut* way to look at it. Only three of us at Promise Lodge have lost our mates, while the other adults have their spouses and families close by," she said pensively. "*Denki* for offering to share Lester's burden. I hope he takes you up on your offer."

Marlin turned to follow the progress of the lone figure that was approaching the next house up the hill. "We'll see what he says. You can lead the horse to water—"

"But you can't count on him having any horse sense," Frances finished matter-of-factly.

Marlin's laughter echoed beneath the roof of the porch. "See you Saturday morning. Hopefully by then our Lord will have suggested a beneficial solution to this situation."

Frances nodded, watching the preacher leave. As dusk settled over Promise Lodge, the off-white houses reflected the last rays of the sunset and the air became cooler, more serene. It was so quiet she could hear the distant hum of a car on the county highway and the breeze sighing high in the trees. She allowed herself a few moments of peace on the porch before going inside to deal with Gloria.

See what's happened to us in your absence, Floyd? she thought as she watched the sky fade from pale gray to a watercolor wash of blues. *We'd appreciate any guidance you and God can send our way, and any help you can bring your brother.*

Chapter Six

As Irene Wickey descended the stairway Friday night, clutching a plastic bag of pastel yarns, her steps were quick and her heart was light. What a joy it was to join the ladies from Promise Lodge for an evening of crocheting baby things for Barbara and Bernice Helmuth! As she burst out the front door, she grinned at the Kuhn sisters, the young Hershberger sisters, as well as at Christine Burkholder and Mattie Schwartz, who were arranging their chairs at one end of the porch.

"This is so exciting!" she blurted out. "I can't tell you how wonderful it feels to live in just a couple of rooms upstairs, surrounded by friends—after a fun supper with Ruby and Beulah. I feel like a free woman!"

The Kuhn sisters laughed as they sat down in their cushioned wicker chairs. "I remember having that same feeling last summer when we moved here, don't you?" Beulah asked Ruby. "It was like we'd found a whole new world where we could be ourselves without the burden of keeping up our brother's house—"

"And without being a burden to our family," Ruby put in with a nod. She picked up the pale-yellow blanket she was working on, and her hook moved quickly along a row of stitches. "We're happy to have you, Irene. What with Mattie,

Christine, and now Rosetta moving out, Beulah and I thought we'd have to make up some imaginary friends to keep us company."

"And just between us girls," Mattie put in softly, "my days living in a lodge apartment were some of the best of my life. It's *gut* to be a wife again, but selling our farms and sticking our necks out to buy this property was probably the most worthwhile thing my sisters and I have ever done."

"Amen to that," Christine chimed in as she sat down beside Mattie. "We had no idea if anybody else would want to live here with us, but we took the chance—and we proved what the power of positive thinking and a whole lot of work and prayer can accomplish."

"And planning for happiness!" Laura chimed in. "Rosetta kept us from getting sucked under by all the drudgery, making sure we took time for fun—and time to celebrate our new home."

Irene chose a chair between Phoebe and her *mamm.* "When I heard you folks had purchased this abandoned campground, I was skeptical at first," she admitted as she took a skein of variegated yarn from her sack. "Who ever heard of three Plain ladies starting up a new community—along with only one man who wasn't even related to them? But every time Truman came home from clearing trees or digging foundations for your homes, he told such wonderful stories that I admired every last one of you."

Irene fastened her yarn onto her hook, chained a few stitches to form a circle, and within moments she'd crocheted the center of a granny square. It had been a few years since she'd picked up her hook, yet her fingers remembered the movements—and she was pleased that her arthritis wasn't bothering her. She felt better than she had for months.

"How are the newlyweds doing?" Beulah asked. She picked up the tiny cap she'd been working on, to see how many more rows of stitches it needed. "Thursday was a wonderful-*gut* day—for them, and for us."

"It was," Irene agreed. "Friends from our church had nothing but compliments about how tasty and well organized the dinner was, and how smoothly the ceremony went, what with an Old Order bishop and a Mennonite preacher both conducting the service," she added. "Truman and Rosetta have a lot to be thankful for. They left this morning to visit a few far-flung relatives near Queen City, to collect their wedding presents from folks who couldn't make it to the ceremony."

"It's an exciting time in their lives," Mattie remarked, crocheting a corner on the blanket she was making. "Amos and I live with a mishmash of furniture from his first marriage and mine—but we both pared way back on *stuff* when we moved from our homes in Coldstream."

"The kids have plenty of *stuff* to deal with," Irene admitted with a laugh. "It seemed like I was moving quite a lot this morning when Monroe and Amos and Roman were loading my furniture into their wagon, but I didn't make much of a dent at the house. That's the way it works when you have pieces left from your parents, and you add another generation or two over the years."

"If they have pieces they don't want to use—pieces you don't want to part with—you can move them into some of the empty rooms upstairs," Christine suggested. "We sisters agreed that we'd keep a few furnished apartments and cabins ready, in case some folks arrived at Promise Lodge without beds and dressers and such. We were glad to have them for wedding guests, too."

"*Jah*, Allen and the Helmuth cousins were mighty glad we had furnished cabins when they came here," Phoebe said.

"We were, too!" Ruby piped up. "It was a relief to leave our brother Delbert's place with just our clothes, my beehives, and the equipment we needed for making cheese."

"*Jah*, that was quite a night when we showed up here with just our suitcases," Beulah recalled fondly. "And the first folks we met were Truman and Rosetta. They didn't bat an eye about two hardheaded Mennonite *maidels* running away from home to come here. We had no idea how welcome we'd feel—or how *gut* it was to belong to a group of like-minded ladies who wanted to live life their way."

Irene blinked back sudden tears, but they were tears of joyful agreement. She'd never burdened Truman with how lonely she'd sometimes felt after his *dat* had died years ago. He was a wonderful son, and he'd looked after her well, so she felt blessed that she could allow him and his new bride some privacy—while she had fun with ladies of her own age!

"You've hit the nail on the head," she said softly, stilling her hook as she gazed at the open, friendly faces gathered around her. "It's *gut* to belong. And it's even better when your friends have a *purpose* to their lives."

Mattie nodded her agreement. "Probably the most valuable thing we Bender sisters have discovered here is that *purpose* doesn't have to center around a man or a family," she said softly. "That idea flies crosswise to Old Order ways. But at our age, with our kids reaching adulthood, we believed there had to be more to life than keeping a husband fed and managing a household. We sisters have developed some remarkable skills—"

"And new businesses," Christine put in with a nod.

"—during the past year, and we discovered strength we didn't know we had," Mattie continued. "Yet we've willingly returned to married life. We know ourselves better now. We know what we can *do*—what we're capable of."

Irene's pulse thrummed as she listened to Mattie's

stirring testimonial. She hadn't realized how much she'd been missing, remaining in the home her family had lived in for generations—not daring to think outside the four walls, the way the Benders had. She sensed she was on the verge of something powerful, something she couldn't yet put her finger on. Surrounded by these women of faith and an independent mindset, she believed that she, too, could find a whole new direction for her life.

"Have you been to Maria's new bakery in Cloverdale?" Phoebe asked after a few moments. "I was disappointed that her business didn't do better here, but Promise Lodge is off the beaten path—probably farther away than her regular customers in Cloverdale wanted to come for doughnuts."

Irene considered Phoebe's question. She'd known and loved Maria Zehr since she was a girl growing up in their congregation, but the pretty blonde's presence had nearly cost Truman his bride. "She seems to be doing well," she replied. "Her building's big enough for a few tables, so folks can come in for coffee and goodies of a morning. She's hired a girl to help her part-time, too, so she's not stretching herself so thin."

"She tried very hard to make a go of it here," Christine remarked as she chose another skein of yarn from her bag. "I'm glad to hear her new shop's off to a solid start. It has to be easier to have customers coming to her, so she doesn't have to deliver most of what she bakes."

"Cyrus, Jonathan, and Allen really miss having her here, though," Laura teased. "They were her best customers!"

The porch rang with gentle laughter. Beside Irene, Phoebe laid her hook in her lap along with a finished white bootie. "Every time I look at that little building Maria left behind, I think there has to be a way to use it," she said in a far-off voice. "The ovens are still in working order—"

"Your aunt Rosetta would be tickled if somebody took

up baking there again," Christine said. "She bought the place lock, stock, and barrel so Maria would have money to start up fresh at her new place, which means a new tenant wouldn't have to invest in equipment. They could just pay a little rent, I imagine."

Mattie nodded. "Last I heard, Rosetta hadn't decided what she might charge," she said with an encouraging smile. "But that would probably only apply to somebody who wasn't family. If *you* wanted to try your hand at a business in that building, I bet she'd waive the rent as her investment in your future, Phoebe."

Irene smiled. Phoebe's expression remained a bit dreamy-eyed, but beneath her placid surface a youthful enthusiasm shimmered like new green leaves aflutter in the spring breeze. "What would you bake, dear?" she asked the young woman.

Phoebe considered her answer. "Well, I always thought Maria tried to make too many kinds of things. And she baked more than she knew she could sell," she added. "Also, I wouldn't want to compete with Deborah—or you, Laura—if you two decide to sell goodies at Mattie's produce stand again this year. Deborah had Noah install a double oven so she could do that, after all."

"*Jah*, but with a baby on the way, she might change her mind," Laura pointed out.

Irene was pleased to hear that Phoebe was considering so many angles, as though she'd given a lot of thought to what sort of baking business would be best. "Maybe you girls could agree to bake different items," she suggested.

"That way, you could all make some money—and you could focus on what you enjoy baking the most," Christine agreed with a nod. "Last summer, folks snapped up all your goodies as fast as you could bake them, so no matter what each of you decides to make, you'll do well."

"*Jah*, there were days when I was wishing my veggies had sold as well as your breads and brownies," Mattie put in with a chuckle. "It's just my opinion, Phoebe, but your piecrust is perfection. You use the same recipe most of us do, yet your crust is always tender and the edges are evenly crimped and golden—never too brown or hard."

"It's the way you handle the dough," Irene murmured. "I had a dear friend whose pies were the envy of all of us because they always sold first at our bake sales—and the local cafés and markets even asked her to bake pies for them."

Phoebe's eyes lit up. "Maybe I could talk to your friend about how she managed her baking and delivery and—ah." Her smile dimmed, and she placed her hand on Irene's arm. "Your face is telling me that she's gone. I'm sorry."

"Oh, we should never feel sorry about Etta Mae," Irene said, patting Phoebe's hand. "She lived a full, useful life and met her Maker at the ripe old age of a hundred and two. But *I'd* be happy to tell you how she organized her baking. The places where she sold her pies are still in business, so maybe they'd like having somebody new they could count on for homemade pies."

Irene felt everyone looking at her and Phoebe, maybe because her voice had risen and her words had come out in such a rush. She wasn't one to brag, but now that Etta Mae was gone, her own pies were the first ones to disappear at church suppers and bake sales.

"Homemade pies are going the way of dinosaurs in the English world," Beulah put in. "If you opened a pie shop, Phoebe, and only made pies you took orders for, you'd already be headed for more success than Maria had while she was here. Truth be told, you have a better head for business, anyway."

"Oh—*oh* but I like that idea!" Phoebe blurted. "Mamm, what do you think about me opening a pie shop?"

Christine slung her arm around her daughter's shoulders. "I think you can do anything you set your mind to, young lady. Do your homework—figure out the cost of your supplies and how you'll get your pies delivered—so you can charge enough to make some money," she suggested with a smile.

"The key to our little cheese business—besides using the fresh milk we get from Rosetta's goats and your *mamm*'s cows—was putting pencil to paper before we bought a single piece of our equipment," Ruby added as she held Phoebe's gaze. "We checked out a lot of different packaging materials, and we wrote down all our expenses for ingredients and utilities and such. We know exactly what it costs us to make a pound of each variety of our cheese."

"And we multiply that cost by three when we figure our prices," Beulah put in as she clipped her yarn to finish the cap she'd made. "When we first saw that figure, we both thought *nobody* would pay so much—"

"But we have yet to throw away any cheese that didn't sell," Ruby continued. "Folks think our cheese is better than what they find in the grocery store—because it's always fresh, and because most of them get a kick out of chatting with a couple of cute Mennonite ladies."

Irene chuckled, along with everyone around her. She had a feeling the Kuhns' customers returned as much to spend time in their delightful presence as to purchase their cheese.

"Never underestimate the advantage of being an Amish woman selling her homemade pies," Beulah stated as she gazed at Phoebe. "Make sure your labels—and the name of your shop—tells customers they're getting the quality they associate with Plain baking."

Irene's thoughts raced as she listened to the Kuhns' advice. If Phoebe decided not to open a pie shop, she might well run such a business herself! "See what I mean about

Promise Lodge?" she said. "Where else could you get such down-to-earth advice, from experienced ladies who are willing to share what they know?"

Phoebe tucked the booties, her yarn, and her hook into her sack. Her lips were twitching with a grin and she rose from her chair. "I'm going over to poke around in the bakery building while I think about all this information," she announced. "Who's going with me? Laura? Irene?"

"*Jah*, I'll take a look," Phoebe's sister said as she sprang from her chair. "There's some fun stuff stuck away in there."

Irene's jaw dropped as Phoebe extended her hand. Had Phoebe read her mind? Did she want a woman who was older than her *mamm* in her pie business, or was she just looking for company—or information about where Etta Mae had sold her pies?

What difference does it make? She asked you! *It's only a walk across the lawn—and it might be the path to a whole new adventure.*

Chapter Seven

Marlin closed his eyes as he bit into a frosted bar that resembled a sugar cookie with sprinkles on it. He was enjoying coffee and goodies at the bishop's kitchen table with Monroe, Amos, and Eli before the two Lehmans arrived, sensing they were in the calm before a Saturday morning storm—unless Lester had changed his tune about moving in with Frances.

"You must like those bars, Marlin," Monroe teased as he chose a brownie from the tray on the table. "I think that's your third one, but I may have lost count."

Marlin chuckled. "Who knew a cookie without any chocolate or nuts could be so addictive? Please let Christine know how much I've enjoyed them."

Amos's lips curved. "Surely Minerva bakes goodies, *jah*?" he queried. "Harley's not exactly wasting away from her cooking."

"Harley loads up on meat and potatoes and gravy," Marlin explained. "Minerva's watching her weight—and she keeps too busy teaching the kids to bake much—so sweets don't show up as often as they probably do at your house, Troyer."

"Might be time to find yourself a wife, eh?" Amos shot

back. "Rumor has it you were working on that after the wedding on Thursday."

Marlin had suspected Amos might bring that topic into the conversation, so he made a point not to snap at the bait. He stood up to look at the road through the kitchen window, to be sure Frances wouldn't walk in on man talk that would upset her. "What *I* want to know," he said carefully, "is whether you folks at the party were passing around binoculars while Frances and I were walking. Harley gave me an earful, as though he'd been able to discern our facial expressions—and it's quite a distance from the lodge to this hill."

Eli and Amos bit into their cookies to camouflage their telltale grins.

"Truth be told," Monroe replied as he fetched the percolator from the stove, "somebody found a set of bird-watching binoculars—probably Ruby's—on the windowsill of the lodge's mudroom. I tried to convince Harley to put them down, to let you and Frances have your privacy, but he was watching you as intently as Queenie follows his sheep in the pasture."

Marlin sighed—and then he caught sight of her. Frances had crossed the yard to chat with Christine, who was cutting dandelions from her new garden plot with the corner of her hoe. "Frances doesn't need to hear about that," he said, pointing purposefully in her direction. "And we don't need to be giving Lester any ideas about spying on her, either. Even without binoculars, he can look right into her house because there aren't any trees to block his view."

"I agree," the bishop said as he set the hot coffeepot on a trivet by the cookie tray. "The last thing we need is for neighbors to be peering at each other in secret. It's childish, it's invasive, and it's not a *gut* way to foster relationships built on honesty and trust."

As Monroe went to the door, Marlin prayed that their meeting would solve more problems than it created. Lester was coming up the road with an expression that could curdle milk, looking even more determined to press his point than he had on Thursday.

"*Gut* morning, Frances," the bishop was saying at the doorway. "Come in for cookies and coffee. Looks like we'll get down to business pretty quickly, as Lester's not far behind you."

"*Denki*, Bishop. It's kind of you to help us Lehmans sort this matter out."

Marlin let Frances's voice settle into his ears before he turned to greet her. She sounded rested and upbeat—gracious rather than grouchy about dealing with an overbearing brother-in-law. When he turned from the window, her quick smile told him she was pleased to see him, even though she spoke to the other men first.

"Amos and Eli," she said cheerfully. Peterscheim was pulling out the chair to the bishop's left, and she took it. "I'm thinking you fellows must be getting your *dawdi* acts together, *jah*? It's exciting that the Helmuth babies will be here in June, and then we'll have Noah and Deborah's first wee one to look forward to in the fall."

The two preachers were all smiles as they exchanged pleasantries about their expanding families—until Lester entered the kitchen like a house afire.

"I hope you men have figured out that I'm acting in Frances's best interest, doing my duty by her," he said without greeting anyone. He raised his eyebrows at Frances as he took the chair across the small table that was the farthest away from her—the seat where Marlin had been sitting. "Maybe we can all help her see the light this morning, while none of the other hens are here to cluck their two-cents' worth."

Marlin frowned, already irritated by Lester's attitude.

What had gotten into this man? When Lester had installed the windows and siding on the Kurtz house and was helping other families with their homes, he'd been such a congenial neighbor. Marlin sensed it would only fuel Lester's fire that the remaining chair was beside Frances—but he took it anyway.

Monroe resumed his seat at the head of the table. "Let me be sure I've got this straight," he said, leaning forward to hold Lester's gaze. "You've told Frances you intend to move into her home, but you've said nothing about marrying her. That's wrong, Lester, and you know it."

Lester raked his black hair with his fingers. His unkempt beard, hat-flattened hair, and wrinkled shirt—not to mention the dark circles under his eyes—gave him the appearance of a man possessed. "Okay, fine, I'll marry her!" he blurted out. He looked at Frances, shrugging in exasperation. "I was gonna be a bit more discreet about it, but these men are pushing my buttons, Frances."

Her face remained expressionless, as fresh and smooth as the petals of a rose despite the emotions that had to be churning within her. The bishop, Amos, and Eli shifted uneasily, as though they each had something to say but were waiting for someone else to go first.

After several moments of silence, Lester's eyes widened. "We'll keep to separate beds in separate rooms, if that's the way you have to have it," he continued doggedly. "It could be a marriage of convenience, in name only—which is no big deal, since you're already a Lehman—soon as Monroe wants to conduct the service. You've had plenty of time to think it over, Frances, so I deserve the courtesy of an answer."

Frances rose slowly from her chair, her mouth pressed into a tight line. Her gaze was so sharp, she could've drilled a hole between Lester's eyes. "I refuse to be any man's *convenience*," she stated softly. "My answer is *no*, Lester. Don't ever talk to me about this again."

As she walked toward the door, Marlin almost went with her, to settle her nerves. But he thought better of it while Lester was present.

Settle her nerves? Who are you fooling? his inner voice needled him. *Frances has more nerve than any man in this room.*

Monroe waited for the door to close behind Frances before he spoke. "Seems to me Frances has resolved this issue," he said softly. He poured coffee into a mug and handed it to Eli to pass to Lester. "Now we need to consider how we can help *you*, Lester. You're in a bad way, my friend. If you continue down the emotional path you're on, I'm concerned that you'll hurt yourself—or other folks. First let's talk about getting you some help with your meals and your laundry."

Marlin nodded, agreeing with the bishop, but he wasn't fully focused on the conversation. In his mind, he kept seeing the way Frances had tempered her frustration with utmost grace, considering Lester's outlandishly rude proposal. She hadn't cried—or struck out in anger—and she hadn't pleaded with him or the other men to take her part.

Frances held herself together—didn't speak to you, but that was so Lester wouldn't make things even more difficult and embarrassing. She stated her case in a roomful of men and walked away. What a woman!

Marlin placed his elbows on the table, tenting his hands in front of his face so nobody would notice that he couldn't keep from smiling. Amos said he would organize a schedule so the ladies could take turns bringing Lester's meals, and Eli thought they could see to his laundry and housekeeping chores the same way. Monroe gently suggested that he and the preachers would visit Lester a few evenings a week and keep him company as he worked through his grief.

Marlin nodded but remained quiet. In his mind, he was following Frances down the road, wherever it might lead.

What a woman!

Frances didn't stop walking until she'd gone all the way down the hill, past her home, and crossed the grassy lawn that surrounded the lodge. As she stepped through the back door into the mudroom, she felt like a teakettle at a rolling boil, ready to spout off and whistle full-blast.

But she paused. Her friends deserved better than an emotional explosion, just because Lester had acted like a horse's backside at the bishop's place.

As she took a deep breath, she caught the clean scent of the soap Rosetta made from her goats' milk. The neatly arranged rows of soap bars drying on a screen helped her put her thoughts in order. She was also aware of the mouth-watering aroma of chicken coming from the kitchen, which reminded her that she hadn't eaten anything this morning. The voices she heard were calm. Someone was cheerfully whistling "You Are My Sunshine"—probably Beulah—and Ruby started singing along.

Frances felt the tension leave her shoulders. She had the sudden urge to move into one of the apartments upstairs—to put her house up for sale—and to commit to that decision before she went home to tell Gloria what she'd done. She'd felt a little guilty, bypassing the house to avoid dealing with her daughter's tragic air of desperation—but not guilty enough to go home.

"Knock, knock?" she called out as she went to the kitchen doorway.

The Kuhn sisters turned toward her from their places at

the big stove, while Irene and Phoebe glanced up from papers they were studying at the worktable. Laura, who was mixing a bowl of pale-yellow batter, flashed her a bright smile.

"Frances! Come in and join our Saturday brunch," the young blonde said. "We're fixing up some corn bread, and some creamed turkey to spoon over it—and you're just in time to eat with us."

Frances sighed in sheer gratitude. "Oh, but I love corn bread," she murmured. "And your creamed turkey smells like heaven itself. I—I'll be happy to stay. How can I help?"

"The teakettle's about to sound off," Ruby said, gesturing toward a back burner. "If you'll fill the big crockery teapot, we'll be set as soon as the corn bread's baked."

"Put in lots of tea bags—from that canister in the corner," Beulah said. "When I drink tea, I want to drink *tea* rather than just colored water!"

Frances eagerly took up the task they'd assigned her, delighted to be included in their plans. The frustration she'd felt about Lester began drifting away like the steam from the hot water as she filled the pot and placed five tea bags in it—and then added three more for good measure. Irene and Phoebe, seated side by side at a paper-strewn worktable, were looking at catalogs and pointing at items with the tips of their pencils as they talked.

"Looks like you two are hip-deep in something pretty serious—and interesting," she remarked as she approached their table. Photos of aluminum pie plates and huge rolls of foil and plastic wrap were spread in front of them, as well as price lists from the bulk stores in Forest Grove and Cloverdale.

Phoebe smiled at Frances, nodding eagerly. "You're witnessing the planning stages of Promise Lodge's newest business," she said. "Irene and I are partners, and we're going to open a pie shop in the bakery building that belonged to Maria."

"We're calling it Promise Lodge Pies," Irene chimed in. "We went around this morning getting these price lists for our supplies, and we've already gotten orders to provide pies for the grocery store and the Skylark Café in Forest Grove, as soon as we can start baking them!"

"What a great idea—congratulations," Frances said as she squeezed their shoulders.

"Meanwhile, Deborah and I are going to keep baking goodies to sell at Mattie's produce stand—which reopens for the season next week!" Laura exclaimed as she poured her batter into a glass pan. "We're going to be busy bees!"

If only Gloria would take an interest in doing something, Frances thought. *She wouldn't be so hung up on Allen—or so aware that her sister and her friends all have meaningful ways to spend their time while she mopes at home.*

She knew better than to suggest that Gloria might help them with their baking, however, because the girls were well aware of her daughter's cooking failures. It occurred to Frances that if she lived at the lodge, she and her daughter could become involved with whatever projects these ladies took on, while remaining surrounded by their good humor and friendship. Wouldn't that be a welcome alternative to living in a house where so many rooms rang with empty silence? Irene had moved into an apartment only a day ago, and already she was caught up in a new business venture— and she looked and acted ten years younger.

Frances helped Laura set six places at one end of a dining room table. Soon they carried out a steaming bowl of creamed turkey, the pan of hot corn bread, some cranberry salad, and two pie plates that held pieces from several pies. When they sat down and bowed for a moment of silent prayer, her thoughts were whirling.

Lord, I see so many possibilities here! Help me to know how to proceed—and denki *for helping me stand up to Lester's proposal. He needs our help, Lord. And I need all the patience You can send me as I deal with him.*

After she opened her eyes, Frances began taking food as though she hadn't eaten for weeks. It was almost embarrassing when she realized she'd split *two* squares of corn bread and covered them with creamed turkey, which was chock-full of carrots, onion, celery, and peas.

"My word," she murmured as she spooned ruby-colored cranberry salad alongside her main course. "You'd think I've been working in the fields or felling trees, the way I'm eating. This food smells and looks so wonderful-*gut*!"

Beulah chuckled. "You're doing us a favor, Frances, helping us clean up the last of the wedding leftovers. It's *gut* to see you this morning."

"My appetite's improved a lot since I've moved in," Irene remarked as she filled her plate. "Food's more appealing when you've got friends to cook it, eat it, and clean it up with. I bet it gets kind of quiet at your place."

Frances nodded. She figured these ladies already knew about her stroll with Marlin—and they would certainly understand her frustration with Floyd's brother. "If Lester had his way about it, he'd be moving in with me," she began softly. "I'm grateful to Bishop Monroe and the preachers for meeting with us this morning to set the poor man straight about how he'd need to marry me first. I'm even *more* thankful that they didn't expect me to say yes to the preposterous proposal he blurted out."

All eyes around the table widened as forks hung suspended in midair.

"Lester proposed to you?" Ruby muttered. "In front of four other men?"

"And before that he'd been thinking he could just *move in*?" Irene demanded incredulously.

Beulah laughed and reached for the pie plates. "You deserve first pick of the dessert for enduring what had to be the most humiliating moment of your life, Frances."

Frances nodded, awash in the relief of sharing her ordeal with compassionate friends. "Now that it's behind me, Lester's proposal was almost funny," she admitted. "He was desperate enough to settle for a marriage in name only, but I told him that I wanted no part of anything he was suggesting—and that I refused to speak of it again. And then I walked out," she added with a shake of her head. "I'm amazed that none of the preachers called me on it or came after me."

After they ate in silence for a few moments, Beulah was the first to speak. "I'm not Amish, so I'm no authority on this," she began in a thoughtful tone, "but from what I've seen, your preachers here—and Bishop Monroe—aren't as uh, *domineering* as other Old Order leaders I've met. They allow for some practicality and insight rather than following every jot and tittle of the rules the Amish have followed for centuries."

"*Jah*, let's remember that most Amish fellows wouldn't have allowed Rosetta to offer apartments to single women—much less to us Mennonites!" Ruby put in.

"Maybe you and Gloria should move into the lodge!" Laura suggested.

"Laura and I liked living here so much that we still spend a lot of time in this kitchen, even though we have nice rooms at the house with Mamm and Monroe," Phoebe said with an emphatic nod. "And besides, if you had an apartment here, Lester couldn't pester you about sharing your house."

"We can go upstairs after we finish eating and show you

all the rooms you could choose from!" Ruby said brightly. "If Christine's or Mattie's apartments—or Maria's—aren't to your liking, we have several other rooms that can be fixed up the way you want them. It would be so *gut* to have you here amongst us, Frances!"

The eager expressions on the five faces around the table nearly brought Frances to tears. "Oh my," she whispered. "Truth be told, I've considered moving in—I'd come in a heartbeat, but I'm not sure I could afford any rent until my house sells. And we have to have new folks move to Promise Lodge for that to happen."

"Maybe Harley and Minerva would buy it," Laura speculated aloud. "Then, if things work out between you and Preacher Marlin, you could move into *his* house!"

Soft laughter erupted around the table as Phoebe elbowed her younger sister. "It's too soon after Bishop Floyd's passing to be playing matchmaker," she warned Laura softly. "Even if we all agree that Marlin's awfully nice—"

"And sorta cute, for a guy his age," Laura added. She smiled kindly at Frances. "I didn't mean to be a smart-aleck. I just want you to be happy."

"We all do," Irene agreed. "I can't speak for Rosetta, but under the circumstances, I bet she'd let you move in without paying, until you could afford to."

"Or she might think of ways you could work around the lodge in exchange for your apartment," Beulah said. "Now that she lives on the hill with Truman, she might be happy to let somebody else oversee the day-to-day upkeep."

As she got caught up in the excitement these ladies were generating on her behalf, Frances's pulse accelerated. She couldn't wait to go upstairs and look around. If she moved into an apartment, she'd have a lot of furniture and belongings she would no longer need. And if she found a way to sell those things, she'd have several months' rent. . . .

"This brings up an interesting point," Irene said in a pensive tone. "What if we started a fund for ladies who come to Promise Lodge and need help with rent money? Sure, your church has probably established an aid fund for when residents have a lot of medical bills, or their house burns down, but what about a cash reserve just for unattached gals who might need to stay here for a while?"

"Maria was a case in point," Beulah remarked. "She wasn't the best business manager, but she was only in her twenties and supporting a younger sister—didn't have any family to fall back on. It could happen to any of us."

"I think that's a fabulous idea," Ruby said, scraping up the last of her gravy-saturated corn bread with the tines of her fork. "A lot of our businesses earn enough that we could donate, say, five percent of our profits. As long as it's voluntary, I suspect Rosetta and her sisters would be in favor of such a fund—"

"Because it goes along with the very reason they moved to Promise Lodge," Phoebe put in eagerly. "I'm willing to donate to that fund from the get-go of our new pie shop! How about you, partner?"

"I'm in!" Irene replied. "Plain women have always stashed their egg money or baking money in a coffee can to cover special gifts or unforeseen family emergencies."

"Let's call it the Coffee Can Fund! I'll even donate retroactively from what we've earned at our cheese factory," Beulah crowed. "Since it's your idea, Irene, I nominate you to manage it for us. I feel really *gut* about having an organized way to help our friends over a rough spot."

"Hear, hear!" Phoebe said as she smacked the table. "I say we celebrate our idea with pie—and you get first choice, Frances."

Frances didn't know what to say. In the blink of an eye, just because she'd mentioned being short of rent money, these friends had devised a fund to cover such a need—for her, but also for other women who might find themselves in desperate circumstances.

"You're amazing—every last one of you," she murmured as she looked at the glowing faces around the table. "I'm proud to call you my friends, and I'd be pleased to live here amongst you."

"*Gut*, it's settled!" Ruby said. "We'll be happy to have you for a housemate."

Frances couldn't recall the last time she'd felt so excited. She chose a slice of red raspberry pie and passed the plate to Laura. By the time they'd all finished second slices of pie, she felt stuffed—but emotionally full, as well. Phoebe and her sister volunteered to clear the table and do the dishes, so the Kuhns and Irene took Frances upstairs to look at apartments.

"When I saw the view from Rosetta's corner apartment at the front of the building, I snapped it up," Irene said as she swung open her door. "I don't have all my stuff in place yet, but you're welcome to look around, Frances."

"When the Bender sisters took over the lodge, all the rooms were for individual campers, but we've had some modifications made," Beulah explained. "Most of us have combined a couple of the rooms—"

"And you couldn't ask for better workmanship than you get from Amos, Monroe, Marlin, and our younger fellows," Ruby put in.

Frances's first thought was that downsizing from a whole house to a couple of rooms would be a major adjustment. And yet, as she went from Irene's apartment into the ones Christine and Mattie had recently vacated, she felt ready to rethink the housing lifestyle she'd known all her life. "Why, it won't take but fifteen minutes to clean these places!" she remarked.

"I think that's what I'll like best about living here," Irene said with a big smile. "That, and the fact that I have a view of my old house—and so many trees around the lodge to shade the place in the summer."

When Frances stepped into the rooms that had belonged to young Maria, she did a double take. "Oh my—these pink walls with the paint that gets lighter toward the ceiling would take some getting used to."

"Wait till you see the sky-blue bedroom ceiling with the clouds," Beulah said with a chuckle. "But it's only paint. Easy to change."

"I suspect Gloria would really like this apartment, though," Frances said as she peered into the other rooms. As they continued around the U-shaped hallway, she noted that some of the rooms were made up with beds and chairs, ready for guests—or ready for her to stay in while she decided which furnishings to bring with her. The empty rooms were freshly painted and some of them overlooked the front lawn, the cabins, and had a view of the Helmuths' new landscaping nursery.

"You've given me a lot to think about," Frances said as they descended the stairs. "I'll go home and tell Gloria about our move right now. We might be back this afternoon so she can choose a place she likes."

"I'd see no problem with her having a room or apartment of her own so you could have a separate place," Beulah said. "She's of an age where sharing two rooms with her *mamm* might feel a bit cramped. The Hershberger girls did that."

As Frances walked through the lobby and out onto the lodge's big wraparound porch, she already felt at home. She inhaled the scent of the lilac bushes that were in full bloom out by the road, grateful that such an opportunity had opened for her just when she needed it. Her short walk back to the house gave her time to think about what she'd say to

Gloria—who, at twenty-three, would probably adjust to new surroundings a lot faster than Frances would.

It'll be just the thing to help you move forward now that Floyd's not around to maintain the house, she told herself as she approached the big ivory-colored home they'd moved into less than a year ago. *You'll be so much happier having friends your age and of like mind to spend your time with.*

When she entered the front room, Frances realized she'd have some trouble parting with the big walnut hutch that had been her mother's, not to mention the lovely dishes and the bone china cups and saucers she'd received for birthdays when she'd been young. But she could take her time deciding what to do with the roomfuls of pieces that had furnished her married life. It would all work out.

She found Gloria upstairs in her room, absently staring out her window. When her daughter turned, Frances could tell she was upset. "What's happened, dear?" she asked softly. "Tell me what's wrong, and then we'll talk about the big decision I've made."

One of Gloria's eyebrows arched. "The way Uncle Lester tells it, you've decided *not* to have anything to do with *him*," she snapped. "He said you were cozying up to Preacher Marlin, already so sweet on him that you'll marry him as soon as he asks you!"

Frances nearly choked. Lester had obviously been here stirring up the pot in her absence. "I told your uncle I wouldn't marry him—because it's not the right thing for me to do, and because he wants to marry me for all the wrong reasons," she said in the strongest voice she could muster. "I'm sorry Lester has filled your head with notions that there's anything romantic going on between Preacher Marlin and me—"

"But you went for a walk with him after the wedding! I saw you myself," Gloria countered. "How do you think it makes me feel that Mary Kate hitched up with the guy I really liked, and now *you* are pairing up with somebody?"

Frances regretted the sense of rejection that enveloped her daughter like a heavy black cloak. There was no telling Gloria that someday the right man would come along for her—especially after Lester had already contaminated her attitude. "I am not pairing up with anyone," she said firmly. "Matter of fact, I've decided to take an apartment at the lodge, where we won't need Lester—or any other man—to look after us. I think you'll enjoy living there, too, and you could even have your own apartment. You can't tell me you really *want* me to hitch up with Lester."

Gloria's mouth dropped open. She looked ready to cry. "Why would I want to live amongst all those—those biddy hens?" she demanded shrilly. "And why, after I've just lost my *dat*, do you expect me to leave my home, as well? I had no idea you were so hateful, Mamm! So selfish."

Frances's heart sank like a stone.

She silently counted to ten as she considered Gloria's accusations. *Had* she been selfish? Hateful? It was true that she hadn't consulted her daughter about moving into an apartment—but then, Floyd hadn't asked anyone's opinion about moving the family to Promise Lodge, either. As the head of the household and a compassionate parent, he'd done what he'd felt was best for Mary Kate and her baby.

What most folks didn't know was that in order to move away quickly, before Mary Kate's condition became apparent to his congregation, Floyd had sold their property in Sugarcreek for a lot less than it was probably worth. He'd invested that money in their new Promise Lodge home, so they hadn't had much of a cash cushion. Her husband had been a proud man, beholden to no one, and he'd figured to replenish their finances when he and Lester reestablished their window and siding business in Missouri—but the medical bills from his stroke had eaten up most of their remaining savings.

Now that Frances was a widow and a single parent, she saw the sale of their property as a prudent financial decision that would keep her from having to depend on Lester or any other man until she could remarry by choice rather than out of necessity. Gloria was old enough to understand these matters, but she was in no frame of mind to see reason. Backed against an emotional wall, she resembled a trapped animal—as though her mother was holding her there by force.

Frances sighed. "Please understand that the money from selling the house would support us for a long time, considering that neither of us has an income," she pointed out. "Roman has been helping us with the chores, but I won't ask him to pay our bills or buy our groceries."

She paused to allow time for her words to sink in. Her daughter's tearful, desperate expression gave Frances all the more reason to stand firm on her decision. "Unless *you* come up with a better idea to generate an income by the end of this week," she said in a purposeful tone, "we're going to follow my plan—not because I'm selfish, but because it takes money to keep us going. I've told Lester he's not to speak to me again about marriage, so please don't encourage him—and don't consider that as an option."

Steeling herself against Gloria's sob, Frances went downstairs. She'd done her share of crying since Floyd's death, and wringing her hands—adding her tears to her daughter's wouldn't accomplish anything. With pen and paper in hand, she sat on the sofa to decide which furnishings and belongings she could part with and which pieces she would take to an apartment in the lodge.

Chapter Eight

"Steady now! Little higher . . . higher—got it!" Allen crowed as he and his *dat* positioned the pre-built dormer on the roof of the tiny home he was constructing. He grinned at Bishop Monroe and Preacher Marlin, who stood on the ground beside the horse-drawn pulley system that had raised the dormer. "By the time you move your horse to the other side, we'll have this dormer secured and we'll be ready for the second one. Once I hang the door, this baby's all closed in!"

Monroe smiled up at him. "I'd be bumping my head every time I turned around in a little house like this," he said. "But it's cute, in a munchkin sort of way. And it went together a *lot* faster than a regular-sized house."

"That's because his old man suggested that he build all the walls and dormers first, and then join them together, like we build a barn," Dat put in with a laugh. "It might not be a house an Amish man would live in, but Plain ingenuity still applies."

"Okay, so I owe you for your advice," Allen admitted. He held the dormer in place while his *dat* rapidly bolted it down with his battery-powered screwdriver. "And just this once, you were right."

The men's laughter buoyed Allen's spirits. He probably

could've constructed his little house by himself, or with assistance from Cyrus and Jonathan, but he was glad he'd invited his *dat* to help. Truth be told, the structure had come together much faster than if he'd worked independently: the four of them and a horse had raised the walls and attached the roof in just a couple of hours, and the two dormers would be in place by lunchtime.

"This home's on wheels, so does that mean you plan to travel in it?" Marlin asked as he unhitched the young Clydesdale.

Allen shrugged. "It's a possibility—and that would be a way for me to get orders to build more of them," he replied. "Right now, though, I figure to stick around while I build a couple of display models in different styles. You can talk about square footage and built-in features till the cows come home, but most folks can't visualize how a tiny home works until they step inside one."

Marlin nodded. "I'm looking forward to seeing this place when it's finished. I could imagine living in a tiny home all by myself, but with a family there'd be no getting away from the wife or the kids—"

"*Jah*, there'd be too much togetherness," Dat agreed as he stood up. "And Mattie would be hard-pressed to serve dinner in a place that didn't have room for a regular-sized table."

"It's a matter of readjusting your priorities and expectations," Allen explained. "Since I don't own a full-sized table, or any furniture to speak of, it won't be as much of a challenge for me to live small."

"It'll be an adventure," Monroe said as he shifted the scaffolding and pulley system to the other end of the building. "I hope customers see your display models and decide then and there to have you build them new homes, Allen. It's *gut* for all of us to be around young fellows who think outside the box and have fresh ideas."

"I agree completely," Marlin chimed in. "This sort of home is also a lot more affordable than the houses we Amish live in."

"*Jah*, once again Dat came in handy," Allen joked as he shot his father a smile. "He came up with enough shingles and lumber and window glass—and other odds and ends left from building your places—that I've only had to invest a few hundred dollars in materials for my house."

"Not to mention some free labor," Dat put in with a laugh. "But it does my heart *gut* to have you living and working here, son. I'll be happy to help you with every house you build, if it means you're sticking around to be a part of our family again."

A shimmer of emotion made Allen glance away. When he'd been a kid finishing school, he couldn't wait to move away from the domineering man who'd made him toe the line and attend church, and who'd lectured him about every little thing he'd done wrong. Had Dat mellowed, or had his own attitude changed?

Allen chose not to think too hard about the answer to that question. For now, it felt nice to bask in his *dat*'s smile and to be the recipient of his expertise.

Within twenty minutes the second dormer was attached. Allen clambered down with the box of bolts and then steadied the ladder while Dat descended with his screwdriver, level, and hammer dangling from his tool belt.

"*Denki* for your help, fellows," he said as he shook hands with Monroe and Marlin. On an impulse, he slipped an arm around his father's shoulders and gave him a quick squeeze. "I'll see what the Kuhns have rustled up for lunch, and then I'll shingle the roof and install the solar panels and the door. It's been a great day!"

Preacher Marlin inhaled deeply and turned around. "My nose is telling me Irene and Phoebe have fired up the oven for their new pie shop," he said, gesturing toward the small bakery near Christine's dairy barn. "Might have to mosey over and see if they have any samples."

"Might have to put in your order," the bishop corrected. "The way I've heard it, they're only baking what they've already sold, which seems like a smart way to do business— not that any of us would allow unclaimed pies to go to waste!"

Allen watched the three men stride past the cabins toward the road, holding a lively conversation as they walked. He noticed that none of them went to the bakery, even though the irresistible aroma of pastry filled the air. Something made him step inside his cabin and wash up. He checked his hair in the small bathroom mirror—*curiosity*, he told himself as he grabbed his wallet.

What would it hurt to order a pie for Dat as a way of thanking him for his time? And pies for Marlin and Monroe, while he was at it? He had a few minutes before Ruby and Beulah would be putting the noon meal on the table, anyway.

As Allen approached the bakery, he inhaled appreciatively. When he stepped inside, the two long tables covered with freshly baked pies made his stomach rumble—and the sight of Phoebe did something funny to his insides, too. She wore a dark blue kerchief over her blond bun and her face was pink from the heat of the ovens as she deftly swept the floor behind the front counter. Irene was spooning fruit filling into a large lidded container. The two of them worked in a companionable silence that suggested they'd had a busy, successful day.

When Phoebe caught sight of him, her smile lit up the whole building. "Allen!" she called out. "What do you think of our day's work? All of those pies are going to the bulk market and the Skylark Café in Forest Grove this afternoon!"

Allen stepped closer to the tables, pretending to inspect

the pies. They'd been baked in disposable aluminum pans, and some of them had lattice tops while other crusts had leaf-shaped slits cut out of them. About a dozen butterscotch and dark chocolate pies awaited a whipped cream topping. It took all of his strength not to grab a pie and dig into it with his fingers.

"I'm impressed," he admitted. "You ladies have baked a whopping lot of pies today, and every one of them looks perfect."

"Phoebe does the crusts and I do the fillings," Irene put in cheerfully. "I have a feeling I'm going to collapse tonight after we deliver all those pies, but it was a wonderful-*gut* first day."

Allen nodded. "You're taking them in a wagon? Won't the jostling make them shift around—and maybe break the crusts?"

"Irene's got a van, because she picks up friends to take to church on Sundays," Phoebe replied. "We'll fold down the back seats for today, but we'll have to figure out a way to stack them if our orders increase."

"What if I built you some pie shelves?" Allen asked on an impulse. "It wouldn't be that difficult to make them square, say, five or six pies deep—or whatever you think you could lift without their being too heavy."

Irene and Phoebe gazed at him as though his idea had just won first prize at the fair. "Wow, that would be perfect!" Phoebe exclaimed.

"We'll buy your materials and pay you for your time," Irene insisted. "We decided from the get-go that we won't maintain a business based on the *gut*will of our friends."

A smile eased across Allen's face. "What if I tally up what those shelves cost and take my pay in pies, over time?"

"You're on! What kind of pie do you like?" Phoebe grabbed a scratch pad and scribbled something across the top of it. "We'll set you up with a standing order for—what? One or two pies a week?"

"Let's shoot for two," he said, already tasting the pleasure of cutting into his own private pie each evening. "And what kind? Surprise me. I never met a pie I didn't like."

Phoebe's laughter filled the little bakery. "If you say that, you might end up with two or three kinds of fruit filling in the same crust, left over from what we've baked for the restaurants," she teased as she scribbled on her pad. Then she looked at him, winking. "But for you, Allen, we'll set back the first pie we make so it'll be ready whenever you come by for it. Will Mondays and Thursdays work?"

"*Jah*, Fridays are going to be really busy, what with stocking the store and the restaurant in Forest Grove for the weekends," Irene put in with a nod. "We've already decided to take Wednesdays and Saturdays off—and Sundays, of course. Life's too short to be cooped up in a hot kitchen more than four days a week, no matter how successful we get."

"You ladies are amazing," he murmured. He wanted to approach the counter, to stand closer to Phoebe and chat a bit longer—except he didn't want Irene to think he was flirting with her partner. "I'll have your pie shelves made before your big delivery on Friday. Is that your black van parked behind the lodge? I'd like to measure the back with the seats down."

Irene nodded. "It's unlocked, whenever you want to take your measurements. *Denki* for offering to build us those shelves, Allen!"

"We believe in paying it forward, so we'll bake your first pie tomorrow," Phoebe put in.

Allen nodded, suddenly aglow with goodwill. "May I receive some of my pay as a pie apiece for Bishop Monroe, Preacher Marlin, and my *dat*? They were a great help today. My tiny home went together in just a few hours."

"It's all finished?" Phoebe asked. "Now *that* would be something to see!"

Allen swallowed hard. How had he known this young woman for most of his life yet never realized how pretty she was—or how huge and blue her eyes were? "I still have to install the door and do the shingles, the detail work, and the painting," he clarified, "but the building's together and the roof's on. It's an amazing little place, if I say so myself."

"We'll have four pies ready for you tomorrow," Irene put in kindly. "I think it's exciting that so many of us here are creating new jobs—with the help of our friends. We accomplish so much more as a community than we ever could if we were going it alone."

"You're right about that," Allen said. He sensed he'd better leave before he gawked at Phoebe any more or said something stupid. "*Denki* again. I'll let you get back to your work—and congratulations on getting so many pie orders!"

As he stepped outside, he took a deep breath to settle himself. Why did he feel so exhilarated, like a can of soda pop that had been shaken? Allen started across the lawn toward the lodge with a sense that the sun was shining more brightly than usual in a cloudless sky that was the exuberant blue of a morning glory. Beyond Noah and Roman Schwartz's homes, Rainbow Lake shimmered serenely— tempting him to stretch out on the dock to catch some rays and listen to the lapping of the water, except that he was excited about finishing his new home. On this first day of May, Promise Lodge felt like the absolutely perfect place to be.

When Allen spotted Cyrus and Jonathan—and Gloria— standing outside his tiny home, his euphoria came to an abrupt halt.

He sighed. Even from a distance, his friends' expressions told him Gloria was pestering them about something—or trying to ingratiate herself so one of them would ask her for a date. Allen *almost* felt sorry for her. She would never possess the poise or the common sense and self-control that came as second nature to Phoebe.

Since when are you so high on Phoebe?

Allen laughed, at himself mostly. He kept walking toward his home, figuring to rescue Cyrus and Jonathan. As he passed the cabins closest to the lodge, he winced at Gloria's shrill, insistent voice.

"So, are you guys doing really well at Sam and Simon's nursery?" she was asking them. "Look at all those cars and buggies in their parking lot!"

"We move a lot of inventory," Cyrus responded, edging away from her.

"Matter of fact," Jonathan put in, "we should probably get back to work—"

"Allen!" Gloria called out when she spotted him. Her eyes widened flirtatiously. "Looks like your tiny home business is off and running! Are you getting any orders for them yet?"

Allen sensed an ulterior motive behind Gloria's bright smile and questions. "I'm going to live in this tiny home while I work out the kinks and construct a couple more display models. Why do you ask?"

His direct question startled Gloria into momentary silence. As she looked away, he was afraid she might start crying to play on his sympathy.

"I need a job," she murmured miserably. "Mamm says if I don't come up with an income by the end of the week, she'll move us into a lodge apartment and sell our house. Isn't that the most horrible idea you've ever heard?"

Allen exchanged a questioning glance with Cyrus and Jonathan, who seemed as surprised by Gloria's outburst as he was. "Considering some of the low-rent places I lived while I was going to plumbing and electrical school," he replied calmly, "an apartment in the lodge sounds pretty homey. That aside, I think your *mamm* has to consider all her options."

"*Jah*, we're mighty glad to be renting cabins and to have Rosetta for a landlady," Cyrus put in. "For a bit extra, she includes our meals and our laundry."

"The Kuhns take *gut* care of us, too—like a couple of *maidel* aunts would," Jonathan remarked.

Gloria planted her hands on her slender hips. "Don't you get it?" she demanded. "My own mother is forcing me out of my home unless I can make some money! You could be paying *me* to fix your meals and wash your clothes! Or—or you could put in a *gut* word with Sam and Simon so I could hire on at the nursery."

Jonathan and Cyrus seemed at a loss for a response, so Allen decided to bring this deteriorating conversation to an end.

"What sort of work would you do for the Helmuths, Gloria?" he asked. "Your best bet would be to speak to them yourself—to tell them your qualifications and the experience you've had working with plants and trees, or with customers."

"You guys are all alike!" Gloria blurted out. "Mean and—and *clueless*. You don't care a *fig* about what happens to me, or you'd—you'd take care of me!"

Gloria stalked off across the lawn in another of her snit fits. Allen sighed, feeling sorry for any unsuspecting fellow who might fall for her looks and marry her before he knew what he was getting into. Gloria reminded him of a little terrier—cute, but always yapping about something, and likely to bite anyone who suggested something she didn't agree with.

"That's the first I've heard about Frances wanting to sell her property," he remarked as he followed Gloria's progress up the road. "Unless another family moves to Promise Lodge soon, she might not have much luck with that."

"She's more likely to sell her place than Gloria is to get a job," Jonathan said with a shake of his head. "I'm not even going to mention her idea to Simon or Sam."

"And we all know better than to let her cook or do laundry for us," Cyrus said. He glanced at the little house on wheels, smiling. "We really should get back to work. Just wanted to tell you how cool your new place is looking."

"*Jah*, we'd just stepped inside it when Gloria showed up. We knew better than to get trapped inside with her," Jonathan put in with a knowing nod. "We'll catch you later, Allen."

Allen nodded, watching his two friends jog past the lilac bushes that formed a boundary between the nursery's back parking lot and the yard where the cabins sat. As he screwed the hinges of his door into place, he wondered how Gloria's dilemma could be resolved—but within moments he was envisioning Phoebe instead. She seemed to succeed at every project she undertook, whether it was the painting she'd done inside people's homes and the lodge or establishing a pie shop with Irene. While Gloria created crisis and drama at every turn, Phoebe attracted positive progress.

Phoebe attracts you, *Troyer. What are you going to do about that?*

Allen smiled, humming as he hung the door. If he played his cards right, building portable shelves and accepting his payment in pies might become the happiest arrangement he'd made in a long while.

Chapter Nine

"Look at all these pies we've baked this morning!" Phoebe said as she and Irene placed eight more on the table to cool. "We did fine yesterday, but I think we've perfected our system now. The baking went faster and smoother today—"

"And I'm not nearly as tired as I was yesterday at this time," Irene remarked gratefully. "After lunch, we'll put the plastic domes and labels on these and deliver them—and tomorrow's our day off!"

Phoebe laughed as she slung her arm around Irene's shoulders. "You had a fine idea, taking a day midweek to do something other than bake. Which four pies shall I set aside for Allen?"

Irene studied their selection of fruit pies and cream pies, chuckling. "Truth be told, dear, I think you could bake one of your shoes into a pie and Allen would be gazing at you so intently, he wouldn't notice."

Phoebe's eyes widened. "Are you kidding? When we were kids in school, he didn't say so much as hello to me— didn't even see me," she recalled. "But I know better than to mess with his dessert. At our common meals after church, he's always chosen two slices of pie before he fills his plate."

Irene smiled knowingly. "You're not a schoolgirl anymore, Phoebe," she pointed out. "And you've obviously been paying attention to his habits even though he considered you invisible. But he's got his eye on you now."

Phoebe waved her off. "Nope, trust me. If we were baking bread or helping the Kuhns with their cheese business, he wouldn't have come in yesterday," she insisted. "It's all about the pie."

"Time will tell." Irene stepped closer to the pie-covered table. "I suggest you choose this lattice-top cherry, and this apple with the streusel topping, and—and a lemon meringue, and a gooseberry," she said as she pointed to each one. "That'll give him plenty of choices, far as which pie he keeps and which ones he gives away."

Phoebe carried each of the pies Irene had chosen to the counter. "Before we deliver our pies this afternoon, we should check our supplies," she suggested. "Now that we have a better idea of how much we'll be baking, we can order our ingredients more efficiently."

Irene laughed out loud. "Change the subject all you want, missy," she teased. "Allen's going to find every possible excuse to come into our shop, and I see some romantic buggy rides in your future—among other things."

Phoebe went behind the counter to start cleaning up. "Not if Gloria has anything to say about it!"

Irene shook her head good-naturedly as she began putting flour, sugar, and aluminum pie pans back into the cabinets. When the countertops were spotless and the floor had been swept, they headed to the lodge for lunch with Ruby and Beulah. It felt good to sit down to a macaroni casserole and the green salad the sisters had made before they'd started the day's work in their cheese factory.

"I'll fix our lunch tomorrow," Phoebe offered, "since you ladies were nice enough to look after us as we started our baking business."

"How'd it go today?" Ruby asked as she spooned casserole onto her plate. "Beulah and I could already smell your pies when we fetched milk from Christine's barn first thing this morning."

"We like to start early—and we're finished baking for the day," Irene replied with a satisfied smile. "It'll be fun to see how many of the pies we took in yesterday have sold—"

"And fun to collect our checks from the bulk store and café owners for today's pies!" Phoebe put in with a chuckle. "Irene wins the prize for insisting that we only bake what we've taken orders for."

Beulah nodded as she poured dressing over her salad. "I can see you two make a fine team. It's *gut* when one partner has experience and the other one has youthful exuberance and energy."

"That's why you and I succeed at selling our cheese and honey, sister," Ruby put in with a chuckle. "You're older and wiser, while I'm young and cute."

"*Jah*, something like that!" Beulah crowed as they all shared a good laugh. "That's not gray hair tucked up under your *kapp*, it's tinsel, right?"

After they'd all eaten second helpings, Phoebe washed the dishes. It felt good to be done with her day's main work by one o'clock. By two, she and Irene had put the plastic domes on their pies and were heading to Forest Grove.

When they entered the bulk store, Phoebe was speechless. The display rack was empty! All twenty of their first day's pies had sold, and the owner, Elvin Plank, handed Phoebe a price list along with a check for the fresh pies they'd brought.

"When folks saw that a couple of local Plain gals had made those pies, they flew out the door yesterday!" he said with a big smile. "I'd like you to bring us thirty on Thursday, and I'd better have thirty-five or forty on Friday to get us through Saturday when we're the busiest. I hope it's all right that I've offered you some discounted prices for your fruit and other baking supplies, now that we're doing business together."

Phoebe's eyes widened when she noted the regular retail price of the various ingredients they used, and the lower amounts Elvin had written beside them. "You've deducted ten percent—"

"And over time, that saves us a *bundle*," Irene put in quickly. "This is very generous of you."

Elvin glanced over toward the woman who was running the cash register. "My wife, Dorcas, couldn't resist buying one of your rhubarb pies yesterday. She said it was the best she'd ever tasted—flaky, tender crust and plenty of filling. We'll be recommending them to our customers, believe me."

After she and Irene bought the ingredients for more pies, basking in Dorcas's praise as she checked them out, Phoebe nearly floated out of the store. "Was this an amazing delivery, or what?" she exclaimed. She removed the ten pies they'd baked for the Skylark Café before they loaded their groceries into the back of Irene's van.

"*Amazing* doesn't half cover it," Irene replied. She threw her arms around Phoebe and hugged her tight. "*Denki* for asking me to be your partner, dear. I feel like a new woman, even if I'm a tired woman!"

Phoebe rested her head on Irene's, sighing gratefully. "I couldn't have done any of this without your knowing the people to call and how we should organize our business," she pointed out. "When we get home today, let's figure out how to work more pies into our schedule while we keep making them just as *gut* as folks say they are."

Allen fastened the final bolt that held his foldaway kitchen table to the wall, and then raised and lowered it a couple of times to be sure it worked the way it was supposed to. As with a lot of the features in his tiny home, the table—large enough to seat two—could be tucked away when he wasn't using it. *A place for everything and everything in its place* would be his motto once he moved in, because there wasn't room for anything extra, or for accumulating any clutter.

When he stepped over to his new sink, all thoughts of carpentry and efficient living flew out the kitchen window. Phoebe was crossing the lawn with a double pie carrier in each hand, as though she was heading for an ice cream social or a family gathering. He'd eaten a big noon meal at the Helmuths' house with Cyrus and Jonathan, yet the thought of having four pies delivered made his mouth water in anticipation.

It's not about the pies, and you know it.

Allen blinked. Where were these thoughts about Phoebe coming from? Was she aware of a shift in the atmosphere between them, or was it all in his head? In a grayish-blue dress he'd seen dozens of times, along with the white apron and *kapp* all the girls wore, Phoebe looked the same as ever, yet he saw her differently. He swung his door open as she approached, hoping he didn't appear as adolescent as he suddenly felt.

"*Denki* for remembering my pies," he said. "I should've come over for them so you didn't have to make a special trip."

Phoebe shrugged in that offhand way she had. "I wanted to see your new place. How's it coming?"

"My new table's just the right size for those pies," Allen remarked as she stepped inside with him. He raised the wooden surface and snapped its single leg in place, aware of how Phoebe's presence filled the whole space with a nervous energy he wasn't sure how to handle.

Fortunately, Phoebe was too busy looking around to notice his emotional state. "So you have a built-in microwave and a two-burner electric cooktop?" she asked immediately. "And light fixtures instead of lamps—like you're living English."

Allen smiled at her astute observations. "They run off the solar panels on the roof," he explained. "Bishop Monroe—not to mention my *dat*—will probably call me out on using English conveniences, but I'm not on the grid."

"I suppose you have to have English features in place so your potential customers will see how they fit into the overall home." Phoebe focused on him, smiling. "And, since you've not joined the Old Order, you're still free to live the way you please. I have to admit that electric appliances appeal to me every time I catch a whiff of gas or the pilot light goes out in an oven."

And since you've not joined the Old Order . . .

Allen held her gaze, grateful that her words held no accusation or judgment. It suddenly mattered to him that Phoebe had taken her vows to the Amish church years ago, which made him look like a slacker by comparison. Beyond that, however, he was impressed by her comment about appealing to his potential clientele.

Phoebe placed her pie carriers on the table and looked up. "So you have a loft area, and a very compact ladder leading up to it," she said. "Where will you sleep? Are you getting one of those sofas that makes out into a bed?"

Allen got hot around the collar, even though she hadn't intentionally asked a suggestive question. "Nope," he replied, pointing into an upper corner. "That's a built-in bunk, and the door beside it opens to the clothes closet and the storage area. The bathroom is above us, so the water pipes join with the ones in the kitchen."

"Ah. It takes a special kind of organization—a different way of thinking—to arrange so many features in such a compact space," she murmured with an appreciative nod. "But it'll be a snap to clean!"

Allen laughed. "Not that it'll be spic and span once I'm living here," he said. "I'll have to keep my clothes picked up and my dishes washed a lot better than I do in the cabin. It'll take some retraining of my inner slob, if this is to be a display model customers will be looking at."

Phoebe's brow furrowed but then she smiled again. "*Slob* isn't a word I associate with you, Allen," she said as she removed the metal covers from the pie carriers. "To me, you've always seemed methodical . . . meticulous about your work. Instead of going about plumbing and wiring in a slapdash way, you went to school for your license even though your *dat* disapproved. It was the right thing to do."

Allen's heart thudded so hard that his rib cage vibrated. His entire being thrummed with an unfamiliar intensity. Phoebe had been a few years behind him in school, and he hadn't paid any particular attention to her when they'd been growing up in Coldstream.

She's got your attention now, though, so what're you going to do about it?

He focused on the four aluminum pie pans with their shiny plastic domes—anything to avoid falling headfirst into emotional waters so deep he'd never be able to swim to safety again. "What do we have here?" he asked in a voice that sounded strangely thin.

Was it his imagination, or did Phoebe's smile seem shy now?

"Irene suggested that I bring you a cherry pie, a lemon meringue, an apple with streusel topping—and a gooseberry!" she added with a laugh. "I figured you could keep the one you liked best and give the rest to—"

"I like them all best," he whispered. He stepped closer for a better look at the four pies, which positioned him within inches of the young woman whose presence was making him delirious. "I might have to sample a slice of each one before I decide. Or maybe I need a taste of . . . this."

Ever so slowly, so he didn't scare Phoebe—or himself—Allen moved in for the kiss he needed as surely as he required air and sunshine. Her blue eyes widened but she didn't bolt, didn't appear shocked—didn't do anything but study him intently until moments before his lips met hers. She closed her eyes, sharing one soft, exquisite kiss. He wanted so much more, yet he backed away before his euphoria and hormones pushed him too far—

But Phoebe placed her fingers against his cheek and kissed him again. Her sigh spoke volumes.

When they stepped apart, Allen was grinning like a lovesick fool and Phoebe was breathing as quickly as he was. "I hope I didn't—"

"Oh, but that was nice," she murmured.

Allen squeezed her hand gratefully. "*Jah*, it was."

At twenty-three, he'd kissed plenty of girls, but this time it felt different. He knew better than to rush into any assumptions, or to say anything that would give Phoebe the idea they were a couple—

But that would be all right, wouldn't it? She's not the type to chase after you or make demands. She's got a life of her own—and she's smart, the voice in his head pointed out. *Isn't that why you like her?*

"I should let you get back to your work," Phoebe said

softly. "*Denki* for showing me your little home—and I hope you enjoy whichever pie you keep."

Allen nodded. "I'm thinking the lemon meringue has my name on it, but I could change my mind," he added with a chuckle. "Would it, um, be all right if we went for a walk sometime soon? Or maybe sat out on the dock? Or got a rowboat out of the shed for a ride around Rainbow Lake?"

Phoebe's blue eyes lit up. "I forgot about the boats! How about a trip around the lake tonight? Irene and I are taking the day off tomorrow, so—that would be great fun!"

Allen's heartbeat shot into a full gallop. "Shall we meet at the dock, say, seven thirty? If we row to the far side, we'll have the lake to ourselves without anybody watching us from their houses, *jah*?"

"*Jah*." Phoebe held his gaze for a long, lovely moment. "I didn't see this coming, but—but I'm really glad it did, Allen. See you later."

Allen's pulse was pounding so loudly it drowned out all thoughts of working. He should check the rowboats and choose one that was watertight, and he should clean it out, and there were any number of things he should do to ensure his first date with Phoebe was everything they both hoped it would be. "See you later," he echoed as he opened the door for her. "*Denki* again for bringing my pies."

Phoebe started toward the lodge with her empty pie carriers. When she turned to wave at him, Allen felt deliciously delirious. His mind was already spinning ahead to other ways they might spend time together in the future—

"I saw what you did," a familiar voice accused from the direction of his kitchen window. "You and Phoebe were *kissing*—alone together inside your little house. And the bishop's going to hear about it!"

Scowling, Allen stuck his head out the door as Gloria came around the side of his home. Her face was contorted with jealousy as she tugged her shawl more tightly around her shoulders. "You had no right to spy through my window!" he snapped. "After all the times I've told you I'm not interested in—why are you stalking me, Gloria?"

She stopped in front of him, looking ready to bite him and cry at the same time. "What was I supposed to do?" she demanded. "I came over to ask your advice about looking for a job, and what do I see but you and Phoebe in a lip-lock, as though you might not stop at that!"

"That's an exaggeration and you know it!" he shot back. "Really, Gloria, this is the last straw. What gives you the right—"

"Maybe if you invite *me* inside, I won't need to chat with the bishop," she hinted in a sugary voice. "And maybe you'll forget all about Phoebe."

Allen's jaw dropped. Did Gloria really think he'd fall for that line? "Tell Bishop Monroe whatever you want," he blurted out. "He's likely to say you were sticking your nose where it didn't belong!"

Gloria glared at him. "We'll just *see* what he says, won't we?"

As she pivoted and ran between the trees, Allen sighed. He had a feeling he was going to pay for yelling at Gloria, but he was at wit's end about how to handle her. He hoped she didn't go after Phoebe to repeat the same accusations—

But Phoebe will see through Gloria's bluster and deal with it like the mature young woman she is.

Whatever happened next, he and Phoebe would handle it together. And they would go on about the business of discovering each other, leaving all thought of Gloria far, far behind.

Chapter Ten

Marlin walked beneath the white metal entry sign to Promise Lodge, gazing ahead to the Lehman place as he pulled his loaded cart behind him. He was hoping to catch Frances alone when he delivered the surprise he'd bought her at the Helmuths' nursery, so the sight of her slender figure made him smile. White sheets billowed in the breeze as she hung them on the clothesline that ran between the back of her house and a large tree several yards away.

He hurried past the dairy and the lodge, hoping to catch her before she went inside. As Frances raised the clothesline with a notched pole to keep the sheets from dragging on the ground, Marlin called out, "*Gut* afternoon, Frances! Have you got a minute?"

When she turned toward him, her smile was bright. "Preacher Marlin! It's a lovely day to be outside—and it looks like you've been shopping," she added as she picked up her laundry basket.

Marlin crossed the lawn, pleased that Gloria wasn't nearby. He wasn't avoiding her, because Frances's older daughter was someone with whom he needed to get better acquainted, but he craved a few moments of uninterrupted conversation with her mother. "I stopped by to see how Bernice and Barbara are doing, and to take advantage of the

Helmuths' sale on Knock Out roses," he said. "We had some bushes like these at our home in Iowa. I liked them because they bloom all season without requiring much attention."

"*Jah*, they're not nearly as fussy as old-fashioned roses," Frances agreed as she approached him. "You've chosen a couple of nice, bright colors, too."

"Which do you like the best?" Marlin asked without missing a beat.

Frances glanced at him as though she suspected his ulterior motive. "All of these plants look full and healthy, with lots of blooms," she hedged. "Color-wise, I've always preferred deep pink to red—"

"So the pink ones are for you!" he interrupted excitedly. "Find a sunny spot and I'll plant them for you within the next couple of days, all right?"

Frances's smile turned shy. "Oh, Marlin, that's very kind, but you didn't have to—"

"I didn't," he agreed. "I wanted to."

Her cheeks turned as pink as the rose blooms. She glanced up the road and then toward her kitchen window. "What a lovely gift—especially the planting part," she added with a chuckle. "You realize that when Gloria sees them, she'll fuss about the attention you're paying me."

"She—we—will deal with that," Marlin said as he stepped closer to her. He hoped his next words came out right, because he was out of practice at asking a woman for a date. "What with the full moon, it should be a pleasant evening for a buggy ride—if you'll join me, Frances. Maybe we could wait until Gloria's gone to bed—say, ten or ten thirty?"

Frances chuckled. "Are we slipping out like teenagers who think their parents won't be aware of their comings and goings?"

"We are—this time, anyway," Marlin replied. "I'm also avoiding the static Harley will give me, you see. It'll be nice to escape the prying eyes tonight, but we'll eventually spend time together with our families—if that's something you'd like to do."

When Frances gazed at him full-on, Marlin's heart floated like a butterfly on a breeze. "I'd like it a lot," she murmured. "Folks will talk, because Floyd's only been gone—"

"Folks are already talking," he pointed out gently. "If you're honoring Floyd's memory by remaining in mourning, I'll respect that. I just thought I'd ask."

"And my answer is yes, Marlin."

His pulse raced like a thoroughbred heading toward a finish line. Would Frances give him such a direct answer if, in due time, he asked her to marry him? He'd considered that possibility ever since she'd marched away from the meeting at Monroe's house. "See you tonight, then. Shall I toss gravel at your bedroom window so you'll know I'm here?" he teased.

"I'll be watching for you, listening with my window open," she said, pointing demurely toward an upstairs room on the corner. "Pull around back and I'll be out directly."

Marlin nodded, suddenly high on anticipation. "Where shall I put your rosebushes until I can plant them?"

She gestured toward the front yard. "Let's make a flowerbed in that sunny spot. I've already found some pretty rocks for a border, and now you've provided my plants! *Denki* for your thoughtfulness, Marlin."

After he placed the pink rosebushes where Frances wanted them, Marlin headed up the road toward home. As he passed the Burkholders' pasture, he was pleased to see that his son Lowell and his best friend, Lavern Peterscheim, were putting a couple of Clydesdale yearlings through their paces under the bishop's watchful eye. He was grateful to Monroe for working with the boys, and pleased that Lowell was showing a real aptitude for horsemanship.

At least one of my sons is happy these days, Marlin mused as he continued toward the house he and the younger kids shared with Harley and Minerva. When he spotted Harley walking the sheep pasture's fence line with Queenie, looking for weak spots, he waved—but he got no response. Perhaps his son didn't notice him from such a distance.

And maybe he's still in a snit after quizzing me about whether I was buying rosebushes for Frances when I bought my own, and I said he'd given me a fine idea.

Marlin laughed and kept walking. Harley was entitled to his opinion about Frances, but that wasn't going to stop him from spending time with her. He hadn't felt so young and lighthearted in a long time, and his adult son's objections weren't going to keep him from pursuing a new future.

When Gloria's wails filled the front room and she slammed the door behind her, Frances looked up from dusting the dishes in the china hutch. "What's the matter, sweetie?" she called out as her daughter started up the stairs.

"I'm not your sweetie! I'm *nobody*'s sweetie," Gloria retorted as she yanked off her shawl and tossed it over the newel post at the top of the steps.

Frances sighed as her daughter's footsteps echoed loudly in the upstairs hallway. She closed the hutch's glass door, allowing Gloria's emotional roller coaster to run its course. Was it normal for a young woman of twenty-three to react so vehemently to every perceived provocation? Were Gloria's upheavals fueled by grief for her *dat*, or should Frances seek help for her despairing daughter's tantrums?

As she ascended the stairs, Frances prayed for wisdom and guidance. She sighed about the shawl draped so haphazardly over the newel post, but she left it there—she'd only cause more anxiety if Gloria thought she was getting lectured for leaving her clothes strewn about.

When she entered her daughter's room, Frances nipped her lip. Gloria was at the window, gazing trancelike over the front lawn without really seeing anything. No matter what encouraging words she said, they wouldn't change the fact that none of the young men at Promise Lodge liked Gloria enough to ask her for even one date. Frances did her best to contain her elation about Marlin's rosebushes and invitation to go for a ride with him that evening.

"What can I do to help?" she asked softly. "What can I make you for supper—"

"How can you think of food at a time like this?" Gloria retorted.

Frances allowed a few moments to go by. "What's happened now?"

With an exasperated sigh, her daughter crossed her arms tightly. "After you announced that we'd be moving to the lodge unless we—*I*—came up with some sort of income," she began in a voice that rose with emotion, "I asked Allen and the Helmuth cousins about working at the nursery, and they laughed in my face. So I went back today to see if Allen would help me, and—and he had Phoebe inside his little house, *kissing* her."

Frances barely had time to raise an eyebrow before Gloria started off again.

"That's *wrong*, Mamm!" she blurted with a fresh torrent of tears. "They're not supposed to be alone together that way, and—and when I tell Bishop Monroe about it, I'm going to be sure he calls them up for a kneeling confession at church."

Frances frowned. Young people had been kissing in secret for centuries, no matter what sort of guidelines their elders and their church rules spelled out. "I'm not sure that's a *gut* idea—"

"Why not?" Gloria demanded tearfully. "If we see folks on the path to perdition, we're to lead them away from temptation, ain't so?"

"It would be different if Allen were English, but he's moved here to live closer to his *dat* and his family," Frances pointed out quickly. "Maybe you should examine your motives for tattling on them. Maybe you're upset because *you* want to be with Allen—"

"See there? You're no help at all, taking his side—and Phoebe's," she shot back. "Why don't you just leave me alone?"

Frances sighed. "If Allen had been kissing *you* in his house, you wouldn't have seen a thing wrong with it, ain't so?" she pointed out softly. "And if Phoebe had been watching you through the window, you'd be plenty upset about her spying on you."

"Puh," Gloria said bitterly. "Allen will never be kissing me, so stop rubbing my nose in it! Don't bother making me supper. Leave me be."

Frances turned to go, more brokenhearted for her daughter than Gloria would ever know. She reminded herself that when Mary Kate had fallen victim to an English stranger and borne his baby, she and Floyd had thought their happy family had been shattered—but God had led them to Missouri to start fresh. The Lord had also provided a decent, loving young man in Roman Schwartz to make things right for their younger daughter. Surely the Lord had a plan for Gloria, too . . . even if she tried His patience with her scheming to make love happen her way instead of waiting for it to unfold.

Who could've guessed at the possibilities Marlin is bringing into your life? the happy voice in her head asked.

You did nothing to attract him, yet he's buzzing like a bee around a blossom.

Frances couldn't suppress a giddy smile as she went downstairs to the kitchen. After he'd so thoughtfully brought her those rosebushes, it seemed only right to make a snack to take along on their evening ride. If they were slipping out like a couple of kids, it seemed appropriate to make something quick and crunchy and spur-of-the moment that didn't require utensils—because sometimes the snacks she whipped up from whatever she found in the pantry turned out to be her family's favorites.

She opened the cabinets where she kept her baking staples. Without thinking too much about it, Frances pulled out a bag of chocolate chips, a bag of butterscotch chips, a jar of peanuts, and the canister of raisins. She also grabbed an open box of apple-flavored cereal rings—and laughed when she saw that Gloria had opened a new bag of M&Ms, closed it with a twist tie, and then hidden it behind the flour canister. Frances tossed these ingredients into a large bowl and stirred them together, adding more until the blend looked right. Snack mix wasn't a recipe so much as it was an answer to all the salty, sweet, crunchy, and chewy cravings it would satisfy with a single handful—not that anyone stopped with one.

Frances filled a lidded container to take along on her ride with Marlin, and placed the rest of the mixture in a large jar on the table. Gloria wouldn't make herself a meal—or even a sandwich—after she'd calmed down, but she'd probably soothe her soul with snack mix as soon as she spotted it.

Frances made a bowl of oatmeal for her supper and carried it out to the porch swing. *If you and Marlin start seeing each other, you'll have to cook full meals again*, she realized—and she would enjoy having an appreciative man to cook for again. After she tidied the kitchen and put coffee and water in the percolator—in case Marlin wanted to come in after their ride—she went outside to take the laundry from the clothesline. The sheets smelled like sunshine, and Frances laughed as the breeze blew them around her like hugs.

As she was lifting her laundry basket, she spotted two lithe figures clasping hands, crossing the grassy area around Rainbow Lake. *Allen and Phoebe,* she thought as they headed for the shed where Preacher Amos had tumbled from the roof last fall . . . and where Floyd had called for Jesus to send His angels to catch Amos, but had ended up breaking the preacher's fall with his own body.

That moment had been the beginning of the end for her husband. Since his passing, Frances had told herself not to dwell on it—nor on the fact that angels hadn't appeared. Had Floyd's unusual outburst meant that he was delusional? Or had God ignored his cry for help?

Frances sensed she'd never have an answer for that. There were mysteries that mere mortals weren't meant to understand.

But it's no mystery how Gloria will behave if she spots Allen and Phoebe together, Frances realized with a sigh. She hoped her daughter was still in her bedroom on the front side of the house, where she wouldn't see the young couple out having fun.

As she went inside, the house was blessedly silent. Frances folded the laundry, deciding it was best to go about her household activities as though nothing unusual was going to happen around ten thirty.

Had Gloria fallen asleep? Frances didn't want to risk rousing her by peeking into her room at sunset. She lit a lamp and picked up the yellow blanket she was crocheting for one of the Helmuth babies, steeped in peacefulness marked by the quiet chiming of the mantel clock on the hour and half hour. Through the window she'd opened slightly, she heard the calling of birds as they settled into their nests.

As dusk deepened into a clear evening and the glorious full moon bathed the front room in its light, Frances's crochet hook flew across the rows of the yellow afghan. She smiled as she imagined sitting beside Marlin in his buggy, enjoying his sense of humor and the timbre of his low voice. At nine thirty, she put away her needlework and turned off the lamp. She slipped out of her shoes to climb the stairs, and padded down the hallway to her bedroom.

While changing into a clean dress, Frances dared to consider wearing a color other than black someday soon—a startling thought for an Amish widow so recently bereaved. Was she being wicked, accepting Marlin's invitation to a moonlight ride? Would her neighbors—and her girls—think she'd forgotten Floyd and was no longer honoring his memory? Marlin would understand if she told him she didn't want to slip away with him this evening—

But that would be a lie. You want to go.

Frances blinked. The voice in her head had gotten more insistent lately, and it wasn't necessarily telling her what Bishop Monroe or Preachers Amos and Eli might advise. Hadn't Eve fallen for the serpent in the Garden of Eden because she'd listened to her own yearnings rather than following God's commands?

Marlin's a preacher. You could ask him about this tonight.

She clapped her hand to her mouth when a laugh bubbled up inside her. Frances doubted that matters of religion would be a topic of conversation on their first date—and she resolved to talk to God about these matters when she returned home without anyone being the wiser about her moonlight ride. As she turned out her bedside lamp and raised the sash of the window, Frances realized that it had been years since she'd felt so alive with secret joy.

She stood absolutely still, listening carefully. Did she hear buggy wheels, along with slow hoofbeats that were muffled by the grass? Amish beaux who arrived after dark knew better than to drive a rig on gravel or a paved road if they wished to keep their courting private. Sure enough, Frances spotted a horse and then an open courting buggy—the sort of vehicle young couples used so they would be in full view of passersby, even if they drove into secluded areas on their dates. When Marlin smiled up toward her window in the moonlight, Frances thought she might pass out from the sheer excitement of what she was about to do.

"I'll be right down!" she called softly through her open window.

With her shoes in hand, Frances quickly left her bedroom. She held her breath as she passed Gloria's room in the darkness, reminding herself to remain calm as she descended the wooden stairs—and to step near the railing on the third one down, to keep it from squeaking. At the top of the stairway she paused so her eyes could adjust to the way the moonlight was shining on the bottom few steps while the top ones remained in the shadows.

One, two—step over, she counted slowly, inhaling deeply to control her runaway heartbeat. *Back to the center—four—*

When Frances's foot landed on something soft, she cried out as she slipped and fell backward. Her shoes clattered on the wooden stairs as she instinctively grabbed for the railing—missed it—and then clutched at spindles. The weight of her airborne body wrenched her arm muscles mercilessly, and when she kept slipping, struggling in vain to find a foothold on the stairway, the pain in her hands was so severe, she screamed and let go. Down the steps she bumped, feeling each riser as it bruised her bottom and her left side. When she finally hit the floor of the front room, she landed in a dazed heap.

"Frances? Frances, what happened?" a male voice called from the kitchen.

Frances was too stunned to move. She heard rapid footsteps, and then Marlin was leaning over her with a worried look on his face.

"You fell," he said softly, cradling her head between his hands. "Where's a lamp, so I can see—"

"Mamm? What's going on?"

Frances closed her eyes in abject misery. Her body felt like one huge, throbbing bruise and her hands and arm muscles were on fire—and now Gloria had caught her sneaking out to be with Marlin, who was lighting the lamp beside the recliner.

So much for our secret date. Gloria will never let us live this down.

Chapter Eleven

Marlin returned to Frances's side, setting the lamp a few steps up on the stairway so he could see how badly hurt she might be. "Did you hit your head?" he asked quietly as he held up his hand. "How many fingers do you see?"

Frances blinked rapidly to clear the tears that had sprung to her eyes. "Three," she murmured. "The way I feel—the way I remember it—I must've hit just about everything except my head. It all happened so fast—"

"Mamm, what were you doing?" Gloria demanded. She remained in the shadows at the top of the stairs, clutching her nightgown around her. "Why is Preacher Marlin here at this time of night?"

Marlin bit back an irritated remark. It would be useless to ask Frances's daughter why he'd made it to her mother's side before she had, but as he looked away from Gloria, something in the shadows caught his eye. "Is that your shawl on the steps, Frances? Is that what you slipped on?"

Her brown eyes widened. "Gloria's shawl," she whimpered. "I should've taken it to her room—"

"Gloria's shawl," Marlin repeated, loudly enough for the young woman at the top of the stairs to understand her part in Frances's accident. "Let's figure out what to do, so you won't hurt yourself any further. Don't get up—but as you flex your legs and feet, does anything feel broken?"

Frances pressed her lips together and gingerly did as he suggested. "I think I'm just sore," she replied. "It's my arms and hands that hurt like the dickens, from grabbing the spindles when my feet flew out from under me."

Marlin was watching her face closely. Its paleness told him she was in more pain than she was admitting to. "Shall I call an ambulance?"

"No!" she blurted out stubbornly. "I'll be all right if I can sit up for a minute . . . get my wits about me again."

Her response didn't surprise him. Frances was slim, but she was as hale and hearty as any hardworking woman. "How about if I help you—"

When he slipped an arm beneath Frances's shoulders to help her sit up, her heartrending yelp told him that her arms had indeed sustained some damage. "Can you wiggle your fingers, honey?" he whispered. "Can you move your arms, or does something feel broken? I don't want to touch you any more than I have to—much as I hate saying that," he added in a voice Gloria wouldn't hear.

Frances seemed to understand what he'd meant. She focused on her hands and arms, bravely trying to move them. "Hurts pretty bad," she admitted. "If you'll help me sit up so we can figure out what to do, I promise not to scream or cry."

Marlin's heart rose into his throat. He knew then, beyond the shadow of a doubt, that he loved this woman—and that he would move heaven and earth to restore her to health. Although Amish folks often moved around after dark and in the wee hours without lighting lamps, it was his fault that Frances had been trying to sneak down the stairs to go riding with him.

"Okay, here we go," he said as he knelt to gently pull her close. "On the count of three. One, two—"

With a groan and a grimace, Frances allowed him to lift her torso upright and then perch her on the bottom step. She was blinking rapidly when he released her. Despite the weight of Gloria's accusing gaze bearing down on them, Marlin thumbed away a stray tear.

"I'm taking you to the emergency room," he told her quietly, even as his mind raced around the possible ways to get her there quickly without hurting her further. He looked up to meet Gloria's gaze. "How about if you call Truman—*please*—and ask him to drive us to the nearest hospital."

"But I'm not dressed—"

"Put on a barn coat on your way out to the phone," Marlin cut in quickly. "And please pick up your shawl so you don't fall on it. I'll look the other way."

Gloria's eyes shot him daggers, but after he turned his head her bare feet thumped down the stairs. She went around him and Frances in a whirl of white nightgown and unbound hair before she sprinted toward the kitchen. He held his tongue until he heard the mudroom door close behind her—not that it would help Frances if he expressed his impatience with her daughter.

"Honey, I'm so sorry you fell," Marlin murmured as he sat on the step beside her. "If I'd asked you to come with me in broad daylight, in front of God and everybody—this wouldn't have happened."

Frances had folded her arms against her waist. Her *kapp* was askew and her dress was disheveled, but she was trying to regain control of her emotions. "Don't blame yourself," she murmured. "I went along with your plan to slip out in the night because I was *so* excited about—well, there you have it," she added with a rueful laugh. "*Jah*, Gloria should've put away her shawl, but in my planning for my secret escape with you, I should've realized it might slip onto the stairs and trip me up. So we all share the blame, ain't so?"

Marlin's mouth dropped open. "If I were the one who'd slipped on that shawl, I wouldn't be nearly as patient and kind," he remarked. He inhaled deeply, thinking carefully before he plunged ahead. "*Love* is patient and kind, Frances, so you surely must be made of pure, unadulterated love. Don't argue with me on that," he added quickly.

Her eyes widened, brown and doe-like. "Just this once I'll do as you say, Preacher Marlin—but only because my hands hurt too badly to smack you for ordering me around," she teased.

He smiled. It was a good sign that Frances was joking with him—and that she hadn't clammed up when he'd talked about love, even though it had been a compliment rather than a declaration. Behind them, Gloria entered the kitchen. After a few moments she came into the front room wearing a knee-length barn coat over her nightgown.

"Truman will be here in fifteen minutes," she said as she crunched on a mouthful of something. Gloria studied them as they sat together on the step, as though assessing what this whole situation might mean. "What do you think they'll do to you at the hospital, Mamm? I mean, your arms aren't broken or anything."

Marlin wanted to reprimand Gloria for the sharpness of her tone, but he allowed Frances to answer.

"I don't think they are, but it might be a while before I have full use of them," Frances put in. "You should be prepared to do our cooking and household chores for a while—"

"I'll tell Mary Kate what's happened," Gloria interrupted. "*She*'ll know what to do."

Marlin couldn't believe what he'd just heard. Most Amish daughters of Gloria's age were in full charge of households and raising young children, yet this young lady sounded ready to shove all responsibility for Frances's well-being onto her younger sister's shoulders. "I'll ask Minerva to check on you, too, Frances," he volunteered. "And I'm sure the other women will be happy to assist with whatever needs doing."

"I'm not worried about it." Frances suddenly sounded weary and subdued by her pain. "I just want to find out what's wrong and get back to full strength again soon, so folks won't have to wait on me."

It was after five in the morning—more than six hours after she'd fallen on the stairs—before Frances returned home from her long ordeal at the emergency room. Both of her arms were wrapped snugly in elastic bandages and suspended in slings, so she needed Marlin's help to get out of Truman's truck without falling.

Without somebody's help for the next month, I can't even get dressed or go to the bathroom, she thought despairingly. All because a shawl had slipped from the newel post before she'd gone down the stairs in the dark.

"I'll help you get settled, Frances." Rosetta's voice broke through her gloomy thoughts. "Do you want something to eat—tea and toast, or breakfast, maybe?—before you go to bed?"

Frances sighed. She was so tired she didn't know what she wanted. "I can't thank you enough for coming along, Rosetta," she murmured as they started for the back door of the house with Marlin. "You and Truman were a godsend, and now it's nearly time to get up so Truman can go to his work site, and neither of you have gotten any sleep." She glanced ruefully at Marlin, who opened the door for them. "I kept you out all night, too—and we didn't have any of the fun we were planning."

"I'm just glad I heard you holler when you fell," Marlin put in gently. "Otherwise, I would've assumed you'd changed your mind about our ride and I'd have gone home. But we *will* take that ride," he added softly.

She blinked away tears of exhaustion and pain. As Rosetta lit the kitchen lamp and Marlin pulled out a chair at the table, it was all Frances could do to sit down without bawling like a terrified child. It was one thing to endure the pain of her sprained arms and wrists. It was another thing altogether to be so helplessly dependent upon other people to do every little thing for her. Without the use of her hands, she couldn't eat or bathe or change into her nightgown— or do any of the normal, everyday activities she'd always handled without even thinking about them.

Useless. I feel totally useless.

With a sigh, Frances roused herself from her funk. "You might as well light the burner under the percolator," she told Rosetta. "The least I can do is feed you folks some break- fast and coffee before you go—even if you have to fix it yourselves," she added wearily. "But if you want to go on home and get your day started, I'll understand—"

"I'm staying right here," Rosetta said gently. "I suspect Gloria's still asleep, so I'll at least get some food into your stomach so you can take something for your pain."

Frances was grateful that no one was asking why Gloria hadn't gone along to the hospital—and why her daughter wasn't here in the kitchen helping. Sadly, she suspected that even if her fall hadn't involved a date with Marlin, Gloria wouldn't be much of a caretaker. Some folks just weren't cut out to be mindful of others' personal needs. Even Floyd, if he were still alive, would've soon become frustrated with the level of attention his wife was going to require for the next several weeks.

Marlin, however, sat down beside her at the table and immediately reached for the jar of trail mix. "Want to share some of this?" he asked her as he poured some mix into the jar's lid. "When I see this stuff, I lose all track of how much of it goes into my mouth."

Frances managed a smile as he fetched a spoon. "There's a whole container of it on the counter by the door," she said, nodding toward it. "It was to be our snack for the road, so you might as well take it home with you."

Marlin gazed into her eyes before raising a spoonful of M&Ms, peanuts, raisins, and chocolate chips to her lips. "*Denki*, dear, I'll do that," he said. "After you have a chance to chew this mouthful of *gut* stuff, let's review what they did in the emergency room so I can tell Minerva. Being a midwife, she's the one amongst us with the most medical knowledge."

Nodding, Frances allowed the crunchy peanuts, sweet raisins, and chocolate to soothe her as she chewed. Truman, bless him, was assisting Rosetta with making some toast and eggs to go with the coffee that burbled in the percolator—and he brought over the cup of hot water and the tea bag his wife had prepared.

"I think it's a *gut* idea for my *mamm* and Rosetta's sisters to know what sort of care you'll need, too," Truman suggested. "It's more than Gloria—or any one caretaker—can handle for the length of time you'll be laid up."

Frances swallowed her trail mix, feeling a little better. "The doctor said the muscles of my hands and wrists and arms got sprained when I grabbed the stairway spindles, because the weight of my falling body shot everything out of alignment," she explained. "I'm to rest for the next couple of days, and my arms and wrists need to be on ice for ten minutes at a time. Between icing sessions, I'm to keep everything wrapped—probably for a couple-three weeks. And that's all I remember," she admitted tiredly.

"Your instructions are on these papers we brought home with you," Rosetta said as she held them up. "Let's keep them on the counter where your helpers can see them. You're also to elevate your arms on pillows so the fluid won't gather in them—and if you're not feeling better in a couple days, or if you're feeling a lot more pain, we're to take you back to the doctor."

Frances shook her head sadly. The aroma of frying eggs was reviving her—and when Marlin held the mug of tea to her lips, she was even more aware of how helpless she'd be for weeks to come. She took a grateful sip, trying not to cry.

"We'll get you through this," Marlin whispered. "It'll be everyone's reminder of how we all need each other when the chips are down—"

"Right now my life seems like one big *cow* chip," Frances muttered. "How am I supposed to sit around and do nothing? I can't even mark off the days on the calendar."

Marlin gently laid his hand alongside her cheek. "You might discover the power of prayer in a whole new way," he said softly. "I suspect that once your pain has subsided, you and your helpers will find plenty to chat about. And when you're lying awake in bed, you'll find relief in talking with God. The Frances Lehman I know doesn't let life's burdens grind her down. This, too, shall pass, sweetheart."

A tear trickled down her cheek. Marlin was being much more patient and resourceful than Floyd would've been— but Frances set aside that thought about her late husband.

With all of her present health concerns, she didn't need to add to her emotional burden by dwelling on Floyd's shortcomings.

And who can think about Floyd while Marlin's offering me trail mix with the warmest, kindest brown eyes I've ever seen?

Frances closed her mouth over another spoonful of salty-sweet crunchiness, unable to drop Marlin's gentle gaze. He seemed to be telling her things with his eyes that he didn't want Rosetta and Truman to hear—but her heart understood him perfectly.

And if her heart was on the mend after losing her husband, wouldn't the rest of her eventually heal, too?

Chapter Twelve

After Marlin tended his horse and left the barn, the lamp-light shining in the kitchen window told him Minerva and Harley were starting their day. He braced himself for his son's remarks; reminded himself to remain patient—but honest—if the conversation became confrontational. Even so, he wasn't ready for Harley's remarks as he entered the house.

"Well, well, look what the cat dragged in." Harley was preparing large bottles of formula for the twin lambs that had been orphaned when their mother had died recently. "I hope you're not going to deny that you were out all night with Frances—"

"Matter of fact I was," Marlin cut in tiredly. "After she fell on the steps, we spent the evening and wee hours at the hospital—with Truman and Rosetta," he added purposefully.

"Oh, no! What happened?" Minerva looked up from the pancake batter she was mixing. "Must've been serious, if it took that long to get her taken care of."

Marlin nodded, grateful to hear a sign of support—or at least compassion for Frances—in his daughter-in-law's voice. "She fell on the stairs. Sprained her arms and wrists when she grabbed the stairway spindles as she went down," he explained. "She came home with both her arms in slings, and she'll need help with *everything* for a few weeks—can't even feed or dress herself."

"So you're going to be her nurse?" Harley challenged. "Really, Dat! Why were you sneaking around in the middle of the night at the Lehman place—"

"Because if you'd *known* I was taking Frances for a moonlight ride, you'd have given me the same static you're spewing at me now," Marlin replied tersely. "It won't happen again, because I'll be seeing her in broad daylight—along with all the ladies who'll be helping her for the next few weeks."

Harley let out a sarcastic grunt. "Maybe this was Frances's way of getting your attention. Maybe she took a tumble down the steps so you'd—"

"Harley! Frances is *not* that type of woman—and think about it," Minerva chided him with a fist on her hip. "If both of your arms were bandaged, how would you eat? And you wouldn't tolerate it for five seconds if someone had to help you use the bathroom."

A muffled chuckle made Marlin turn to see Lowell coming into the kitchen, ready for his breakfast—and, at his age, always amused by talk of bodily functions. "Not many folks would want that sort of help," Lowell remarked.

"What sort of help? Who got hurt?" asked Fannie as she came inside with the basket of eggs she'd gathered. She gazed expectantly at everyone in the kitchen, thinking she'd missed out on some juicy gossip.

"Frances fell down the steps and has both her arms in slings," Minerva replied quickly. "She and Gloria are going to need a lot of help, so we'll let the other ladies know about that when we go into the lodge for school today."

Marlin flashed Minerva a grateful smile. Although she'd temporarily diffused Harley's negative attitude, his older son wasn't finished expressing his ongoing grief for his *mamm*. Exhausted as he was, Marlin decided the entire family might as well participate in a discussion about his relationship with Frances.

Because he intended to have one.

"Harley, we've talked about how you feel I've dishonored your mother's memory—or forgotten her altogether—because I've spent some time with Frances," he began. "I'm sorry you feel that way. You probably believe that if I continue to see Frances, I'm doing it to spite *you*, but actually, I've discovered that she's a delightful woman and I intend to court her."

Marlin gazed at his two younger children, gauging their reactions to the topic of conversation. "How do you feel about that, kids?" he asked them softly. "I know you miss your *mamm*—we all do. But as I prepare to move forward with my life, I want you to hear about this from me instead of from the grapevine. I care about your feelings, and your concerns."

Harley poured the warm formula into the big bottles and screwed on the nipple lids with more force than necessary. "I'll say it again, Dat," he fumed. "You have a perfectly *gut* home here with Minerva and me, so you don't need to—"

"Harley, hush." Minerva frowned at him, tilting her head toward the kids to remind him about their sensitive feelings. "It's the right and natural thing for widowed men—especially preachers—to remarry, because the church expects it, and because most men don't do well on their own after—"

"Dat's not on his own!" Harley protested. "He has his three children, and he has you to fix his meals and—"

"If something happens to me, Harley Kurtz, you'll be a basket case before I'm cold in my grave," Minerva shot back, arching her eyebrow. "Let's not pretend you'd live out the rest of your life alone, either—and I wouldn't expect you to."

She tested the griddle, composing her thoughts as she watched drops of water dance on its hot surface. "Your *dat* has a right to some happiness. He's trying to set an example for his family about returning to normal life after his loss," she added in a purposeful tone.

Minerva glanced at Marlin before she began pouring circles of pancake batter on the griddle. "I think it's even better that you're seeing Frances because you *like* her rather than because you *need* her. Lester Lehman's a prime example of what happens to a man who chases after a woman out of desperation."

Fannie's eyes had widened as she followed the conversation. At fourteen, she was at a vulnerable age where the loss of her mother had left a gaping hole in her life. "Would . . . would Frances be moving in with us—if you married her?" she asked hesitantly. "Or would we go to her house?"

Marlin walked over to slip his arm around her slender shoulders. "It's too soon to consider those details—but you've asked a very *gut* question, honey," he assured her. "Whenever a man and a woman remarry, they both have family members to consider. But they're still the parents, and they make the decisions they feel are right. You and Lowell and Gloria are the ones who will be most affected if Frances and I marry."

"But that's gonna be a while yet, ain't so?" Lowell asked. "We'll have some time to adjust to the idea."

"You've got that right, son," Marlin replied. "Nobody's in any hurry—and truth be told, I haven't asked her yet. She turned Lester down flatter than a pancake, so she might say no to me, too."

And you'll be in a world of hurt if she does.

The voice in his head was telling him a truth he already

knew on a gut level. Over the past week, Frances had taken over his imagination and he'd pictured her beside him at the table, and as they rode in his buggy and socialized after church services. He was even carrying on conversations with her in his thoughts.

When she'd fallen, the bun beneath her *kapp* had come loose. He'd yearned to unpin it—a temptation as ripe as forbidden fruit until they were married. His fingers were still itching with the memory of it, and with the need to touch a woman again.

If Frances turns you down, you might as well crawl back into your barrel factory and not come out into the light of day again.

"Well, Frances brings wonderful-*gut* cakes and cookies to our common meals," Lowell remarked with a lopsided grin. "So she can't be all bad—right, Harley?"

Harley rolled his eyes at his younger brother and left the kitchen with a big bottle in each hand.

"She was teaching me to crochet, too," Fannie remarked in a faraway voice. "Ruby tried to show me, but with Frances and me both being left-handed, I was catching on better with her. Might be a long while before she picks up a hook again, by the sound of it."

Marlin let out the breath he didn't realize he'd been holding. It seemed his younger kids had given him their tentative blessing—or at least they hadn't expressed any negativity about Frances. A welcome hint of sunshine peeked through the dark clouds of Harley's attitude.

"Maybe the crochet club—or you and I—could make Frances a prayer shawl," Minerva suggested as she deftly flipped the first batch of pancakes. "We have plenty of time to make baby things for the Helmuths, after all."

"*Jah*, let's do it!" Fannie said as she headed to the mudroom sink with her egg basket. "Frances would crochet—or cook—something for us if we were laid up, after all."

As he took his place at the head of the table, Marlin sent up a quick prayer of thanksgiving. All things considered, the conversation about Frances had gone well—because no matter who might've caught Marlin's eye, Harley would dislike the idea of taking her into the Kurtz family. It was a common thing for widowed men and women to remarry and blend their families, but that didn't mean that all of their children willingly went along with it.

"Here you go, Marlin. Hot off the griddle."

Marlin glanced up into Minerva's pretty face and inhaled the aroma of the big platter of pancakes she'd placed in front of him. "*Denki* for taking such *gut* care of me—and for trying to make Harley see reason," he added with a rueful smile.

Minerva laughed. "I doubt the subject of your remarriage will ever sit well with him, but we have to help him understand your situation—and move beyond his grief for his mother," she said. "I can imagine Essie up in heaven shaking her head about her boy's attitude—and shaking her finger at him!"

"She did that a lot when he was growing up—and she also warmed the seat of his pants a time or two when his contrary streak got out of control," Marlin recalled fondly. "It'll all work out. God always sees to that."

"God is *gut*—every day, and to every one of us," Minerva agreed.

When she and Fannie and Lowell joined him at the table, Marlin bowed his head. He had so much to be thankful for, and so many people at Promise Lodge who were helping him move beyond the heartache of losing his dear Essie.

As his eyes remained closed in prayer, Essie's sweet face

filled his soul—and she was smiling at him. Marlin smiled back at her, feeling blessed by her presence.

When Frances awoke from a fitful few hours of sleep, it took her a moment to recall why her arms hurt so much—and why they were propped on a pillow on her chest. The clock on the dresser chimed softly.

It's only seven o'clock and I have no idea how I'm going to make it through this day, she thought wearily. *When a horse is this badly hurt, we put it out of its misery.*

It took all her strength to swing her legs to the side of the bed and sit up. A wave of dizziness and pain made her suck in her breath. How was she supposed to get through this ordeal?

"Gloria?" she called out. Surely her daughter was out of bed by now.

After several moments of listening to the absolute silence of the house, Frances began to worry. "Gloria?" she cried out again. "Gloria, please! I need your help!"

After a few moments, Frances heard footsteps. Was she hallucinating, or had Gloria rushed past her bedroom door? She was trying to figure out how to leave the room without falling—and how to use the toilet without being able to lift her nightgown—when her daughter appeared in the doorway.

"Now that you're awake, I'll go fetch Mary Kate," Gloria said with a frantic expression on her face. "I didn't want to leave until you knew where I was going."

Before Frances could get another word out, her daughter's rapid footsteps were echoing in the stairwell.

When Frances sagged against the pillows in her lap, pain flared like wildfire in her arms. How was she supposed to unwrap her bandages when her hands were bound up?

Surely it was time to put her arms on ice—and how was she supposed to do that? She couldn't expect her friends to stay with her and keep track of the time she had her arms on ice and the time she was to wait before she iced them again and—and all of those other bothersome procedures listed on the papers she'd brought home.

Like a giant snake, despair wrapped itself around her heart and squeezed until she could hardly breathe. Her bladder felt way too full.

"Frances? I'm coming upstairs," a vaguely familiar voice called out. "Don't worry—I'll be right there."

Don't worry. Wasn't that what the angels in the Bible said when they appeared to humans?

No, they said "fear not." But it seems like the same thing.

Frances also recalled that in spite of the angels' reassurance, the people in those Bible stories felt frightened anyway—so she burst into tears. She'd been brave at the emergency room and while Marlin, Rosetta, and Truman had been helping her, but now that the floodgates had opened, she was wailing like a terrified child—and she had a feeling she couldn't stop anytime soon.

"Oh, Frances, I'm sorry this has happened," the voice said as it reached her doorway. "I've come to help you, dear. I bet everything hurts, doesn't it?"

Through her tears, Frances saw Minerva, the midwife. When the young woman sat down beside her on the bed and gently took her in her arms, Frances cried even harder. "I—I'm sorry I'm such a—*mess*," she wailed.

"We'll make it better," Minerva said as she carefully kept her arms around Frances. "When I got here, Gloria was dashing out the back way like a ghost was chasing her. What was that about?"

Frances took a deep breath, trying to control her sobs. "She went for her sister. Gloria's a *gut* girl and she tries so hard—but she was never meant to be a nurse," she added with a shaky laugh.

"A lot of folks aren't," Minerva remarked. "We'll figure out other ways Gloria can help you, but meanwhile shall we head down the hall to the bathroom?"

Relief flooded Frances's soul. Minerva was a midwife, so she was no stranger to helping women through all manner of messy, embarrassing situations. As Marlin's daughter-in-law helped her to her feet, Frances felt a thin ray of hope shining through the gloom that had overwhelmed her.

It took a lot longer than usual for such ordinary chores as using the toilet and getting her face washed and her teeth brushed, but by the time Frances emerged from the bathroom, she'd regained control over her emotions.

"Your instructions from the emergency room say you're to rest in bed for a day or two so you don't overdo it," Minerva said as she helped Frances back to the bedroom. "It'll be easier if you stay in your nightgown today while we begin your ice therapy—so we won't have to move your arms to get you into a dress," she pointed out.

Frances grimaced. "*Jah*, it was no picnic for poor Rosetta, getting me out of my dress and into this gown," she recalled. "The way I was yelping, it's no wonder Gloria wants no part of taking care of me."

"I found Rosetta's note on the counter, along with the supply of ice packs she stashed in your freezer," Minerva said, settling Frances into the armchair near the bed. "How about if I bring those upstairs with some of the breakfast casserole the Kuhns tucked into your oven—and some coffee. Caffeine is a pain reliever and a stimulant, and I think we could both use some."

As Frances waited for Minerva to return, she pondered what she'd just heard. Rosetta had left a note in the kitchen?

And Ruby and Beulah had already brought over food? How had word of her injury gotten around the neighborhood in the few hours since she'd returned home?

How much did Marlin tell his family about my fall? This is all so embarrassing. . . .

When Minerva carried a breakfast tray and a tote bag filled with frozen ice blocks into her room, another question occurred to Frances. "Aren't you supposed to be with the scholars at the lodge? Who's teaching classes if you're here tending to me?"

The young brunette smiled as she held up a forkful of hash brown potatoes smothered with ham and cheese. "After Marlin told us what happened to you, I stopped by the bishop's house on my way here," she explained. "Laura was delighted to cover the lessons today, and Christine offered to start up a list of ladies who'll bring food and come in to help you. Even if Gloria was *gut* at caretaking, your ice therapy and general care are a lot for any one person to take on."

Frances swallowed her food with a forlorn sigh. "I despise being such a burden."

"The way most of our friends see it," Minerva put in gently, "it's a chance to come over and visit with you, Frances. Everyone helped when Amos was laid up after his fall—and we'll be there for Bernice and Barbara when they've given birth. So don't worry," she repeated. "We all take our turns at caring and being cared for."

By the time she'd eaten her breakfast and sipped a cup of coffee, Frances felt better. When Mary Kate entered the bedroom, her smile lifted Frances's spirits, as well. She slipped behind the armchair to gently hug her mother.

"Roman's downstairs with little David—but I don't guess you want a lot of men around while you're in your nightie," Mary Kate observed. She gave her mother a mystified smile.

"Gloria tells me you slipped on the stairs while you were sneaking out with Preacher Marlin last night. You never cease to amaze me, Mamm!" she added with a laugh. "How can I help?"

"You're just in time to see how to unwrap your *mamm*'s arms so she can put them on ice to keep the swelling down," Minerva replied as she loosened the end of the stretchy bandage on Frances's arm. "Gloria should watch this procedure, too."

Mary Kate shook her head. "She's mad as a hornet about Mamm seeing Marlin," she said. "Maybe we should have Gloria help in other ways—so she won't leave Mamm on ice too long or rewrap her arms so tight that she cuts off the circulation."

Minerva nodded. "How about if you bring a couple of old, thin bath towels, so your *mamm*'s skin won't be directly against the ice packs?"

When Mary Kate left on her errand, Frances lowered her voice. "See what I mean about Gloria? Are members of your family that upset about Marlin wanting to see me?"

Minerva blessed Frances with a radiant smile. "*I* think it's a fine idea for you two to have fun together, and Fannie and Lowell seem okay with it, too. Harley's a pickle of a different color, though—angry at his *dat* for seeming to forget about his *mamm*," she replied in a pensive tone. "You can't please everybody, so you might as well please yourselves, ain't so?"

After her daughter returned, Frances sat in the armchair with carefully arranged ice packs in towels beneath her arms and on top of them. After ten minutes, Mary Kate gently rewrapped Frances's arms as Minerva coached her. Frances still didn't enjoy feeling so helpless, but at least she knew she'd be getting the proper care.

Mary Kate glanced at the clock. "I'll be back in time to

give you your next ice treatment," she said. "I'm going home to stick some things in a duffel so David and I can stay here with you."

"But you have things to do!" Frances protested. "There's no need for you to—"

"*Jah*, there is. You're my *mamm*—and you certainly looked after me when I was carrying David and when I delivered him," Mary Kate insisted. "So don't give me any more arguments. Besides, David can be your resident ray of sunshine."

Mary Kate had only been gone a few minutes when Frances heard other footsteps and voices in the stairwell. Christine, Mattie, Irene, and Ruby peeked into the room, flashing their friendly smiles.

"My word, you're all wrapped up like a mummy!" Mattie said as she came to put her arm around Frances. "And I'm sure you don't like it one little bit."

"We, um, heard you've *fallen* for Marlin," Irene put in with a chuckle. "*Gut* for you!"

"Looks like a great time to get our licks in while you can't smack us!" Ruby teased. "But we bring you *gut* tidings of great joy from the lodge—"

"And a list of the days and times your helpers are going to be here," Christine put in as she waved a sheet of paper. "We left our pans of food downstairs with Gloria. She seemed so relieved to see us, I suspect she'll be happy to answer the door and handle the housework and warm the food your friends bring over."

Frances shared a smile with Minerva. "We all have our purpose, and I think we just found one for Gloria," she said with a chuckle. "Oh, but it's *gut* to see your cheerful faces, ladies. I feel better already."

Chapter Thirteen

"We've got the last of today's pies in the oven," Irene remarked as she started putting away the baking supplies. "How do you think our first week in business has gone, Phoebe?"

Phoebe smiled brightly. "Who knew that we'd do so incredibly well? We've doubled the number of pies we baked on Monday—and between the Skylark Café and the bulk store, we'll deliver sixty pies this afternoon!"

"Just my opinion, but I don't want to take on any other outlets," Irene said. "What with also baking Allen's pies and the occasional pies our neighbors might ask for, I think we've hit our limit. I don't want our quality to suffer because we're in a hurry or we're feeling tired by week's end."

"I agree completely. There's more to life than pie and work, after all."

Irene smiled to herself. Her joints and muscles were complaining about all the time she'd spent on her feet this week, but Phoebe was hinting that other activities were occupying her time—as well they should.

"If that means you're seeing Allen, I'm glad to hear it," she said gently. "When he invited the Kuhns and me to look at his tiny home after supper last night, I was impressed with his workmanship. I couldn't live in such a small space, but Allen puts every square inch to *gut* use."

"His tiny home is amazing," Phoebe agreed. "He's hearing from folks who want to come look at it and possibly order one, so he'll be building a tiny home that's a different design next week."

Irene nodded as she closed the big canisters that held their sugar, shortening, and other ingredients. Mattie, Christine, and the Kuhns were keeping their excitement under their *kapps*, but they were extremely pleased that Allen and Phoebe were dating—it meant two of their fine young people would most likely stay at Promise Lodge. When the door swung open, Irene couldn't help but notice that Allen's brown eyes immediately settled on Phoebe and took on a shine as hot as coffee.

"It's not even noon and you two are cleaning up for the day?" he teased. He held up a wooden object that resembled a plant stand—except it had a handle on the top and square shelves inside its four legs. "I've made sixteen of these to fit inside your van, Irene, and they'll hold six pies apiece. Will that work?"

Phoebe brushed flour from her apron as she went to look at the carrier Allen had brought. "That's ninety-six pies," she replied quickly. "We'll be delivering sixty this afternoon, so we'll only have to put four or five pies in each unit. That'll make them easier for us to lift down from the van and carry—don't you think, Irene?"

Irene laughed. "You did that math so fast my head's spinning, but *jah*, they'll work beautifully. You made those carriers quickly, Allen, and we appreciate your help."

Allen nodded as his gaze returned to the young woman a few feet away from him. "I don't have them painted yet, but I can do that this weekend. Is it all right if I use up some leftover paint my *dat*'s got?"

"That'll be perfect." Phoebe set the carrier near the table where the pies were cooling. "So this hinged side opens, and you slide the pies onto the shelves, and then you fasten the side, *jah*? I like the raised edges on the shelves, too— so the pies won't slide out while the van's moving!"

Irene watched, fascinated, as Phoebe put six pies on the shelves, fastened the hinged side, and picked up the carrier. "That's the best thing since sliced bread!" she said. "Will you and I be able to lift a loaded carrier out of the van?"

"Oh, *jah*—easy peasy. It's not as heavy as it looks," Phoebe replied as she raised it to shoulder level. "Think of how many trips it'll save us, carrying five or six pies into the store instead of two. Allen, you're a genius!"

The young man's cheeks flushed. "No, it's you ladies who fit that description. Looks like Promise Lodge Pies is already an amazing success." He studied the array of warm pies on the table. "Which one of these is mine?"

"Any pie you like," Irene replied quickly. "The bulk store and the café have specified the number of pies they want for the weekend, but not the fillings—and we baked five extra today."

"Lucky me," Allen said as his hands closed around a lattice-topped pie with deep pink filling. "Today, rhubarb's my favorite—but I can't go wrong. Soon as I take this to my cabin, I'll bring the rest of your carriers so you can load them whenever you're ready." With a wink, he whispered something that made Phoebe nod and nip her lip in anticipation.

Irene returned to redding up the baking area so the young folks wouldn't think she was eavesdropping. But then, she didn't need to. Their shining eyes told her they'd be seeing each other again soon, and that Mattie and Christine would probably be planning a wedding before the end of summer.

* * *

Marlin closed his *Ausbund* as the final note of the last hymn lingered in Bishop Monroe's front room, bringing them to the end of the church service. He was eager to eat and then slip out to visit Frances, who hadn't attended church because she was to continue her frequent ice treatments for a few more days.

After Monroe delivered the benediction, he made announcements, as usual. "We're keeping Frances Lehman in our prayers as she recuperates from a nasty fall," he reminded everyone as he gazed at both sides of the room. "Mary Kate and Gloria are assisting her, as are most of our ladies, and I'm sure she'd welcome other visitors later in the week. Whenever your life seems difficult, consider how limited Frances feels while both of her arms are wrapped and confined in slings."

Folks nodded sympathetically, murmuring to one another. On this warm spring day, everyone appeared ready to leave the pew benches and set up for the common meal, which would be held picnic-style in the bishop's backyard.

"Are there other announcements?" Monroe asked.

Within a heartbeat, Gloria stood up. "*Jah*, I've got one, Bishop," she said in a voice that thrummed with purpose. "If Phoebe and Allen haven't confessed to you about wandering from the straight and narrow, we should hear their story right now. They were alone together in Allen's tiny home—and they were *kissing*."

Marlin winced. He'd hoped that Gloria's role in her mother's accident would quell her tendency to point her finger at others, but it seemed she was even more determined to call them out.

Beside him on the preachers' bench, Preacher Amos chuckled. "That's really *gut* news about my son," he murmured, "but apparently Gloria's still not taking the hint."

Bishop Monroe raised his hand to silence the chatter that filled the room. "Gloria, you probably feel you're doing the right thing by pointing this out," he said, "but proper procedure calls for notifying one of the preachers or me if you have a grievance against someone in the congregation. Then we can discuss the matter in private, rather than demanding an on-the-spot confession."

Gloria's eyes widened as though she believed the bishop had missed her point. Before she could protest, however, Allen rose from his place near the back of the men's side.

"Phoebe and I did nothing out of line—nothing that courting couples haven't done for centuries," he insisted in an irritated tone. "And besides, with you peering through the window at us, we weren't exactly alone, ain't so?"

As laughter filled the room, the color rose in Gloria's face. Before she could speak again, however, Phoebe stood up. She appeared a bit embarrassed, but determined to set the record straight.

"If I understand the timing correctly, after Allen told you to mind your own business, you rushed past me on your way home," Phoebe recounted. "Is that when you threw off your shawl? And then your poor mother fell on it going down the stairs that evening?"

"She wouldn't have fallen if she and Preacher Marlin weren't sneaking out like thieves in the night!" Gloria blurted.

"*Jah*," Lester chimed in vehemently, "and that whole episode wouldn't have happened—and Frances would be just fine—if I'd been there with her. But *no*, you preachers wouldn't let me take care of her, like I wanted to."

"Whoa! Things are getting out of hand." Bishop Monroe held up both hands to stop anyone else from throwing a conversational rock. He focused on Gloria and then Lester. "I'd like to speak to you two when we break for dinner. Maybe

I'm calling it wrong, but I think the green-eyed monster has gotten ahold of you—and we need to straighten that out."

"Green-eyed monster?" Gloria demanded. "All I said was—"

"Jealousy," Marlin put in as he, too, felt compelled to stand up. "As Allen pointed out, there's nothing going on that courting couples haven't engaged in forever—nothing improper. I'm sorry you and Lester are unhappy about my feelings for your *mamm*, Gloria," he added in a gentler tone, "but your accusations only make me more inclined to shower Frances with the happiness she deserves."

"Amen!" said one of the women near the front. "What a man."

When Bishop Monroe turned to give him a purposeful gaze, Marlin sat down. His heart was thundering like the hooves of a runaway horse, yet he felt exhilarated. He'd probably spoken too soon—all the more reason to visit Frances before she heard about his feelings secondhand. But he'd told the truth.

Preacher Amos elbowed him playfully. "Stick to your guns," he whispered. "Monroe and I can tell you how a second marriage gives a man a whole new lease on life."

"Congratulations, Marlin," Preacher Eli said as he leaned in front of Amos. The other folks in the big room were standing up, and their chatter covered what he was saying. "You called it right, saying that Lester and Gloria are acting out of jealousy. They deserve our prayers and encouragement, *jah*—but sometimes a verbal kick in the pants is what's really called for."

Marlin's elation swelled as other men of the congregation flashed him a thumbs-up or clapped him on the back while they were carrying pew benches outside to the tables in the yard. As he watched the women taking out platters of sliced ham and bowls of salad, he missed seeing Frances among them.

Beneath a tree several yards away from the tables, Monroe stood with Lester and Gloria. His hands rested on their shoulders and his expression was earnest as he spoke with them. Marlin sensed that neither of them felt sorry for the remarks they'd made—but at least Gloria had been gently, publicly put in her place, so she had nowhere else to take her objections to Allen and Phoebe's courting. Lester, too, had exhausted his opportunities to protest the way Frances had rejected him, so maybe he would finally accept the situation for what it was.

"I think you and Frances make a lovely couple." A light voice drew Marlin out of his thoughts.

"*Jah*, and *you* deserve some happiness, too," an identical voice chimed in from his other side.

Marlin thought he might be experiencing double vision, because Barbara and Bernice Helmuth were smiling at him with identical dimples, freckled faces, and brown hair tucked under their white *kapps*. Because his daughter-in-law—the midwife—had given him some clues, however, he could tell the twins apart.

"Barbara, I appreciate your support," he said to the young woman who was somewhat larger because she was carrying twins. "That goes for you, too, Bernice, and I wish you both all the joy and excitement of having your first children. The day Harley was born was a game-changer. When Fannie and Lowell came along, they each made my world spin in a different direction, too."

"We're getting pretty excited," Bernice admitted as she grasped her sister's hand. "By this time next month, we'll probably be holding our babies."

"*Jah*, and we're mighty glad you brought Minerva to Missouri with you," Barbara put in. "Now we can have home deliveries, rather than having to go to the hospital amongst strangers. It means a lot."

By the time he'd eaten a quick meal, Marlin had heard encouraging words from nearly everyone in the crowd—except for Harley, Lester, and Gloria, of course. Even if folks hadn't been happy for him and Frances, he would've felt right about expressing his feelings for her publicly. He sensed that several knowing gazes were following him as he walked down the hill toward the Lehman place, which was all the more reason to speak with Frances on this fine, sunny day—before anyone else did.

No more sneaking around like thieves in the night, he thought with a chuckle. *But after Frances is feeling better, we need to take that moonlight ride we missed.*

As he approached her house, he was pleased to see Frances sitting on the front porch with Mary Kate. He waved—and then realized she was unable to wave back. Marlin jogged across the front yard, energized by the way she watched him. "How are you today, Frances?" he called out as he went up the walk to the house.

"I think I'll survive!" she replied pertly. "I've got two of the best nurses in the business."

"I can see that. Hello, Mary Kate," he said as he smiled at Frances's daughter. He grinned at the sturdy little boy who was lying on a blanket on the porch floor. "David, you're growing like a weed, son. What are you, about three now?" he teased.

David let out a hoot and wiggled all over as he gripped Marlin's finger.

"He was five months as of last week," Frances replied proudly.

On an impulse, Marlin sat down on the porch floor and lifted the little guy into his lap. When two blue eyes focused on him, he felt a *ping*, like Cupid's arrow hitting his heart. If he and Frances were wed, David would be his grandson . . . his first grandchild—because even if Minerva and Harley announced they were expecting, Marlin sensed he and Frances would be married before their baby was born.

All the more reason to state your case, the voice in his head insisted. *What've you got to lose?*

Everything, if she won't marry me, a strident voice from his heart replied. *So don't mess up. And don't rush her.*

"I just finished Mamm's ice treatment. Now David's ready for his dinner and maybe a nap," Mary Kate said, drawing Marlin from his thoughts. "I'm pretty sure Mamm's ready for some conversation other than mine, too, as I've run out of gossip."

Marlin laughed, grateful that Frances's daughter was giving them some time to catch up with each other. After Mary Kate took David inside, he stood up and gazed out into the yard to gather his thoughts. "The rosebushes look like they're doing well," he remarked.

"Roman's watering them until I'm able—and they're in the perfect spot where I can enjoy them from the swing. *Denki* for bringing them, Marlin." Frances raised her eyebrows and lowered her voice. "Now come sit by me while we have a few minutes!"

Marlin wanted to cheer—wanted to hug her exuberantly—but he refrained from doing anything that might hurt her arms. He eased onto the swing, grinning like a kid with his first girlfriend. "Feeling better?"

"You're *gut* medicine," Frances replied. "How was church? I hope I'll be able to go in two weeks when we worship next."

Marlin pondered her question. Should he tell her about Gloria's outburst—and Lester's?

Why ruin Frances's fine mood? Stick with the news that makes a positive difference.

To put his words into proper context, he would need to mention that Gloria had started an avalanche of accusations when she'd called out Phoebe and Allen—but who knew how much time he had before Mary Kate came back? Marlin held Frances's gaze as he carefully slipped his arm along the back of the swing behind her. It felt good to sit so close to her as the swing rocked with a comforting creak of its chain.

"I may have spoken out of turn—and too soon," Marlin began softly. "When Monroe asked if anyone had announcements, and Gloria started an onslaught of remarks by demanding a public confession from Allen and Phoebe, I referred to you and me as a courting couple."

Marlin watched Frances's eyes widen. Were her lips twitching to keep her from bursting into a smile, or was she trying not to cry?

He cleared his throat. "Considering how we've not even gone on our first date, I may have put the cart before the horse, so I wanted you to hear it from me before anyone else broke the news," he explained. "I don't want to be like Lester and force my feelings—or my presence—on you, Frances."

When she looked away, a smile was tugging at her lips. "Marlin, you couldn't be like Lester if you tried—or at least not like Lester as he's behaving now, which is so unlike the man we knew before he lost his wife," she added sadly. Her sudden smile was like sunshine bursting through rain clouds. "So we're courting, are we? What did folks say about *that*?"

"What do *you* say about it?" Marlin fired back. "I suppose *no* is one of the potential answers."

Frances didn't waver. "But *yes* would open up a whole new world for us, wouldn't it?" she asked softly. "Yes—to the courting part, anyway. If things work out between us, though, you'll have to ask me all those other big questions up front and proper before you tell everyone else what comes next."

Marlin laughed out loud, and when Frances joined him he felt ten feet tall. "We may have to do something about your sassy mouth, Miss Frances," he teased her. And then the sight of her mouth made him go very still.

He swallowed hard. Was it unfair to kiss her when she couldn't push him away or put her arms around him? Marlin leaned toward her, unable to breathe—unable to think of anything except the need for a kiss that made his lips burn before they even touched hers.

When Frances closed her eyes, she wasn't submitting to him. She was saying *yes* in yet another important way that made Marlin realize she was different from any other woman he'd ever met. When she'd been Bishop Floyd's wife, Frances had given no hint of how funny and direct she could be—or how refreshing.

But she wasn't another man's wife now. And she was letting him court her . . . letting him kiss her, so softly and sweetly that he lost all sense of time and place.

"Oh my," Marlin murmured when they eased apart. "Now we've gone and started something."

"*Jah*, we have," Frances agreed. "My hands are itching to hold yours."

Yearning—and sympathy—shot through him as he looked at her wrapped arms in their slings. "I—I want to hold you, but I'm afraid I'll hurt you," he admitted.

"Well, we have that to look forward to, ain't so?" she asked with a little laugh. "As tingly as I feel, that must surely mean that my circulation's improved and that I'll be healing faster, don't you think?"

Marlin kissed her again. "I like the sound of that."

For several moments they sat contentedly in the swing, swaying forward and back in companionable silence. Marlin couldn't recall the last time he'd felt so exhilarated and energized, ready to take on a new relationship and everything it might bring along with it. It was completely different, marrying for the second time, because—as he and Frances were both finding out—they had children to consider, and two households, and memories from their first marriages that might affect their expectations.

"What did Gloria say about Allen and Phoebe?" Frances asked softly. "Did she make *gut* on her promise to tell the bishop she saw them kissing?"

"*Jah*, and she demanded that they confess before the congregation. Allen and Phoebe fired right back, saying she'd spied on them—and that Gloria had tossed her shawl on the stairs or you wouldn't have slipped on it," Marlin recounted cautiously. "Then Lester claimed you wouldn't have fallen if Monroe and we preachers had allowed him to take care of you, because you wouldn't have been sneaking down the stairs in the dark to be with *me*. It was turning into a circus until the bishop called a halt and requested a private chat with Lester and Gloria."

"Oh my," Frances said with a sigh. "Maybe it's best I wasn't there today."

"You're probably right. I'm hoping now that Gloria's aired her grievance, she'll let it go," he put in matter-of-factly. "Although I suppose I'd see it differently if I were Gloria— or Lester."

Frances gazed into the distance, shaking her head. "If only some nice young man would take a fancy to her—and if only she'd know when to quit making a pest of herself," she murmured. "I—I don't know how to help her. She doesn't listen to anything I suggest."

"That's how it works for most folks her age," Marlin pointed out. "Young people think their parents can't possibly understand their trials and tribulations—or else they feel we're hopelessly out of touch with reality."

He considered his next thoughts, and then expressed them. "For Harley's part, he thinks I'm being selfish—sweeping his mother's memory under the rug to the point of betraying her. He has no idea how much I miss Essie every day, or how I've controlled my grieving so as not to burden him with it."

Frances nodded. "As the parent, you feel you need to be strong."

"And how are you doing with that part?" Marlin asked. "Your emotions are still pretty raw, only a couple of months beyond Floyd's passing."

Frances gazed toward the rosebushes in the yard. "When I . . . when I went to the cemetery last week," she began softly, "I got the feeling that Floyd's spirit was no longer there because I no longer *needed* him to be there for me. But instead of feeling like he'd abandoned me, I felt at peace—as though he'd moved on, so I should, too. Does that make any sense?"

Marlin considered her response as a preacher and a counselor, rather than as a man come courting. "It took me a long time to reach that point after Essie passed, maybe because her death was sudden and unexpected," he replied. "Everybody's different. Grief can be like a boomerang—when you think you've tossed it off and you're doing fine, it comes flying back at you."

"It does," Frances agreed. "I knew Floyd was failing after

his fall with Amos, so I had a chance to prepare myself, I suppose. My I ask how your Essie died?"

Her question caused such an unexpected welling up of sadness, Marlin had to wait a moment for it to pass. "She went in her sleep. I woke up late that morning and realized something was terribly wrong when she didn't open her eyes," he replied with a hitch in his voice. "When the doctor offered to do an autopsy, I didn't see the point of cutting her open because it wouldn't bring her back—and we believe God has His reasons for calling folks home."

"*Jah*, He does. I'm sorry for your loss, Marlin," Frances murmured. "*Denki* for answering my painful question."

I'm sorry for your loss. It was the customary remark folks made when they didn't know what else to say, yet coming from Frances, the words sounded compassionate and sincere—perhaps because she knew about such a loss herself. When Marlin sighed, her sigh mingled with his as though their thoughts and feelings were already in sync.

Once again he knew he loved this woman, for reasons that probably wouldn't make sense to anyone but himself.

When has love ever made any sense? Is there a rule book—a checklist—you're supposed to follow?

The voice in his head made him smile and want to change to a lighter topic of conversation—although dipping into a soul's darkness, walking through the valley of the shadow, was a necessary part of coming into the light again. "I'm glad we can talk this way, Frances. I don't want to rush you into this courtship thing," Marlin said softly, "so I'm depending on you to tell me if I go too fast."

Her face lit up with mischief. "What's the point of the rides at the amusement park if you don't go fast?" she teased him. "It's *gut* to stretch beyond your comfort zone from time to time, ain't so?"

"I love you—for saying that," he blurted, as though qualifying the statement excused his outburst. "And here I go, racing ahead when I've said I'd give you time—"

"Ah, but the best words—the true words—usually come flying out because our heart knows things that our mind hasn't yet caught up to." Frances held his gaze with eyes as warm and dark as melted chocolate. "Maybe your family should come over and have dinner with mine, to give everybody a taste of what it'll mean to blend together. That way, we're right out in the open where all the kids can see us," she added in a knowing tone.

"Are you sure you wouldn't rather come to our place, since you can't be in the kitchen—"

"No," she interrupted with a purposeful shake of her head. "I'm more comfortable here at home, considering I may need to slip away for an ice treatment while you're all here. Mary Kate's perfectly capable of fixing the dishes we've always liked best—and how about if Minerva brings a few things that you folks enjoy?" she asked with a lift in her voice. "It'll be a potluck, of sorts. Nobody has to do all the cooking, and everyone will have familiar food on the table."

The screen door swung open and Mary Kate winked at them. "I think that's a fine idea, Mamm," she said. "I've put David down for his nap, so how about if we talk about our family get-together while I give you your next ice treatment?"

Marlin laughed, grateful that Frances's daughter had overheard them with such an open mind. "Maybe I should leave, so you won't feel odd with me looking on—"

"Stay right where you are," Frances insisted. "It's easier if I sit in the wicker chair, so its arms can support me. If you keep talking to me, my ten-minute treatment will seem a lot shorter. The clock stops when my arms are bundled up in towels and ice packs."

It did Marlin good to watch Mary Kate care for her mother—and to see the way Frances moved from the swing to the wicker chair without any assistance. After the upsetting evening she'd had at the emergency room earlier in the week, he was pleased to witness Frances's recovery. Her resilience and bright ideas were further proof that she wanted to spend time with him as much as he craved her company.

When Mary Kate had finished arranging the towels and ice packs around Frances's arms, he thought it would be a good time to address an issue she might see differently than her older sister did.

"Mary Kate, are you concerned that your *mamm* might be taking to me on the rebound—perhaps too soon after your *dat*'s passing?" he asked softly. He watched her face closely for signs that her reply didn't express her true feelings.

When Frances appeared ready to answer for her, Mary Kate gently squeezed her shoulder. "I suppose to a lot of folks, it seems she hasn't had long enough to mourn Dat's loss," she said in a thoughtful tone. "But once he refused medical help—and had a stroke—we all knew how the story would end. We had some time to prepare ourselves."

Marlin nodded. Although Mary Kate was the younger daughter, she was far more mature than Gloria, and she did what needed to be done without hesitation.

"Mamm has always known her own mind. She's found ways to follow her heart and God's leading even when my *dat* the bishop might not've agreed with her," she added with a chuckle. "Roman and I want her to be happy and to feel loved. As long as you give Mamm a chance to change her mind if your courtship starts feeling uncomfortable, we're *gut* with it. Folks had their doubts about Roman and me, too, after all."

"You two have made a fine home for baby David," Frances said softly. "Once again, it was Gloria who protested the relationship, because she wanted Roman for herself."

Marlin nodded, satisfied that Mary Kate's response was honest—and pleased that she'd discussed the matter with her husband. Now that his courtship of Frances was public knowledge, he preferred that folks express their opinions in ways that were constructive rather than contentious.

The rest of the afternoon passed quickly, and Marlin didn't leave the Lehmans' porch until it was nearly time to tend the horses. "When shall we Kurtzes come for dinner, ladies?" he asked as he rose from the swing.

After a moment, Frances replied, "Let's make it Thursday evening after Roman's finished his milking. I have an appointment with the doctor on Wednesday—so maybe after that, I won't have to fit my day around my ice treatments."

Marlin nodded. "Need a ride? I can take you."

"*Denki*, but we've got her covered," Mary Kate replied. "Our neighbors have taken *gut* care of us, bringing meals and such, so Roman and I will drive her to the clinic. It'll get us out to do a bit of shopping."

Marlin could understand why a trip to town would be something to look forward to, after a week of being confined by Frances's treatments. "I'll let my clan know to be on their best behavior for Thursday night," Marlin teased. "Meanwhile, I'll be checking on you—so let me know how I can help."

As he strolled up the hill toward home, Marlin whistled cheerfully. Was it his imagination, or was the sun shining more brightly on trees that seemed greener? The surface of Rainbow Lake glistened like a million diamonds in the distance, and all around him the property of Promise Lodge reflected the wonder and glory of God's creation.

Lord, I'm so glad You led my family here, he prayed as he gazed up at the brilliant blue sky. In the west, the sun dipped toward the far horizon, yet to Marlin it felt like the dawning of a new era rather than a sunset that marked the day's end. When he glanced back at the Lehman place, the three new rosebushes were bathed in rays of sunlight.

Best investment I ever made.

Chapter Fourteen

Allen sat at his new kitchen table Thursday afternoon, jotting down the details of the next two tiny homes he would build. An English fellow who lived near Forest Grove had brought along a friend, and by the time they'd examined Allen's home and had studied the three different floor plans he'd shown them, they were reaching for their checkbooks.

Gazing at the two checks he'd received as down payments, Allen felt giddy. It was a day to celebrate, and he knew just how he wanted to do it. He glanced at his handwritten contracts, thinking he probably needed a more official-looking order form. This time, however, the two fellows' checks had sealed the deals, and they'd been satisfied with the handwritten spec sheets he'd signed for them.

He had money, he had materials to order, he had work to do—and his business was off and running. For a few moments, Allen sat at his table grinning like a kid who'd won the grand prize at the county fair.

As he headed across the lawn toward the little bakery, he was bubbling with the news he wanted to share with Phoebe before anyone else heard about it. Aromas of pastry and sweet fruit filled the air. The bakery windows were open, so he could hear Irene and Phoebe talking.

"What about that gal who left her number with Elvin at

the bulk store?" Irene was asking. "If we say yes, we'll be baking another two dozen pies tomorrow."

"Or, we could make an exception to our schedule and whip them up early on Saturday morning," Phoebe responded. "It's a one-time event—and maybe we should allow for special orders."

"Maybe we need to ask your sister or Deborah to help when we take on more baking than we'd planned," Irene fired back.

Allen smiled as he grasped the handle of the screen door. It sounded as though Promise Lodge Pies was already more of a success than its proprietors had bargained for.

"We can ask them, if you'd like," Phoebe replied. "Or, if you don't want to work on Saturday morning, I could bake them myself—but it won't be the same without you to make the fillings."

"*Jah*, but even if you do the baking, we're also talking about another delivery."

As Allen stepped inside, Irene was sweeping the floor behind the counter while Phoebe placed plastic domes over the pies that covered the big worktable out front. "I'll be heading into town on Saturday," he put in. "If I can use your new shelves to take the pies in my wagon, you won't have to drive, Irene."

"Allen! You're just in time to pick out your pie," Phoebe said with a lilt in her voice.

"You want to join me on that trip to town Saturday?" he asked quickly. "I uh, sold two tiny homes today, so I've got some celebrating to do."

"*Two* of them?" Phoebe rushed over to hug him. "You've had a wonderful-*gut* day!"

"Congratulations, Allen!" Irene called out. When she came out from behind the counter she was beaming at him.

"So tell me—what sort of person buys a tiny home? Or *two* of them?"

Allen laughed, pleased with their reactions. "Two different fellows ordered them," he clarified. "One guy saw my ad on the Forest Grove mercantile's bulletin board, and he brought a buddy along to check me out. They've got hobby farms, and they want to put small, affordable homes on them—"

"What's a hobby farm?" Irene interrupted with a puzzled frown. "Every farmer I know considers his farm a full-time job—a lifestyle rather than a hobby."

Allen nodded at her observation. "Seems a lot of English folks want to get out of the city, so they buy five or ten acres to live on and then they commute to their jobs," he explained. "These two guys are probably in their late twenties or early thirties, not married. They don't want big houses to maintain, or pricey mortgages hanging over their heads for years."

"Ah." Irene nodded and began sweeping the main room. "If they have jobs in town, you'll most likely get paid in regular installments rather than having to wait for them to sell some cows or crops."

Allen smiled. Irene was every bit as sharp as her younger business partner. "Actually, they gave me down payments today. Within the next couple of weeks they'll pay me half the price we agreed on, with the final balances coming due when I've finished their homes."

"Wow," Phoebe murmured as she continued putting domes on pies. "They must be pretty well off, if they don't have to go to the bank for loans."

Allen stepped closer to the table—and Phoebe—to decide which pie he wanted. "I don't know how they're coming up with the money—that's their business," he added as he studied the rhubarb, gooseberry, and cherry pies. "I don't want to get involved with banks and loan processes—all that paperwork and legal stuff—so I'm just accepting cash. These guys seemed happy to pay for my Amish craftsman-ship and to seal the deal with a handshake."

"That's how everybody used to do business," Irene re-marked as she hung up her broom. She held Allen's gaze from across the bakery. "It's one thing for Phoebe and me to sell our pies for cash, but a house is another matter alto-gether. May I ask how much money we're talking about? You can tell me to mind my own business if you want to," she added quickly.

Allen laughed at her jovial tone. "It depends on the square footage and the grade of materials a buyer wants, along with the detail work," he replied. "Neither of these guys wants high-dollar walnut or anything much fancier than I have in my place. The smaller house is going to run about twenty-five thousand, and I'm charging thirty-five thousand for the one that'll be about half again as big as mine."

Phoebe's smile made Allen's insides shimmer. "Well then, Mr. Moneybags," she teased as she tweaked his cheek, "maybe Irene and I should ask you for a loan to expand our bakery!"

"Don't listen to her!" Irene said with a laugh. "We've al-ready reached the work limit we've set for ourselves. Too much of a *gut* thing can cause trouble, especially if you take on more work than you can do your best on."

"I agree completely," Allen said. "I'm marking a wall calendar to allot the time I'll need for each house I've agreed to build, so folks will know they may have to wait a while for their homes. I'm allowing myself time for the finer things of life—like this fabulous gooseberry pie," he said as he picked it up.

"And time to spend with you," he whispered to Phoebe.

Her blush made Allen desperate to kiss her, but he didn't want Irene watching them.

"It'll be *gut* to go into town on Saturday, away from spying eyes," she murmured.

When Phoebe turned back toward Irene, her expression was caring yet resolute. "Let's call that lady and say her pies will be at the store on Saturday afternoon. If you want, you can mix up the fillings tomorrow. Laura and I can bake the pies while you're making our delivery tomorrow, or on Saturday morning."

Irene appeared satisfied with these options as she removed her fruit-smeared apron. "We can make that work," she agreed. "I'll fetch the van so we can load today's delivery."

Allen watched Irene through the window as she walked briskly toward the lodge building. "She reminds me of my *mamm*," he remarked wistfully. "Works hard, figures things out—and tolerates *me*."

Phoebe nodded. "Your *mamm* put up with a lot when you were growing up," she recalled fondly. "I bet she's glad you've got me keeping track of you these days. Now that you've sold a couple of tiny homes, I can picture her looking down from heaven with a proud smile on her face."

Allen's heart lurched. There was no replacing Mamm—no filling the hole she'd left in his and his *dat*'s lives when she'd died a few years ago—yet things suddenly seemed to be falling into place for him. He *liked* having Phoebe keep track of him, more than he would've admitted even a week ago.

"How about if we leave around twelve on Saturday?" Allen asked. "We'll bank my checks and deliver your pies, and then we'll have the rest of the day and all evening to do something fun."

"We will," Phoebe agreed. "I can't wait."

Chapter Fifteen

As Mary Kate went to answer the front door Thursday evening, Frances fidgeted in a kitchen chair. What had possessed her to invite supper guests when she couldn't help her girls prepare the meal? What if Harley railed about his *dat*'s relationship with her, and the evening became unbearably tense? *Who could've guessed how difficult it is to handle your doubts when you can't use your hands?*

For the umpteenth time, Frances sighed loudly. Ordinarily she'd be setting the table or stirring the meat mixture or filling water glasses—anything to keep busy and release some of her nervous energy before Marlin and his family arrived for their first meal together. But she was stuck sitting at the table.

She felt utterly useless.

Gloria was at the stove, apprehensive for her own reasons. "I'll turn up the fire under this sloppy joe mix so it'll be nice and hot—"

"No!" Frances yelped. "We don't want it to stick to the pan and scorch."

Her daughter shot her a wounded look. "I was only trying to help, Mamm."

Frances hung her head. "I'm sorry I jumped at you, Gloria," she muttered. "It's *me* I'm frustrated with—"

"Wow, something smells really *gut* in here!" Lowell said as he entered the kitchen. As always, his cowlicks sprang to life when he removed his straw hat, and his slender face was alight with a lopsided smile. "Lavern and I worked Bishop Monroe's Clydesdales all afternoon, so I could eat a horse!"

"You *are* a horse—the backside of one," Fannie teased softly as she followed him toward the table. She was carrying a gift bag with bright pink tissue paper sticking out of it, and she shyly approached Frances. "Minerva and I made you a little something. I—we hope you'll like it."

Frances's eyes widened. "Oh, but you didn't have to— well, you'll have to show it to me, dear," she added apologetically. "With my arms in these slings, I can't reach into your sack."

"Hope it's all right that we brought a layered salad and a jelly doughnut cake," Minerva said as she carried a glass bowl to the table. "Nothing fancy."

"It's not like we made anything special, either," Gloria put in as she replaced the skillet's lid with a loud *clang*. "I wouldn't have chosen sloppy joes for a company supper, but it's what Mamm wanted."

Frances bit back a grimace at her daughter's tone, and she noticed Minerva's and Fannie's bewildered expressions, too. Lowell was all smiles, however.

"Sloppy joes? Awesome!" he crowed as his sister removed the tissue paper and lifted something from the gift sack. "I'll probably eat four or five!"

Fannie eyed Lowell as though he'd come from another planet. Then she focused on Frances again. "It's a prayer shawl," she explained as she unfolded it. "We hope it makes you feel better while you recuperate, Frances."

Frances nearly burst into tears. "What a thoughtful surprise. That shade of green reminds me of grass under a shade tree in the summertime," she said as she gazed at the triangular-shaped shawl. "You've made my day, Fannie and Minerva. I—I feel better already."

"Glad to hear it," Marlin said as he entered the kitchen with Mary Kate and Harley. He set a covered cake carrier on the countertop and came over to stand by Frances. "What did the doctor say at your check-up yesterday? Looks like you got the wrappings off your arms—that's progress!"

"*Jah*, I suppose," Frances replied with a shake of her head. "I wasn't any too happy when he told me I'll be slung up for another couple of weeks, doing more time on ice, before I can start physical therapy. I go back again next week."

Marlin perched on the chair closest to her, smiling tenderly. "I'm sorry it'll be a while before your arms are free," he murmured. "I'd go absolutely insane if I couldn't use my hands and arms. We'll all help you through this, Frances."

"Patience is a virtue—but right now, it's not one of mine," she muttered. She managed a smile for Gloria and the guests gathered in her kitchen. "It's nice to have company around my table again. We'll eat as soon as Roman's back from checking a cow that's ready to calve."

"I'll give him a hand," Harley said, quickly heading for the mudroom door.

Frances was glad the two young men would have each other for company this evening. When Mary Kate and Minerva set a basket of sandwich buns, a fruit salad, and a large baked bean casserole on the table, Frances realized she'd left Fannie hanging. "How about if you put that pretty shawl on the arm of the recliner for me, so I won't get food on it?" she asked. "*Denki* again for such a lovely gift, Fannie. You've come a long way with your crocheting!"

The girl's face turned a pretty shade of peach as she took the shawl and the gift bag to the front room. Marlin leaned closer and lowered his voice.

"She worked like a trouper on that shawl—had to rip out some stitches and redo them a few times," he murmured. "I suspect she was praying for patience as much as she was praying for you while she was making it."

"I wasn't much help with Fannie's left-handed technique," Minerva put in as she filled the water glasses. "But she kept at it."

"It was awfully sweet of her to think of me," Frances said in a voice that was tight with emotion. "I can use every prayer she stitched into that shawl."

When Roman and Harley returned from the barn, everyone chose a place to sit. After Marlin scooted Frances closer to the table, he looked to her for guidance and she nodded toward the place to her right, at the head where Floyd had always sat. The arrangement seemed normal, to her way of thinking—even if Gloria's expression soured as they all bowed in prayer. The whole point of the meal was for everyone to sample what it might be like to become a family, after all.

Lowell dove into the food with an enthusiasm that made everyone relax. He immediately loaded two buns with the sauced hamburger mixture, and his first big bite left traces of tomato sauce around his mouth.

"Sooo *gut*," he murmured. Lowell's smile as he took a second huge bite won Frances's heart.

"Slow down, son. Your food's not going anywhere without you," Marlin teased gently. "Frances will think Minerva never feeds you."

Mary Kate sat to Frances's left, placing food on both of their plates. Once again Frances felt helpless. She regretted that she was like another baby Mary Kate had to feed—because David's high chair was at her other side. Roman was an old hand at helping with his son's meals, however . . . and

Frances enjoyed watching everyone eating, even though she couldn't pick up her own sandwich.

She blinked when a forkful of bun and fragrant meat appeared in front of her. Marlin was holding it, smiling as he waited for her to close her mouth around it.

As she accepted the bite he offered, her gaze locked into his. For a moment it seemed that only the two of them sat at the table—until Frances quickly sat back to chew. Could the kids hear her hammering heartbeat? Did they find it offensive that Marlin had fed her with his own fork?

"See there?" Mary Kate murmured as she offered Frances a bite of the lettuce salad. "Being unable to use your hands might have some unexpected advantages, *jah*?"

"No washing dishes, for example," Minerva remarked with a chuckle.

When Marlin held up another bite of her sandwich, Frances saw Harley's expression stiffen—but he held his tongue. She suspected his *dat* had given him a pep talk before they'd arrived. Frances knew exactly how difficult it was for a parent to ask an adult child for cooperation.

"Mamm, really!" Gloria blurted out. "Do we have to watch him *feed* you? That's gross."

Frances almost choked on the bite she'd just taken. She could've pointed out that during the nine days she'd been unable to use her arms, she would've starved had she waited for Gloria's assistance with her food—but she didn't want to fill the sudden silence in the kitchen with such a negative remark.

Lowell's second sandwich stopped several inches short of his mouth. His face fell as he struggled with his emotions. "Why are you so mean to your *mamm*, Gloria?" he asked in a voice wracked with adolescent agony. "I—I would give *anything* to have my mother back."

Frances swallowed hard, deeply touched by the boy's

words. Minerva and Fannie blinked back sudden tears, while Harley looked off into the distance. Mary Kate appeared ready to reprimand her sister, but instead she gripped the table's edge when thoughts of her father made her face pucker.

After several intensely uncomfortable moments, Marlin cleared his throat. "We all miss her, son," he murmured. "And Gloria's family is missing her *dat*, too. When a loss hits us this hard, sometimes our grief makes us cry, and sometimes we lash out in our pain. It's part of the process, and we're blessed to have our families and friends so we don't have to go through it alone."

The kitchen seemed to sigh around them as the *tick-tick-tick* of the battery clock marked off several more seconds of tight silence. Gloria rose from her chair, her face stricken. "Excuse me," she muttered before she hurried from the room.

Little David squawked, calling to her, but Gloria didn't turn around. After a few moments, the slamming of a bedroom door above them was a sharp reminder of how Gloria felt about having the Kurtzes in her home . . . and about the relationship that was blossoming between the two parents at the table. Frances wondered what she, as the hostess, could say to alleviate the tension that lingered in the kitchen.

She leaned forward to smile at Lowell, who appeared flummoxed by the drama he'd unwittingly caused. "I'm sorry you've lost your *mamm*, Lowell—and I'm really glad you like the sloppy joes," she added in the most upbeat voice she could muster. "Comfort food feeds our souls as much as it feeds our bodies. For me, sloppy joes are all about the soft buns and the tangy sauce—the sloppier, the better."

Lowell smiled, repositioning his sandwich in his hand.

"*Jah*, I'll probably be needing another napkin. I'm always the messiest one at the table."

"We all find a way to distinguish ourselves," Fannie put in with a playful roll of her eyes.

The meal continued without any further outbursts. With a helper on either side of her, Frances made her way through all the food on her plate. When Minerva cut her a slice of the jelly doughnut cake, Frances wished she'd saved more room for dessert.

"Oh, but this looks scrumptious," she said as she inhaled the cake's aroma. It had been baked in a tube pan, so it resembled a doughnut on the platter—and it was veined with a thick layer of strawberry preserves. "If you served this for breakfast, I suspect everyone at the table would be happy."

Minerva's eyes lit up with laughter. "Now you're giving them ideas!" she remarked as she glanced at Harley and Lowell. "Luckily, it's a very simple recipe, and you can use whatever sort of jam you have handy."

"Simple things are best," Marlin said softly. He cut a forkful of cake and held it in front of Frances. "I hope you like it, dear. When Bernice brought this to the common meal last Sunday, I think every man there asked his wife to get the recipe—right, Harley?"

The size of the slab Harley was cutting for himself answered his *dat*'s question. "It's become my mission to try this cake with a different kind of jam each time, so I can decide which is my favorite," the younger man said with a chuckle. "I'm thinking leftover pie filling would work, too."

"Probably so," Frances agreed. When she closed her mouth over her first bite of cake, she was immediately struck by its dense, moist texture—and the way Marlin was watching her enjoy it.

"Every bit as *gut* as it looks," Frances murmured as she held his gaze.

His lips twitched. "*Jah*, you are, sweetheart," he mouthed, so no one else could hear him.

Her heart hung suspended in her chest as his words sank into her lonely soul. Floyd had been a wonderful husband, but he hadn't been particularly romantic with his words even when they were a young courting couple. Hearing so many endearments and receiving such close attention from Marlin gave Frances a heady rush—a sense that she could do no wrong, and that she couldn't possibly dissuade him from falling for her.

How was a woman in her late forties supposed to handle a handsome man who waxed romantic even in front of their family members?

"I didn't mean to embarrass you," Marlin said as he gave her another bite of cake. "Would you like me to be quiet—or to leave?"

Mary Kate and Marlin's kids could hear what he was saying—and they had to be aware of the way he was gazing so directly at her—but Frances dismissed her qualms about having so many witnesses. "Stay," she whispered. She told herself her voice sounded husky from swallowing a big mouthful of cake.

Marlin's smile made her heart flutter wildly. Somehow she got through the rest of her dessert without floating up off her chair.

When she'd finished eating, the girls shooed her out into the front room so they could clean up the dishes. Harley, Lowell, and Roman left to check on the cow again, so Marlin accompanied Frances to the sofa. He picked up the prayer shawl Fannie had crocheted and gently draped it around her shoulders before he sat down beside her.

"That color of green suits you," he said, sounding a little preoccupied.

"It's a lovely gift, and I'll treasure it always," Frances said as she admired it. "I—I wish I could touch it."

Marlin glanced over his shoulder toward the kitchen. Then he focused on her again. "I'm sorry Gloria feels so uncomfortable—and I can still see the resentment in Harley's eyes," he began in a tight voice. "I'm determined that we can make this work, Frances, but if you'd rather not pursue a relationship, or if you think we should wait a while, I'll understand."

"Let's stick with it," she blurted without missing a beat. "I see this time of my life as an opportunity to make a whole new future for myself—regardless of how Gloria feels about it," she added quickly. "I'd like you to be a part of that future, Marlin. You make me *happy*."

She thought he might cry, but then his handsome face lit up like the sun in the western sky. "I'm so glad you said that, Frances. Even after I lost Essie, I still believed in the healing power of love. And I believe in *us*."

Frances blinked. He sounded so sure, so purposeful, as though they were already a couple deeply in love—but then, the statements she'd made had sounded just as committed and sincere, hadn't they?

This is moving too fast, the voice in her head warned. *You barely know this man, yet you sound ready to hitch up with him.*

"We—we can't stop believing," Frances murmured despite her misgivings. "It's our belief in things seen and unseen that gets us through the tough times—but don't assume that I'm handling my situation very well, Marlin. For me, the most difficult thing in the world is feeling so *useless*."

He settled back against the sofa, pondering what she'd said. Frances found it heartening that Marlin didn't feel the need to fill the silence with talk, or to have the last word. As she sat mere inches away from him, however, she was acutely aware that she couldn't touch him or hold his hand—and that there was no easy, proper way for him to touch her, either.

Chapter Sixteen

"Is that a new shirt, Troyer?" Cyrus called through the window of the nearest cabin. He let out a loud wolf whistle.

"Is that cologne I smell?" Jonathan immediately teased from the adjacent cabin.

Allen glanced toward the Helmuth cousins, who remained blurs behind the dark screens of the windows he was passing. Most likely, they'd taken their lunch break and would soon head back to the nursery to help Simon and Sam with the brisk Saturday business. "What's wrong with a clean shirt and cologne?" he shot back at them. "I don't see the girls beating down your doors, begging for dates."

"Ohhh, listen to the big shot, going into town to deposit his checks and impress his woman," Cyrus heckled good-naturedly.

"Guess I'd better have my Sunday best clothes at the ready," Jonathan put in, "because we'll be going to a wedding any day now!"

Allen waved them off, walking more quickly toward the barn at his *dat*'s place, where he kept his horses and the wagon. It was a perfect May afternoon, and he was determined that nothing would keep him from having a wonderful time with Phoebe. As she stepped out of the bakery carrying a loaded pie shelf, he waved at her. Her smile told him that she, too, was ready to enjoy their time in Forest Grove.

By the time Allen had hitched his horse to the wagon and driven to the bakery, Phoebe and her sister were standing alongside the loaded wooden pie shelves awaiting his arrival.

"We had an extra chocolate pie when we finished our baking," Laura piped up, "so we left it in the fridge for you."

Allen smiled. Phoebe wouldn't have had ingredients left over by accident after she'd made the pies for her special order, so she'd been thinking of him all along. "I'll put that pie to *gut* use," he assured them. "Since I've been collecting my two pies per week, not a scrap has gone to waste."

In short order, Allen lifted the pie carriers into the wagon. As he arranged them near the wagon seat and secured them with bungee cords, he inhaled the aromas of pastry and sweet fruit. He wondered how early Phoebe and her sister had begun their baking, to have two dozen pies baked and cool enough to transport by noon—but he didn't ask. No reason to talk about work when he wanted to focus on having fun.

He helped Phoebe onto the wagon seat and then vaulted up beside her. "See you later!" he said to Laura as he urged his horse forward.

"Have a really *gut* time!" she called after them.

Allen waited until he'd driven under the white metal Promise Lodge sign before he shifted closer to Phoebe. "How was your morning? Was it a lot different baking with your sister than with Irene?"

Phoebe settled comfortably near him, rocking against him as the wagon swayed. "Laura and I have baked together since we were little girls," she pointed out. "Irene's more organized when she's cooking the fillings for several pies at a time—but that comes with years of experience." She tweaked the short sleeve of his shirt. "Is this new? It's a nice shade of green."

"Mattie felt sorry for me after she did my laundry a couple of times," he admitted. "I suspect you'll soon see Dat wearing a shirt made from the same fabric."

"I've already noticed the dress Mattie made from it— along with dresses for Barbara and Bernice. Now the five of you can dress alike when you go someplace," she teased.

"Not gonna happen!" Allen said with a laugh. "But it's nice that Mattie looks after me."

"Somebody needs to."

Allen's heart lurched at the underlying hint beneath Phoebe's words. He let it go unanswered, however, because they had the rest of this fine Saturday to discuss anything and everything—or to just enjoy each other's company without getting serious. "I was framing in a new tiny home this morning, so I didn't eat lunch," he said as they turned onto the state highway. "Where's a *gut* place to catch a bite after we deliver your pies?"

Phoebe fiddled with a string of her *kapp* as she considered her answer. Her cornflower blue dress accentuated the color of her eyes when she focused on him. "The Skylark Café looks to be a great place, if the aromas coming from the kitchen are any indication," she replied. "I've never eaten at any of the restaurants in Forest Grove, so wherever we go will be a new adventure."

Allen nodded. "The Skylark makes a great Philly steak sandwich, and probably the best roast beef, mashed potatoes, and gravy I've had in a long while."

"As *gut* as what Ruby and Beulah make?" Phoebe challenged.

"Seriously *gut*," he replied. "But don't tell them I said that."

Her face lit up with a childlike smile. "Let's eat there," she suggested. "Truth be told, Laura and I rose before the chickens this morning, and the baby-sized pies we made ourselves from scraps and filling are long gone. I'm ready for some real food."

After they arrived in Forest Grove, it took a while to find a parking spot because lots of shoppers were in town tending to their Saturday errands. Allen felt a deep sense of satisfaction as he followed Phoebe into the store with two carriers full of pies, because the lady who'd ordered them was talking with the manager as they walked in.

"Oh, you must be Phoebe! It's so good to meet you!" she exclaimed. She was probably forty, dressed in denim with a flowery scarf at her neck, and her enthusiasm was contagious. "We're serving some of your pies for dessert at our employee in-service day, and the rest will be auctioned off as part of a fund-raiser for the new homeless shelter in Cloverdale."

Allen enjoyed watching Phoebe chat with the lady before handing her the bill for the two dozen pies. "Where are you parked?" she asked as she accepted the woman's cash. "We could carry your pies to your car instead of unloading them here."

"That would be wonderful," the woman agreed. "My van's at the side of the store—and I took out the back seats so the pies can travel flat."

Once again Allen was impressed by Phoebe's practicality, and her willingness to provide services that would endear her to her customers. After he'd helped load the pies into the big van, they stood aside as the woman backed out of her parking spot.

"You and your husband have a great day!" she called out through her window.

Phoebe returned her wave, a satisfied smile on her face. "That was an interesting assumption," she said.

Allen wasn't sure how to respond as he and Phoebe gathered the wooden pie carriers. "I thought it was even more interesting that a homeless shelter's being opened in Cloverdale," he hedged as he started toward his wagon. "I can't imagine folks in this rural area being homeless—as though they have no families to help them when they fall on hard times."

"I suspect it's an English problem," Phoebe said in a troubled tone. "We Plain folks wouldn't dream of letting someone live on the streets—not that anyone we know would venture so far from their family and friends."

Allen walked to the street ahead of her, watching for traffic. "When I was going to school in the city, I became more aware of the homeless population," he recalled with a sad shake of his head. "I can see how Old Order *rumspringa* kids trying to make it in the English world might fall through the social safety net—especially if they're too proud or stubborn to return home."

When they reached the wagon, Phoebe gazed at him. "I'm glad that didn't happen to you, Allen—glad your sisters stayed in touch with you after the family left Missouri," she murmured. "It makes a *gut* case for joining the church, where you'll always *belong.*"

He didn't challenge her sheltered worldview, but after his stint in the city, training to become a licensed plumber and electrician, Allen knew he could've lived comfortably among the English. For Phoebe—and most Plain girls—however, church membership was a given rather than a decision. "Are you hinting that I need to take my vows?" he asked, keeping his tone light.

Her face turned an endearing shade of pink. "Well, that

day has to come, *jah*?" she asked softly. "How else can you marry and have a family? How else will you claim your salvation, if you don't join the Old Order?"

Once again, Allen could refute her reasoning—the mind-set she'd been born into and had never questioned. He didn't reveal his doubts about religion, however, just as he dodged the topic of marriage.

"When the time's right, we do what we're supposed to do," he replied. When she handed him a carrier, he gently closed his hands over hers. "And right now, we need to get my checks to the bank before it closes, *jah*? Then we'll eat some lunch at the Skylark and enjoy the rest of this perfect day."

The angle of Phoebe's eyebrow told him she wasn't fin-ished with their current conversation, but that she'd go along with him—for now.

After they'd loaded the pie carriers and made his deposit, Allen enjoyed watching Phoebe exclaim over the Skylark's pot roast and mashed potatoes, which were smothered in rich beef gravy. He felt ten feet tall when she slipped her hand around his elbow as they strolled the main street of Forest Grove. It felt good to move among folks they didn't know, free from eyes and ears that wanted to follow every little detail of their time together. When he suggested a ride around the countryside, Phoebe immediately agreed.

"Except for coming into Forest Grove to shop, I haven't gotten away from Promise Lodge since we left Coldstream," she admitted as the wagon rolled past the businesses toward the county highway. She gave his elbow a hesitant squeeze. "Compared to you, I've led a pretty limited life."

Allen shrugged. "Moving a couple states away from your family—or going to trade school—aren't *gut* choices for a lot of Plain folks," he remarked, "but as a preacher's kid, I was feeling pretty pinched when I finished at our school in Coldstream. Dat didn't expect me to take up his carpentry business, but he did insist that I figure out how to make a living. Girls don't get that kind of pressure."

"*Jah*, but I could've been more adventurous," Phoebe countered. "I could've lived with some of Mamm's cousins in southern Missouri as a mother's helper or a caregiver— just to see more of the world. But I didn't even consider it."

"Seems to me you jumped into your new business with both feet, which is a lot more adventure than most Amish girls take on," Allen pointed out. "Buying your own supplies and committing to delivery dates is a lot different from working in somebody else's store or looking after somebody's kids."

Allen smiled to encourage her further. "I think you've put your God-given talents to *gut* use by taking advantage of the building and equipment Maria left behind. And Irene's grateful to you for taking her along on the ride."

Phoebe chuckled. "*Jah*, she wasn't keen on today's extra order, but that's okay. We've allowed each other some flexibility," she said. "When I offered Laura fifteen percent of our income from today's baking, she snapped it up. This afternoon she'll turn another profit from the goodies she's selling at Mattie's produce stand."

"You Hershberger sisters lead industrious lives," Allen observed. They were passing through the lush countryside, where the occasional modest farmhouse, barns, and neatly trimmed lawns told of salt-of-the-earth farm families. He pointed to the left of the wagon. "The fellows who bought tiny homes this week live down that road. After they post photos of their new houses on the mercantile bulletin board alongside my ad, I hope to get even more business."

"*You're* the one who's on a new adventure!" Phoebe said

proudly. "Who knows where this housing trend will take you? God put you in the right place at the right time so you could jump in on the ground floor."

Allen tingled with happiness. Her opinion meant a lot because she wasn't flattering him the way Gloria did, trying to win his favor. Phoebe had a sense of purpose—and she was a much better organizer and record keeper than he was.

"If your business expands, you might need to work someplace other than the area between the cabins and the Helmuths' nursery," she suggested in a faraway voice. "Mamm promised Laura and me each a plot of ground when we moved to Promise Lodge, so . . . if I were to claim my property, you could do your construction work there— even put up a shop building and move your tiny home onto my land, if you wanted to."

Allen's eyes widened as alarm bells went off in his mind. "That's a very generous offer," he murmured. "I'll give it some thought."

Was she making a play for him, offering the use of her property with strings attached? Or was Phoebe only being helpful, knowing he'd need storage space for his building materials—not to mention a place to work during bad weather and the winter months?

Her suggestion made Allen realize that he'd rushed into his new building venture on the excitement of the tiny home craze, without thinking far enough ahead. It hadn't occurred to him to ask Rosetta if he could build his tiny homes on the large lawn beside the cabin he rented—and he needed to get her permission sooner rather than later. He should probably offer to pay more rent, as well.

Allen kept driving, listening to Phoebe's good-natured conversation and putting in an occasional response. He admired her—adored her—in many ways, but her property suggestion had sent him into a tailspin. He set aside his concerns, however, as they drove into Cloverdale to look around. They saw the large white building where Irene attended Mennonite church services, as well as Maria Zehr's new storefront bakery.

After they enjoyed cream puffs and coffee at one of Maria's tables while they chatted with her, Phoebe agreed to Allen's suggestion that they circle back to Promise Lodge on a different road. It was a beautiful day for a drive, and he chuckled as Phoebe recalled Maria's reaction to the successful pie business she and Irene were running in Maria's previous building.

When Allen pulled off the state highway onto the shoulder, he didn't mention that they'd reached the eastern boundary of the Promise Lodge property. He guided Phoebe between some trees and outcroppings of rocks before they reached a hilltop clearing that gave her a whole new perspective of the tract of land her *mamm*, her two aunts, and his *dat* had purchased a little more than a year ago.

Phoebe sucked in her breath. "You can see *everything* from up here!" she said in a hushed voice. "There's Lavern and Lowell in the bishop's training ring with a couple of Clydesdales, and Harley's herd of sheep—with Queenie watching them from beneath that shade tree—and Marlin's barrel factory, and all of our houses! And Rainbow Lake, and Mamm's dairy barn, and Ruby's white beehives in the orchard. *Wow*."

Allen rested his hand at the base of her spine, nodding as her excitement took hold of him, too. "It reminds me of a big table with scenery and buildings for a model train setup," he remarked. "The progress our settlement's made is really amazing, when you consider that before our parents came, only the lodge building and the cabins were there, surrounded by a lot of undeveloped land."

Phoebe stood mesmerized, studying the panorama of Promise Lodge as though she wanted to memorize every fence line and shed. Allen treasured her rapt expression and the closeness of her slender body as she leaned against him. He sensed he'd given her a gift by showing her their settlement from this hilltop vantage point.

"What about that parcel of land tucked behind the Lehman places and the orchard?" she asked dreamily, pointing at it. "From the side of the hill, we'd have a beautiful view of the lake. We'd have to have a road built to give us access to it—but anyone who claimed that piece of property would need to do that. What do you think, Allen? Should I ask Mamm if I can have it?"

Allen's throat closed with the sudden case of nerves her question caused him. *After Phoebe's earlier remark about property, you should've known better than to bring her here!* his inner voice chided. *Now she's planning your future, and she thinks you're okay with that.*

He eased away from her, pretending to look at something near the lodge so she wouldn't see how she'd startled him. Their relationship, which had felt so comfortable over the past week, now gave him the sensation that an invisible halter had been fastened around his head—and that Phoebe was holding the lead rope.

"That's up to you and your *mamm*," he replied cautiously. "She might've had specific places in mind for you and your sister."

"True. I'll have to ask her about it when I get back."

Allen tried not to act as though he was in a hurry to get away from her, but as dusk fell, he drove Phoebe straight home. He'd been looking forward to kissing her, yet when she threw her arms around him—right in front of the bishop's house, where Monroe or her mother might be watching them—Allen tasted Phoebe's confident assumption that his plans for the future meshed with hers.

Claustrophobia engulfed him. He stabled his horse and the wagon at his *dat*'s place, and then jogged behind the lodge and the cabins, relieved to reach his little home on wheels without encountering Cyrus, Jonathan, or anyone else.

Maybe I should hitch the horses to this place and head down the road—tonight, Allen thought as he shut the door behind him.

But he couldn't leave Promise Lodge. He'd already started on the two new homes he was building, and he had nowhere else to haul his materials.

Why didn't you have plan B in place before you jumped into this tiny home business? Or before you showed an interest in Phoebe?

At twenty-three, Allen was no stranger to romance, so he recognized the signs. The adoration on Phoebe's pretty face as they'd passed beneath the Promise Lodge entry sign had told him she was hooked on him—and he'd been happy to go along with that idea until she'd started talking about property. Phoebe was already envisioning a home on the hill overlooking Rainbow Lake, along with the marriage that fantasy implied; she surely wouldn't allow him to move his construction business to her property without expecting something in return. Even if he went along with her plans for a happily-ever-after, he didn't have the money to build her a traditional house that was big enough for a family— or her dreams. The novelty of living in his tiny home would wear off quickly for a young woman who was accustomed to a full-sized kitchen with a family-sized table.

Allen's rueful sigh filled his little house. He had to throw cold water on this situation—had to put out Phoebe's fire immediately—before both of them got burned.

Phoebe rushed toward the kitchen, bursting to talk with her mother—except Monroe was sitting at the head of the table beside her, and they were engrossed in a game of Scrabble. Their faces glowed in the light from the battery lamp, but it was a sense of deep, abiding love that made her mother appear so radiant these days. Rather than inter-rupting them, Phoebe paused in the doorway. More than anything, when she and Allen married, she wanted to feel the fulfillment that filled this kitchen—the sheer joy that always simmered just beneath the surface of her mother's face whenever Monroe was near.

"Nice try, sweetheart, but you can't play *ferhoodled*," Monroe challenged with a chuckle.

"But it's a word, and you know it!" Mamm protested.

"*Jah*, I know all about feeling *ferhoodled*," he agreed, "but just because you muddle my brains every time you touch me doesn't mean I'll allow you a word that's not in the English dictionary we're using. Rules are rules."

"I know just how to touch you so you'll let me play what-ever I want!" her mother teased as her hand slipped beneath the table.

When Phoebe gasped, the couple immediately sat up straighter. "You're home already," Mamm observed with a little laugh. "Did you and Allen have a *gut* time?"

The lamplight danced in Monroe's dark eyes as he pushed out the chair on the other side of him. "If you don't want to share all the details, that's all right—because we don't, either."

Phoebe blushed, but she sat down. Maybe it was best that

Monroe was here, after all, because he was quicker than Mamm to acknowledge her as an adult. Her mother would tell him about her request before the night was over, anyway.

"Allen and I had a fine time—and I've decided on the plot of land you said I could have when we moved to Promise Lodge." The words came out in more of a rush than she'd intended, but Phoebe held her mother's startled gaze. "You still want to do that for Laura and me, *jah*?"

Mamm's eyes got huge as she took a sip of her iced tea. "Of course I do," she replied warily. "What brought this on?"

Phoebe shrugged, fighting a nervous grin. "When Allen and I stopped alongside the highway and looked out over the whole spread of Promise Lodge, I—I spotted a place I've not seen before. It's behind the Lehman places and the orchard, and it has enough rise to it that a house would look out over Rainbow Lake—"

When Mamm shot Monroe an alarmed glance, Phoebe finished her thought. "The moment I saw it, I thought about what a blessing it would be to have such a view—to watch the sun rise over the lake each morning," she explained quickly. "And if I don't speak for it, somebody else surely will."

Monroe nodded. "I know the property you're talking about. We'll need to run a road up to that section—but that will happen anyway, as more folks come here to live," he added in a thoughtful tone. "That piece of ground's too hilly and rocky to be suitable for crops, so it's probably a fine choice for you—unless you're going to take up farming someday," he teased.

He reached for Mamm's hand as a sentimental smile softened his face. "I considered that area on the hill myself," he recounted, "but when I brought your *mamm* to this spot that overlooks the valley, she could already envision big red barns and Clydesdales grazing in the pasture, so I chose this place. She's persuasive that way, your *mamm* is."

Phoebe couldn't miss the shimmer of affection that passed between her mother and Monroe again. She was grateful that he was finding positive things to say, because her mother still seemed tongue-tied.

"If I understand the arrangement correctly," Monroe went on, "you Bender sisters and Amos pooled the money from selling your previous farms to buy this entire tract of land. As each new family moves here, you deposit the money they pay for their property into your management account, *jah*? And—just as Mattie gave her two sons the places they're living on—you're going to provide plots for your girls?"

"*Jah*, that's what we decided," Mamm confirmed. "Because Rosetta wasn't married then, the lodge and the cabins became hers so she could earn an income from them. The rest of us chose the property we wanted—and I took the plot with the barns on it for my dairy herd. We suspect horses were once kept there, for trail riding."

Phoebe admired the way her *mamm* and aunts had dared to invest in the abandoned campground that had become home for so many Plain families. Mamm's sense of accomplishment was shining in her eyes, easing the anxiety she'd shown a few moments ago.

"We've made back our initial investment and we're using the surplus to fund major improvements—like the new roof the lodge needs, and building roads," Mamm continued as she gazed at Monroe. "Truman did a lot of that work for us at a much lower cost than somebody else might've charged, so we've been in the black from the start."

Monroe was following her words closely. "So although we'd welcome more new families, the settlement—and you initial investors—are in *gut* financial shape even if no one else comes here."

"It still amazes me, what we've accomplished," Mamm murmured. She focused on Phoebe, smiling wistfully. "Your question about claiming your land caught me off guard because I figured it would be a few years before you'd want it. Maybe we should ask Laura to choose a place, as well, so Truman can do any road work or other improvements for both of you at the same time."

An immense sense of relief washed over Phoebe as she sat back in the chair. Maybe because Monroe was so supportive, Mamm wasn't going to insist on any details about her request.

"Tell me, though," Mamm continued as she studied Phoebe in the lamplight. "Does this sudden urge to claim your land have anything to do with Allen? Or are you figuring you'll earn enough with your pie shop to have a house of your own someday—so you won't have to live with us newlyweds anymore?"

Phoebe swallowed hard. Should she reveal how certain she was that she wanted to marry Allen? When she thought of a conversational way to sidestep that, she nodded. "Yes."

Monroe laughed out loud. "You can sit on the fence *now*, young lady," he teased, "but soon enough we'll figure out what's going on, ain't so?"

Phoebe scooted away from the table and stood up. "*Denki* for your generosity, Mamm, and for seeing that Laura and I receive the same benefits Mattie gave Noah and Roman," she said lightly. "I suspect it wouldn't have worked that way if we'd stayed in Coldstream."

Mamm's eyebrows shot up. "If we'd stayed in Coldstream," she said, "just think of all the wonderful-*gut* people we wouldn't have met and the businesses we Bender sisters couldn't have started. All three of us would still be single—and miserable."

When Mamm gazed lovingly at Monroe, Phoebe took her cue to leave them to their Scrabble game—and to the speculative conversation they'd have about her and Allen.

But that's all right, she told herself, smiling as she passed through the unlit front room to go upstairs. *Pretty soon, everyone at Promise Lodge will be talking about us, wishing us well as they anticipate our wedding!*

Chapter Seventeen

As Marlin guided Frances inside his barrel factory on Wednesday afternoon, his hopes for the future were high. The low metal building rang with the racket of Harley's hammer as he pounded rings around wooden staves to make new barrels. Harley's pounding meant he couldn't hear what Marlin and Frances were talking about, but he could see them, so he knew nothing improper was going on.

"Harley makes our basic barrels, and then Lowell and I add the other details," Marlin explained to Frances. "A lot of rain barrels are made from big plastic drums, but our clientele likes the look of wood, so that's the only kind we make."

He placed his hand on the small of her back to guide her past some items that were ready to ship. "We sell a lot of these barrels with the checkerboards on top, as well as the shorter porch tables that have storage space inside," he said as he pointed them out. "And these barrels with pumps and potting tables attached are going over to the Helmuths' nursery! We're delighted to have Sam and Simon as new customers."

Frances nodded. She was listening closely, but her brown eyes lacked their usual luster. "So they'll collect rain from the nursery building downspouts, and use that water when they plant seeds for bedding plants and such?"

"*Jah*—and if you haven't seen all of the blooming plants they've got now, I'll take you over there." Marlin smiled, because her question had given him the opening he'd been hoping for. "The greenhouses are a sight to behold, filled with all the colors of their impatiens, coleus, and hanging baskets of geraniums and fuchsia. We could get you some flowers for beds or porch pots or—"

"Not that I could plant them," she interrupted with a sigh.

Marlin kicked himself for not wording his idea differently. Sunday was Mother's Day. He'd considered getting her several flats of plants as a gift—and planting them for her—but her despondent tone of voice raised a red flag. "I'm sorry the doctor said your arms have to stay in slings for another week, sweetheart," he murmured beneath the staccato beat of Harley's hammer. "I know you were hoping to start your physical therapy."

Frances nodded, looking away from him.

"I'd be happy to get you some flowers and plant them for you," Marlin continued, trying to sound upbeat. "They'll be something colorful to look at while you recuperate—and if we get them soon, you can choose what you like best before they get picked over."

Frances remained quiet for a few moments. "My hands are itching to touch warm, moist soil and my arms ache to cuddle baby David," she said sadly. "I had no idea how deprived—how useless—I'd feel with my arms slung up like broken wings. I'd give anything to wash a sinkful of dishes."

Marlin carefully slipped his arm around her shoulders. He played another conversational card, hoping it would lift her spirits. "I was delighted when Lowell and Fannie asked me about giving you a couple of rain barrels for . . . for a Mother's Day gift," he said gently. "And Minerva wants to take enough food for the common meal after church on Sunday so that Mary Kate and Gloria don't have to cook anything. You'll feel a lot better if you come to church and mingle with your friends, don't you think?"

The last thing Marlin expected was Frances's wide-eyed response. She appeared as terrified as a spooked horse, and just as ready to bolt. "I—I'm figuring to come to church on Sunday, *jah*," she replied in a tight voice, "but there's something I really need to say, Marlin. Please hear me out."

Marlin's heart thudded. Frances was swallowing hard, blinking back tears as she tried to pull herself together. When he gently blotted her cheeks with his handkerchief, the swiftness with which she turned away startled him. The past two weeks had been very difficult for her, yet until this meltdown, he'd thought Frances was handling her affliction with more patience than most folks would.

Frances sniffled, sighing loudly. "I—I spoke too soon about making you a part of my future, Marlin," she blurted miserably. "Gloria and Harley will never accept it if you and I marry, and I—I can't deal with their constant confrontations. And maybe they're right. Maybe we Lehmans aren't cut out to blend into the Kurtz family."

Marlin sucked in his breath. Her words had packed an unexpected punch—and it didn't help that Harley had stopped hammering and seemed to be following their conversation from across the shop. "What's changed your mind?" he whispered. "After we ate supper at your place, you seemed so happy—so determined to make this work."

"I was wrong."

He frowned. Frances sounded so certain, so final. "Has Gloria been filling your head with negative—?" Marlin's thoughts whirled as he searched for ideas that would change Frances's mind. "At her age, Gloria won't have to become a

Kurtz if you and I marry. I suspect she'll want to keep her *dat*'s name for a lot of reasons."

A tear dribbled down Frances's face and splattered on one of her slings. "Gloria's not saying much these days. But this was my decision, not hers."

Marlin racked his brain for a convincing comeback. Why did Frances suddenly sound so dead-set against their relationship? "We wouldn't have to live at my place with Harley, you know," he pointed out quickly. "And one of these days Gloria will be moving away to marry—meanwhile, she could probably live at Mary Kate and Roman's place."

He gently tipped up her chin with his finger, praying he could restore her sense of perspective. "Let's remember that you and I are the parents here, Frances. We're in charge of our families, not the other way around," he said softly. "Widowed Amish folks usually remarry, so this is a challenge our kids will need to deal with sooner or later."

Frances shook her head bleakly. "I've thought about this during a lot of sleepless nights, Marlin. You told me early on that if I had doubts, I could call a halt to the courtship. So I am."

Marlin's heart was deflating like a balloon with a slow leak, losing hope with each silent second that passed between them. "Maybe the doctor's report has depressed you, and everything will look better tomorrow," he murmured. "How about if I walk you home and we can talk again—"

"I've said what I needed to say. I'll walk home by myself."

When Frances turned toward the door he'd brought her in, on the far side of the barrel shop, Marlin stepped in front of her. "If you use this back door, you won't have to walk past Harley," he murmured as he pointed at it.

Frances blinked. "*Denki. Gut*-bye, Marlin."

Gut-bye. The word tore at his soul as he opened the door for her. It didn't feel right to let Frances walk home alone, but he sensed his presence—or his desperate attempts to change her mind—might ruin any chance he had of talking with her in the future. With her arms positioned close to her body in slings, she seemed intent on holding herself together, as though she feared falling apart as she walked away from him.

When she'd stepped outside, Marlin made a last attempt—knowing it was the wrong thing to say. "Frances, may we *please* keep our options open? I—I love you," he said as he followed her out into the sunshine.

She stopped, closing her eyes in exasperation. "You've told me that before, and now you're only saying it to butter me up. Please don't—just *don't.*"

Marlin's chest got so tight he wondered if he was having a heart attack.

That's what it is, all right—your heart has just been attacked and you have no idea how to fight back. Not that fighting is the answer.

Marlin watched the retreating figure in the black dress, *kapp*, and apron with a heaviness he hadn't felt since he'd lost Essie. He hadn't lied when he'd told Frances he loved her, but his timing was terrible. She'd lost her husband only a couple of months ago, and she'd lost the use of her arms just a couple of weeks ago. He'd come on to her like a house afire—with the best of intentions, but not a lot of common sense.

What does common sense have to do with it? You love her, and she crushed you like a bug, man.

He had no particular reason to go inside again, because working on rain barrels was the furthest thing from his mind, and he didn't want to deal with Harley's remarks. When he stepped in to fetch his hat, however, his son was standing just inside the door.

"Seems Frances has changed her mind," Harley said with a shrug. "Women do that."

"Don't start with me," Marlin warned. He crammed his black straw hat on his head and walked quickly outside. He had no idea where he was going, but it didn't seem to matter.

Frances stood at her bedroom window staring out into the darkness of another restless night, feeling as jagged as the streaks of lightning that flashed across the sky. After Mary Kate had helped her into her nightgown, she and Roman and David had gone to bed in a room down the hall. Frances knew sleep wouldn't come for her anytime soon, however.

She deeply regretted the things she'd said to Marlin in his shop and the way she'd treated him. He was a good man, a generous soul, and he would make a wonderful husband—but she couldn't ignore her tormented heart.

It's too soon to go from one husband to the next.

If she'd expressed her doubts to Marlin, he probably would've understood, would've given her more time, but in her frustration she'd slammed an emotional door in his face. Frances hung her head, finally free to cry while no one could talk her out of her despondency. She'd always believed in the Bible verse that promised joy would come in the morning, but dark nights of the soul served a purpose. During her forty-seven years she'd rarely passed through the valley of the shadow, yet it seemed a necessary segment of her journey—a time of emotional reckoning and housecleaning.

A time to face reality. You need to figure out how to pay your bills and make a life without depending on a man—if only so you know you can do it.

Bishop Monroe and her neighbors might consider that a prideful notion, despite the way so many women at Promise Lodge had shown independent streaks. Frances knew she was being hard on herself—and on Marlin. The Old Order's marriage-based lifestyle had withstood the centuries because it worked: it guaranteed that widowed women and widowers' motherless children would be looked after.

Deep down, however, Frances didn't want to marry Marlin for the security their relationship would provide. She had the outlandish notion that she would only remarry for love—and that Marlin would surely love her more, respect her more, if she didn't enter the relationship as a needy dependent.

And there's no needier, more dependent woman than one who has both arms bound up in slings, she thought with a loud sigh.

"Mamm? Can—can we talk?"

Gloria's question made Frances brace herself. Had she whimpered or sobbed too loudly without realizing it? Her older daughter hadn't said two words to her since her outburst when Marlin's family had visited, so this late-night visit caught Frances by surprise.

"*Jah*, we can," she replied in a hoarse whisper. The last thing she wanted was to waken Mary Kate, who devoted so much time and energy to her during the day.

Frances remained by the window, wishing her face wasn't wet with tears—but she couldn't wipe them away. After a few moments her daughter padded barefoot into the dark room, stopping a few feet behind her. When her daughter didn't say anything more, Frances finally turned.

"Is something wrong, Gloria? Can't you sleep, either?" she asked softly. She reminded herself to rise above her own misgivings, because bless her, Gloria had never been good at reading other people's emotions.

The next flash of lightning illuminated Gloria's forlorn expression. In her long cotton nightgown, with her dark braid trailing down her back, she reminded Frances of the little girl who'd always been less confident and more vulnerable than her younger sister. Frances's heart softened with sympathy, and she got frustrated all over again because she couldn't open her arms to her daughter. "Oh, Gloria," she murmured. "What's on your mind, sweetie?"

Gloria sniffled. "I—I went over to the nursery today, to ask Sam or Simon if I could work for them," she replied in a stricken voice, "but there were so many customers there, and I—I couldn't get my nerve up to talk to them. And what work could I do for them, anyway?" she added despondently. "I'd probably just mess up and get fired."

Frances's heart shriveled. Had she been wrong to tell her daughter to look for gainful employment? It wasn't as though they were destitute . . . yet.

"Why are you saying we need money?" Gloria asked miserably. "Dat and Uncle Lester's business has always done well, ain't so? And Dat wasn't one to spend money on *anything* we didn't absolutely need."

Frances sighed and kept looking out the window. Gloria had asked for the truth, so it was time to explain their situation—even though it would probably upset her daughter more. "Remember when we learned Mary Kate was expecting—and we knew how much talk it would cause amongst the congregation in Sugarcreek?" she began softly. "And remember how fast your *dat* decided to sell out and come to Promise Lodge because of that?"

Gloria nodded, remaining silent.

"Well, we took less money for our property there in order to sell it quickly," Frances explained as gently as she could. "It took most of our money to build this home and reestablish the window business here in Missouri—and then when your *dat* fell with Amos, and had his stroke, his medical bills took most of what was left. So we don't have much to fall back on."

Frances blinked rapidly. The financial pinch she'd known about for months seemed a lot more pressing—a lot more real—now that she'd told her vulnerable daughter about it. "Until another family buys this place," she continued sadly, "we might have to sell most of our furniture to get by."

That idea sent a tremor of fear through her, but Frances was determined to end on a confident note, for Gloria's sake. "With the help of the *gut* Lord and our friends, we'll be all right," she insisted. "Your *dat* firmly believed that, and so do I. We have our faith, and we have our family—"

"Oh, Mamm, I've made you cry," Gloria interrupted when she finally looked Frances in the face. "I didn't mean to doubt you. Didn't mean to bother you with my—"

"I was already having a little pity party when you came in," Frances admitted with a shake of her head. "I told Marlin not to court me anymore. I hurt him badly, but I had to say it."

She hadn't intended to bare her soul, but it was the shortest path to the truth. No sense in dancing around the fact that she'd rejected a wonderful man who'd said he loved her even after she'd shut him down.

Gloria's eyes widened. "So you're not going to marry him? Oh, my."

Frances was surprised that her daughter sounded sorry about this news, after all the times she'd so strenuously objected to Marlin's presence. "The time's not right," she explained. "I didn't want to marry him just because he could take care of us, Gloria. I wanted to prove we could make it on our own terms—"

"Oh, my," Gloria repeated before nipping her lip. "Well,

since I can't seem to land a job or a husband, and you'll not be able to work for quite a while yet . . . maybe we should move into the lodge and sell the house, like you said before."

Frances's eyes widened. "What's happened to change your mind about that?" she asked. "Last I knew, you didn't want to live amongst those *biddy hens*—and truth be told, maybe I was being harsh, expecting you to leave our home so soon after your *dat*'s passing. I'm sorry about that, honey."

Gloria shrugged, glancing out the window as she composed her response. "Well, besides needing the money, we—I was just thinking how big and empty this house will feel after Mary Kate and Roman and David move back home," she said sadly. "It's not the same here without Dat."

Once again Frances ached to embrace her daughter, but her arms remained pinned against her body in their slings. "*Jah*, you're right about that part."

"It would be easier if you married Marlin," Gloria said with a sigh. "And it would be helpful if I got married—or did a better job of pulling my weight. But in the meantime, maybe moving to the lodge would take off some of the pressure, ain't so? At least we'd have friends to eat our meals with. And it wouldn't be so—so *quiet* all the time."

Frances felt fresh tears dribbling down her cheeks, yet she was smiling. Who could've foreseen this switch in Gloria's attitude? Just the fact that her daughter was giving some serious thought to their situation made her feel more hopeful about their future.

"Let's try to get some sleep, and we'll talk about this again tomorrow," she suggested. "If we figure out what furniture to sell—and how to do that—we could move to the lodge by the time I'm taking my physical therapy. It'll give us a target to shoot for. Something to look forward to."

"All right. Let's do it." Gloria slipped her arm around Frances's shoulders and kissed her cheek. "*Denki* for listening, Mamm. And—and I really am sorry you broke up with Marlin," she added ruefully. "It was easy to see that you were happy together. I just wish I could find somebody."

Frances watched her daughter slip quietly out into the hallway. What had just happened? What had prompted Gloria's change of heart?

Her ways are almost as mysterious as Yours, Lord, she thought as she got into bed. *It's anybody's guess what might happen next, but at least she and I are in this together now.*

Chapter Eighteen

By the end of the church service on Sunday, Allen wanted to flee the big meeting room in the lodge. Phoebe had been gazing at him from the women's side all morning, her blue eyes wide with questions she'd ask as soon as folks got up to prepare for the common meal.

Trouble was, he didn't have answers she wanted to hear.

He'd buried himself in his construction work all week, avoiding her rather than facing her disappointment—but he had nowhere to hide on this sunny Sabbath. Because it was Mother's Day, long tables had been set up outside under the trees, and folks would spend a leisurely afternoon visiting after they'd finished their meal. Even though he hadn't joined the church, he couldn't work today because the two framed-in tiny homes were in plain sight of the picnic tables. Maybe if he slipped out when everyone stood up . . .

"We've got a few announcements before we men serve the ladies their lunch today," Bishop Monroe said as he smiled at the congregation. "First, the bedding plants along the centers of the tables are gifts for the mothers amongst us, courtesy of Sam and Simon."

"And we'd like folks to know that Barbara's now confined to bed rest as she awaits the birth of her twins,"

Minerva put in. "I'm keeping an eye on both her and Bernice for the duration."

"She's feeling fine, though, and would welcome your visits," Sam added with a nervous chuckle.

Allen assumed it was Sam, anyway—he had a hard time telling the redheaded Helmuth brothers apart. He couldn't imagine how stressed those fellows must be, awaiting their first children. Allen was okay with kids once they were walking, talking, and out of diapers, but babies terrified him—and he was pretty sure Phoebe wanted a houseful of kids. Just one more reason to bolt . . .

"That's *gut* to know, and we all share your excitement as you await your new arrivals," Bishop Monroe said. "We also welcome our newlyweds, Truman and Rosetta, to our gathering today, along with Irene. Sundays aren't the same when you Wickeys attend your Mennonite service, so we're glad you've chosen to alternate between the two churches."

From his pew bench in the center of the men's section, Allen was glad to see Rosetta's confident smile across the meeting room. He had some important questions to ask, if he could catch her when she wasn't surrounded by family and friends . . . so it seemed he couldn't slip away, after all.

"Anything else we should know about before the men set out the food?" the bishop asked.

"*Jah*, I—I have a question," one of the ladies piped up.

Folks looked around to see who'd spoken, until Frances Lehman stood up. Allen felt bad for her, with her arms still hanging in slings.

"Gloria and I have decided to move to lodge apartments when I've started my physical therapy, rather than rattling around in our huge house," Frances continued. "I'm wondering how we should go about selling the furniture we won't need anymore."

Allen couldn't miss the way Preacher Marlin's jaw

dropped, or the pain on his face when he leaned his elbows on his knees, as though he was bearing the weight of the world on his shoulders. What had happened? Folks began whispering as though they, too, were surprised that Frances and Marlin didn't appear to be a couple anymore.

"I can help you with that, Frances," Truman offered after a few moments. "I know an auctioneer who'll either conduct an on-site sale for you, or he'll take your furniture and sell it at his auction barn."

"We could use some of your pieces—especially bedroom sets—to furnish more of the rooms in the lodge," Rosetta put in.

Frances's expression wavered. "I'd rather sell it," she said in a faltering voice. "I'm putting the house up for sale, too. If any of you know of a family looking to come here, I'd appreciate it if you'd put in a *gut* word about our place being ready to live in."

The meeting room got very quiet. Bishop Floyd had moved his family to Missouri less than a year ago, so it seemed sad that Frances and Gloria no longer wanted to live in their house now that he was gone. Allen shifted to observe how Gloria was reacting to her mother's announcement. Her air of quiet acceptance surprised him.

"I'd sell my place and move into the lodge, too," Lester piped up, "but I guess I wouldn't fool anybody if I took to wearing *kapps* and dresses so I could live there."

As laughter erupted around him, Allen was pleased to hear Lester's lighthearted joke. Lester left very early on weekday mornings to install the windows at the townhome complex where Truman's company was doing the landscaping, so Allen could understand why he didn't need a full-sized home.

Maybe you could cut Lester a deal on a tiny home if he was willing to install the windows and siding himself, Allen thought. He set this idea aside, however, as everyone around him stood up to prepare for the picnic. Like a lot of Amish settlements, Promise Lodge celebrated Mother's Day by allowing the women to sit and visit while the men did the serving and cleaning up. His best tactic was to busy himself amongst the men, hoping Phoebe would join her *mamm* and aunts outside.

He'd barely made it into the kitchen, however, before a slender hand clasped his elbow.

"Allen, you forgot to pick up your pies this week," Phoebe said earnestly. She pointed to a metal pie carrier on the counter. "I made two fresh ones yesterday, just for you!"

There was no avoiding her, because she was standing so close that Allen could smell her clean clothes and fresh scent. He put on an apologetic smile. "I've been working hard on those two new homes," he hastened to explain, "so I forgot all about pie! I can't possibly eat so much pie myself, so maybe we should set them out today, *jah*? There's no such thing as too many desserts at a common meal."

When Phoebe's smile fell, Allen kicked himself. Her confused expression stabbed at his heart, but he told himself to remain firm about breaking up with her.

She took a deep breath. "I thought maybe after dinner we might walk up to that piece of ground we spotted from the highway—the one overlooking the lake," she added hopefully. "Mamm says I can have it! So if you need a place to move your construction—or to build a shop—well . . . you can use it, Allen."

He didn't know what to say. After several moments of silence, which she surely interpreted as his rejection, Phoebe sighed. "We'll talk later. I guess you men are busy setting out food."

Allen felt lower than a roach. He'd broken up with a

couple of girlfriends while he'd lived in Indiana, but it would be harder to deal with Phoebe's disappointment because they would both remain at Promise Lodge for the foreseeable future. Before he could change his mind, he took a knife from the drawer. Surrounded by the other men, who bustled about unwrapping bowls and looking for serving utensils, Allen focused on cutting the two pies into neat, even pieces.

It took all his willpower not to devour a slice of the lattice-topped strawberry rhubarb pie on the spot, not to slip back to his tiny home to keep Phoebe's pies all for himself. The other pies on the counter didn't look nearly as delectable.

"Son, if you'd like to sit with Mattie and me at lunch, we'd be delighted to have you."

Allen looked up to find his *dat* leaning against the kitchen counter, watching him closely—as though he knew more than he was saying. "Um, sure—that would be fine," he hedged.

Dat smiled like the cat that ate the canary. "None of my business, but I couldn't help noticing that Phoebe left here looking like a kitten who'd been drenched by a bucket of cold water."

Allen sighed. He really didn't want to listen to Dat and Mattie's advice about his love life while he ate, but at this point it would be impolite to sit with Cyrus and Jonathan— or to leave the gathering altogether. "You know how it is when girls get their hopes up and start living in a fairy tale," he said with a sigh.

"*Jah*, that happens," Dat said with a chuckle. "And I might have a secret up my sleeve for the handsome prince in the story."

Allen's eyes widened as his father took hold of the two

water pitchers Preacher Eli was handing him. After Dat headed outside, Allen quickly placed a slice of the strawberry rhubarb pie in the lid of Phoebe's pie carrier and shoved it to the back of the countertop before taking the two pies outside to the dessert table. If the day was about to slide further downhill with Phoebe, at least he'd have one last slice of her pie to sweeten the descent.

After all the food was arranged on the long serving tables and the ladies were lining up to fill their plates first, Allen joined his *dat* beneath a big maple tree near the side of the lodge.

"Mattie's taking plates over to the Helmuth place to eat with Barbara," his father said. "So before we go through the serving line, I thought we might chat."

Allen's stomach rumbled with hunger. He recalled the long, uncomfortable *chats* his father the preacher had often had with him while he was growing up—yet he was intrigued about the secret Dat had mentioned earlier. "How about if we have our dessert first?" he suggested, nodding toward the lodge. "There's a piece of Phoebe's pie in the kitchen calling my name, and I'll share it with you."

Dat chuckled as they headed around the back of the lodge. "Any particular reason you shut her down?" he asked nonchalantly. "Last I knew, the two of you were enjoying each other's company—and truth be told, I was delighted. She's a nice girl. *Gut* head on her shoulders, too."

"*Jah*, but she's got stars in her eyes and marriage on her mind and I'm not there yet," Allen blurted.

"Would your cold feet have something to do with her asking Christine for that plot of ground overlooking the lake?"

Allen stopped short of the kitchen door, staring. "How'd you know about that?"

Dat laughed. "Monroe told me. We guys have to stick

together, you know." He opened the door and gestured for Allen to go in first. "It occurred to me that if the young lady of my dreams was acquiring property, I'd be getting nervous, too. I'd feel like she was the driver and I was the horse."

A ray of hope made Allen smile as he took two forks from a drawer. "You nailed it, Dat," he murmured. "Phoebe means well, offering to let me move my construction supplies to her plot of land—and even build a shop on it so I can work indoors in the winter. But the moment she suggested that, the walls closed in on me." He scooted the slice of pie between them on the counter.

His father nodded as he cut off the tip of the slice. "Mmm," he moaned as he chewed. "You can't argue with the way this girl cooks. But you can choose your own piece of property, son. It was my fondest wish to do the same for you as Mattie did for her boys, but you were going to school in Indiana, so—"

"You had no idea I'd be coming to Promise Lodge," Allen put in. When he stuck a large bite of pie in his mouth, it tasted even more perfect than he'd anticipated. Who could've imagined this turn of events? This opportunity his *dat* was hinting at?

The smile on his father's face shone like the sunrise on a May morning. "Allen, your return to Missouri with your sisters ranks right up there with my finally getting to marry Mattie," he said in a voice that was hoarse with emotion. "Sam and Simon's parents bought the land where the nursery sits as an extension of their business back East, so I funded their house for your sisters' homecoming gift. It's your turn, Allen. Pick out the property you want, and it'll be yours whenever you're ready for it."

Allen felt like a shaken can of soda pop, ready to explode

with pent-up excitement. Having land of his own meant he could park his tiny home and erect a shop very soon, so Rosetta wouldn't be charging him extra rent—or any rent at all! Never had he dreamed that his stern Amish father would give him such a generous gift. Especially because he hadn't committed to joining the church.

Maybe this is his way of persuading you to do that, his thoughts niggled. *Maybe it's another version of the trap Phoebe's setting.*

Allen figured he'd better clarify the arrangement before he got his hopes up too high. "What if I don't join the Old Order?" he asked softly. "Or what if I don't ever marry?"

His *dat* flashed him a knowing smile. "You know my opinions on those topics, but you're my son," he replied as he cut a large bite from the remaining pie. "You need a place to live and work, so it makes sense for me to offer you property no matter what you do with your life, *jah*? It's my way of saying . . . I want you to stick around."

Allen was astounded. While growing up, he'd never envisioned Preacher Amos as a man who'd allow his son a detour from the same life path or the same rigid religious practices he believed in. Life with a leader of the Old Order Amish was like men's Sunday clothing: black and white, with no gray areas or wiggle room for differing beliefs.

Allen had never imagined that beneath his stern exterior, his *dat* had a soft spot for him, either. Had Amos Troyer always been a doting father, or had Allen been too full of himself—too set on getting away from his *dat*—to notice?

"And if I give you land, it takes the reins out of Phoebe's hands—at least until you marry her," Dat added with a laugh.

Allen laughed, too, even though his father playfully laid his fork across the final chunk of pie to claim it. If Allen was to have any more of Phoebe's fantastic pastry and filling, he'd either have to grab a slice of her pie before it had all disappeared from the dessert table . . . or he'd need to give her a reason to keep baking for him.

"*Denki*, Dat," Allen murmured. "You've offered me a generous gift, and I appreciate it."

"You're welcome." His father stood straighter, leaving sentimentality behind. "Where would you like to live? You can have as much land as you like, but I can't see you needing a lot of acreage for raising crops or pasturing animals—although that might change over time."

Allen had a sudden vision of his tiny home parked on the far shore of Rainbow Lake, with a new fishing dock just steps away from his door. If he didn't claim that pretty section of the campground, somebody else surely would. "What if I want the lake, and that adjoining piece of ground that falls between the orchard and the Peterscheim place?"

His *dat*'s forehead wrinkled with thought. "I guess we've always considered the lake as community property—"

"But what if I keep it stocked, so everyone can still fish there?" Allen asked, his voice rising with excitement. "And if they want to ice skate on it, that's fine, too. Truman could run a road along the back side of it that would access the property Phoebe wants, and kill two birds with one stone."

"Sounds more like two birds building a big nest to me," Dat teased.

"Sounds like the perfect place for a tiny home and a bachelor hangout," Allen countered quickly. "Waterfront property is always considered prime real estate. I'm surprised nobody else thought of it first."

His father cut into the last chunk of pie and nudged half of it toward Allen. "I'll run this past Mattie and her sisters, as my business partners, but consider it a done deal. They got first dibs on property when we moved here, and I went along with their wishes, so it's my turn to have a say now, *jah*?"

Dat held up his last bite as a salute. "Isn't it amazing what gets decided over pie?" he asked lightly. "It's like the sugar and fruit and pastry all come together to show folks what really matters. I'll go speak with Mattie and her sisters right now."

Chapter Nineteen

Frances sighed and opened her mouth for another forkful of potato salad—not because it tasted good to her, but because for the first time, Gloria was feeding her. Mary Kate, Roman, and baby David sat across the table, trying to make encouraging conversation. Ruby and Beulah had joined them, too, and sat at the end of the table behind Frances's lawn chair, which was situated sideways so Gloria could feed her more easily.

All around her folks chatted and laughed, enjoying the beautiful weather and the Mother's Day picnic beneath the big trees, but Frances couldn't rise to the occasion. She felt as if she were living inside a big, invisible bubble that dimmed the sights and sounds around her and kept her separate from—and uninterested in—all that was going on. She was happy to hide behind her large sunglasses, so the well-meaning people around her couldn't see how miserable she was.

"I'm going to grab a slice of that cherry pie and some of Ruby's chocolate cake before they're gone," Gloria said. "What can I bring you for dessert, Mamm?"

Frances suspected her smile looked as feeble as it felt. "Oh, I couldn't eat another bite," she insisted. "Without being able to move around, I don't work up much of an appetite."

"You could bring me a couple of those lemon bars, sweetie," Ruby piped up.

"I like the sugar cookie bars best—if there's room on your plate," Beulah hinted.

Gloria pressed her lips into a worried line, but left the table to fetch the desserts. Frances took the opportunity to sink into herself rather than having to make conversation. It seemed that announcing her intention to sell her house and furnishings had sucked all the energy from her. She let her eyes close, giving serious consideration to going home for a nap. It was a relief when Gloria sat down in front of her again and blocked the glare of the sunshine.

"Frances, I'm sorry to hear you want to sell your place."

Preacher Amos's deep voice jolted Frances out of her woolgathering. He was gazing speculatively at her from Gloria's seat, awaiting her response. But what could she say? She felt tongue-tied with his dark eyes focused so intently on her.

"I was also sorry that you and Marlin seem to have parted ways," Amos continued softly. He leaned toward her with his elbows on his knees. "He's crazy about you, Frances."

Her heart thudded painfully in her chest. "It's too soon," she said, looking away.

The preacher considered this. "Maybe so, but why burn your bridges? Marlin's a patient fellow—"

"And he deserves a strong, happy wife," Frances blurted before she could catch herself.

Amos's bushy eyebrows rose. "You sound just like I did after I fell off the shed last fall," he remarked. "Remember how I told Mattie the wedding was off, because she deserved a healthy husband? I'd still be a victim in a wheelchair if Truman and Roman hadn't made me take my medications—because I was so depressed, I didn't know up from down. And I didn't much care."

Amos looked behind him, where Roman sat with David in his lap. "Is that how you remember it, son?"

Roman nodded. "You were in a bad way, Amos. You spent too much time in the dark feeling moody and snapping at folks who tried to help you."

Frances blinked. Amos and Roman had perfectly described her feelings, despite the way she and Gloria had patched things up between them. "I'm sick and tired of feeling sick and tired," she muttered.

"*Gut*!" the preacher said as he gently grasped her knee. "Once you've reached rock bottom, the only way is up, so you're ready to head in that direction, *jah*? When do you see your doctor again about getting out of those slings?"

She looked away again. "They were supposed to come off last Tuesday, but—"

"Well, that explains it," Amos cut in. "Anybody would feel despondent about coming home with her arms still trussed up."

Though Frances wanted the preacher to let her be, he held her gaze through her sunglasses. "What if I take you to your next appointment? We'll ask your doctor about some antidepressants, even if he starts you on your physical therapy," Amos suggested. "I suspect you decided to ditch your house and Marlin during low moments when you weren't really yourself."

"You said that exactly right, Amos," Mary Kate chimed in from across the table. "Mamm's dug herself into an emotional trench lately and we can't seem to help her out of it. Her next appointment is this coming Tuesday, by the way."

"But we want to move to an apartment in the lodge because the house is too big and too quiet," Gloria put in as she returned with her loaded plate. "We both think it'll do us *gut* to have friends to eat with and talk to, now that . . . now that Dat's gone."

Frances's heart lurched as her daughter's words brought tears to her eyes. Was she really so depressed that she needed medication? Why couldn't Amos let her handle her grief the way she wanted to?

"You're probably right about that part," Amos agreed. He focused again on Frances. "But I can't think that selling the furniture and the family belongings that have meaning for you will improve your situation. After you've recovered, you'll wish you had them back."

Frances nipped her lip, noting the way Gloria's expression tightened. Once again she wished people would just leave her alone and stop questioning her decisions. "We need the money," she murmured.

Was it her imagination, or had everyone at the tables around them gone quiet, to listen in on her private woes?

Amos cleared his throat. "I could tell you that God will provide—and He will—but I'm going to do you one better, Frances," he said in a low voice. "If living amongst your friends at the lodge will lift your spirits, do it. But keep your house and your furniture. It was Rosetta's intention from the beginning to take in women who need a place to live—even if they can't afford to pay rent. Accept her hospitality, at least until you can figure out what comes next in your life."

"*Jah*, Frances, we've started our Coffee Can Fund, remember?" Ruby put in.

"And even if we hadn't," Beulah said, "Rosetta wouldn't dream of turning you away, and neither would we. We gals are all in this together."

"Did someone say my name?" a cheerful voice called out behind Frances.

Frances's heart shriveled. She hadn't intended to become the object of anyone's pity or the recipient of charity. Before she could protest, however, Rosetta and Truman came over to the table and greeted everyone. Their hands were clasped and their faces radiated the love they shared. From all appearances, they were the happiest couple on the face of the earth.

Frances envied them. Once upon a time, she'd been happy, too.

Preacher Amos rose to pump Truman's hand. "You're just the folks we want to see," he said jovially. "Frances and Gloria are thinking to live in one of your lodge apartments for a while—"

"Perfect!" Rosetta said. "Truman's *mamm* says it's one of the best things she's ever done for herself."

"—and, Truman, if you've got a minute this afternoon," Amos continued, "I'd like us to figure out the best place to plow out a road that'll run around the other side of the lake and give us access to that tract of land behind the orchard."

"We can do that," Truman said with a nod. "There's already a natural path that runs around the lake and up the hill. Just a matter of taking a dozer to it and adding gravel so it'll support traffic."

"Shall we take a look?" Amos asked. Then he focused on Frances again. "Will you believe me when I say God will turn your life around, and that we'll all do our best to help that happen?"

Frances nodded, mostly so the preacher would be on his way. When he and Truman strode off toward Rainbow Lake, Rosetta slipped her arm around Frances's shoulders and gestured for Gloria to sit in the chair Amos had vacated.

"I'm glad you ladies want to move into the lodge," she said earnestly. "For a while, Ruby and Beulah were worried that they'd be rattling around all by themselves. I have another idea, too—and it concerns a job I think you'd be really *gut* at, Gloria."

Gloria's forkful of chocolate cake stopped in front of her mouth. "A job?" she echoed hopefully. "I could sure use the money."

Rosetta beamed at her. "Well, the job I have in mind doesn't pay—but I'll put on my thinking cap about some gainful employment for you, too."

Gloria glanced at Frances and back to Rosetta. "I'm all ears."

"How would you like to be Promise Lodge's scribe for *The Budget*?" Rosetta asked. "It's a weekly task I took on when we first started our new settlement. Now that I'm married and living up the hill—cooking and cleaning house and keeping up with a big garden and my goats—I don't have as much time to do it." She shrugged endearingly. "You seem like the perfect person to report our goings-on, and to write the weekly piece in a way that will entice more folks to join us here."

Gloria's jaw dropped. "You think I could do that? For the newspaper that every Plain family in the country reads?"

"You'd be really *gut* at that!" Mary Kate put in. "You always have an ear to what folks are doing, and you won spelling awards in school, and—"

"Are you saying I'm nosy?" Gloria teased. "But I suppose that's a helpful trait if you're going to report the news of the neighborhood."

"So you'll do it? I'll let you see copies of the pieces I've sent in, to get you started," Rosetta said excitedly. "And I know of some responsibilities around the lodge and the grounds you could take on for pay, too. Can you give me a day or two to organize my thoughts on that?"

Gloria exhaled in disbelief. "Well, *jah*, if you're sure I won't mess up—"

"Who amongst us doesn't make mistakes?" Rosetta challenged gently. "My life has changed now that I'm not single and living amongst my renters. If I had a manager, I wouldn't have to keep an eye on every little thing myself."

A manager? Is this my Gloria Rosetta's talking about?

Frances shifted in her chair, careful not to let on that she had doubts about her scatterbrained daughter's qualifications for such a position. Gloria's eyes had taken on a shine that Frances hadn't seen in a long while—so why douse the spark Rosetta had kindled with her enthusiasm?

Rosetta beamed at Frances, delighted by the way this situation was playing out. "Would this be a *gut* time to choose your rooms in the lodge?" she asked. "If you like the apartments Mattie, Christine, or Maria lived in, you could pack an overnight bag and sleep there tonight! We could get you settled in tomorrow—or we could start work on whichever rooms you wanted, if you choose some that are unfinished."

"Let's do it, Mamm!" Gloria set her desserts on the table and stood up. "We could start a whole new life right this minute!"

Rosetta slipped her arm gently around Frances's shoulders to steady her as she rose from her lawn chair. "Sounds like you already have a plan for happiness, Gloria," she remarked. "That's the most important qualification any employee of mine could have. Shall we go upstairs and look around?"

Frances's head was spinning from all the new ideas Amos and Rosetta had talked about in the past few minutes. "I—I looked at the apartments a while back, and I really liked Christine's," she said. "But Gloria might have a different idea about—"

"If Gloria's going to be my manager—or even if she decides not to," Rosetta put in, "she'll want her own space. Once we decide on her job description, an apartment will be included as part of her pay. How does that sound?"

"Like a dream come true!" Gloria replied breathlessly. "I'm going upstairs to look around right now!"

Frances watched Gloria take the porch stairs two at a time before rushing inside, letting the screen door bang behind her. "I can't recall the last time I saw her so excited," she murmured. "But are you sure about her being your manager, Rosetta? You didn't have to come up with a job on the spot, just because she's looking for work."

Rosetta's eyes sparkled as she gave Frances a gentle hug. "Seems to me she and I were both in the right place at the right time when the right idea came around, *jah*? If that's not the hand of God bringing us together, what else can we call it?"

Frances blinked back sudden tears. "Might just be a miracle."

Chapter Twenty

Exhausted, Barbara clung to her sister's hand and fought the urge to scream in pain and frustration. "How do women do this again and again?" she asked in a halting voice. "I feel like a wrung-out dishrag after so many hours of pushing and—" She grimaced as another contraction wracked her body.

"One down and one to go, sister," Bernice encouraged as she pressed a cool wet cloth to Barbara's face. "We'll get you through this. Don't give up."

"You'll soon forget about the pain and remember this as the most special day of your life," Mattie said gently. She was holding her swaddled granddaughter, gazing raptly into her tiny face. "You have a perfect baby girl with adorable carrot-colored hair. When I showed her to Sam just now, he was over the moon."

"You're doing fine, Barbara," Minerva assured her from the end of the bed. "How about if you scoot up against the headboard and try from that angle? Before you know it, this part will be over and your little girl will have a—oh, I see the top of a head! Give another *gut* push—"

Somehow Barbara found the strength to bear down again. A wave of euphoria washed over her as she felt her second baby leave her body.

"Another girl!" Minerva announced. "She looks perfect, too. We'll get both of you cleaned up and you can take a closer look at the two miracles you and Sam have made. Congratulations, Barbara."

"*Jah*, sister, you did it!" Bernice exclaimed. "Oh, but it's a big day for the Helmuth family!"

Barbara heaved a sigh of relief. All she really wanted was a dark, quiet room and twelve hours of uninterrupted sleep, yet the little wail that rang out near the foot of the bed rallied her.

Two girls! I have two perfect baby girls and they'll love each other the way Bernice and I always have.

She looked at her very round twin sister, gratefully sipping cool water from the glass Bernice offered her. "Hope I didn't scare you out of going through this," she murmured.

Bernice let out a nervous laugh. "It's a little late for me to back out, *jah*? Truth be told, my back's starting to give me fits—the way yours did yesterday."

From across the room, Minerva looked up from the baby she was washing. "I'll check you over before I leave, Bernice. It amazes me, the way you twins conceived and are now giving birth at almost the same time," she remarked. "If you'll diaper your wee niece, I'll tend to your sister so she's ready for Sam and Simon and your *dat* to visit."

By the time she'd eaten a muffin and had drunk some tea, and Minerva had helped her wash up and change into a clean nightgown, Barbara felt human again. When she was sitting up against pillows in bed, the rush of love that surged through her at the sight of her daughters made her laugh and cry at the same time.

"Oh, but they're wrinkly—and would you look at all that carrot-colored fuzz on their heads!" she exclaimed as Mattie and Bernice stood on either side of the bed with the babies.

The moment she cradled a baby in each arm, gazing at

their tiny faces at last, Barbara was filled with a wondrous sense of awe. She gazed from one twin to the other, noting their identical noses and foreheads and bow-shaped mouths.

"There's a pretty picture," her *dat* remarked as he entered the room behind Sam and Simon. He stopped at the foot of the bed, gazing raptly at her and his new granddaughters. "This takes me back to the day you girls were born," he said softly. "It's another new beginning for our family—a whole new generation, praise God."

Barbara thought she'd never see the day when her stern, strong father might cry, but he was clearly moved as he stroked the girls' tiny cheeks. Sam came up and kissed her temple, appearing awestruck yet a little nervous as he looked at his new daughters.

"Which names did you decide on?" he asked. "We talked about so many that I've lost track of which ones we actually chose."

Barbara mentally reviewed the names they'd considered as she studied the two dozing babies in her arms. "Carol and Corene," she replied. "They seem like a Carol and a Corene to me."

"Then that's who they are," her husband said. "If you've got one to spare, I'd like to get better acquainted."

As Sam lifted Corene to his chest, Barbara looked at the happy, eager faces gathered around her—the folks she loved most in all the world—and she knew the meaning of deep, abiding joy.

She and Bernice had decorated a room that would be the nursery for all three babies. It was situated between the bedrooms they shared with their husbands—but that night she insisted that Carol's and Corene's bassinets be placed in the room with her and Sam so she could keep better track of them. What with the sounds of Bernice, who was now in labor down the hall, and checking on her new daughters,

Barbara didn't sleep a lot that first night. But she'd never felt happier or more blessed.

The next morning as she was feeding Carol in the nursery, Sam sat beside her holding Corene. The loud moans in the adjacent bedroom gave way to a shrill wail. Several minutes later, Simon appeared at the door with a blanketed bundle in his arms. He was exhausted from the long night of Bernice's labor, yet exuberant.

"We have a boy!" he announced. "And we're calling him Caleb."

After Phoebe carried six hot pies to the table to let them cool, she opened the bakery windows wider. "I'm glad we're almost done baking for the day," she said to Irene. "It's only nine o'clock, but my *gut*ness, it's hot."

"*Jah*, the rain shower we had in the night made it more humid, too." Irene pressed her handkerchief to her forehead as she stirred a pot of gooseberry filling. "Maybe we should ask Bishop Monroe about installing a big fan—or even a window-unit air conditioner. It's only the twenty-third of May. By July, we might not be able to keep working—or we'll have to cut way back on our orders."

"An air conditioner?" Phoebe mused aloud. "Well, the building's wired for electricity because Maria was a Mennonite—"

"And I am, too," Irene reminded her. "I'll take Monroe a raspberry pie and see if he'll give his blessing to cooling us down in here. It's not as though we'll be running a TV or a computer or anything else that'll let the outside world into our business."

Phoebe propped the door open so the morning breeze could pass through the building—and stopped to stare. Two Clydesdales were hauling a slate blue tiny home—*Allen's* tiny home—across the grassy yard in front of the lodge. Lavern Peterscheim and Lowell Kurtz were guiding the huge horses from either side, while Allen walked behind the little house on wheels wearing an expression of sheer exhilaration.

"What does this mean?" Phoebe asked as she watched the little parade. She'd done her best to keep her disappointment to herself when Allen had hardly spoken to her on Sunday—and when he'd served the pies she'd baked especially for him at the common meal.

"What do you see, dear?" Irene carried the kettle from the stove burner to the low counter in the kitchen where they put together pies. When she joined Phoebe at the door, she let out a low whistle. "Now *there's* a sight you don't see every day. Where do you suppose Allen's going with his little house?"

Blinking rapidly, Phoebe tried not to let her imagination run to all the places he might be heading. If he were leaving Promise Lodge, surely he would tell her—wouldn't he? "I—I have no idea," she replied with a hitch in her voice.

Irene slipped an arm around Phoebe's waist. "I have a feeling there's been some trouble in paradise, but I don't want to butt in," she said sympathetically. "Allen's a *gut*-hearted young man, but he's seemed skittish lately. Hasn't even come to claim his pies. Is he running scared, with a case of cold feet?"

Running scared . . . cold feet. Phoebe thought back to the delightful day she and Allen had spent in Forest Grove—the day she'd spotted the perfect place for the home she so badly wanted to share with him.

"Why would he be scared?" she asked sadly. "I told him I was going to ask for the land Mamm was giving me, so he could move his construction equipment there—so he could have a shop. I thought he'd be happy to have more work space, now that he's building those two new—"

"Well, that might explain it," Irene murmured with a shake of her head.

"What'd I do?" Phoebe whimpered. "I was only being generous—and I was so excited because nobody had spoken for the land that overlooks the lake. It's the perfect place for a house—"

"And after one date you were seeing yourself in that house with Allen, ain't so?"

Phoebe swiped at her tear-filled eyes. "I thought that's what he wanted, too. I—I felt like things were getting serious between us. After all, we've known each other all our lives."

Irene smiled gently at her. They watched for a few more moments, as the massive horses hauled the tiny home across the road and between the big garden plots where Mattie's vegetables were growing. "I suspect he felt you were getting a little ahead of him, dear," she explained. "Men like to feel they're the providers. They want to have everything in place—a house to take a bride home to—before they pop the question."

"But Allen *has* a house!" Phoebe protested, pointing as the back end of his tiny home disappeared from their view. "I was offering him a place to park it! And now he's taking it somewhere else before Truman's had a chance to build a road to my land."

"Your land," Irene echoed as she returned to the kitchen. "No matter how *gut* your intentions are, dear, if Allen went along with them he would always be aware that he's parked on *your* land."

Phoebe blinked. Had she been too hasty, asking Mamm for a parcel of ground? Had Allen interpreted her invitation to work on her land as an expectation that they would marry soon?

That was your intention, wasn't it? You've been dreaming of your wedding day ever since he kissed you.

Phoebe sighed. Why hadn't she anticipated Allen's reaction? All her life, she'd known that men did the proposing and the providing, yet she'd gotten so excited about the perfect plot of ground that she'd rushed ahead and done things *her* way. She hadn't considered that Allen might think she was putting the cart before the horse, or manipulating him into marriage.

He probably feels you've one-upped him, latching on to property when he doesn't own any.

"Maybe I have some fences to mend," she murmured as she headed back to the worktable.

Irene smiled as she opened bags of frozen blackberries to make more filling. "Fence mending is a skill we all have to work at from time to time," she said gently. "It doesn't get any easier as you get older—or get married—but we have to keep trying. Thinking you love someone doesn't mean a thing if you don't put that love into action."

As Phoebe rolled a ball of dough into a circle to form a piecrust, she hoped Irene had it right. The best ideas often came to her when she allowed her thoughts to wander while her hands worked with dough, so she hoped she'd know what to do about Allen by the time she'd finished the day's baking.

Chapter Twenty-One

When Marlin halted his rig near the Lehmans' front porch on Tuesday afternoon, he had a sinking feeling the ride to the clinic was going to be very uncomfortable. Frances stood on the top step staring at him as though he'd grown horns.

"Preacher Amos told me *he* was driving me to my appointment," she said stiffly.

"Amos and Mattie are helping with their three new grandbabies today," Marlin said as he stepped down from the buggy. He smiled at Frances, hoping his good news would soften her resistance to riding with him. "Barbara had twin girls yesterday, and early this morning, Bernice had a little boy—Corene, Carol, and Caleb are sure to keep the Helmuth and Troyer tribe hopping for a while."

"Everything went well, then?" she asked.

Marlin stopped at the bottom of the porch steps. Frances looked pale and listless in her black cape dress and *kapp*, and he yearned for the sight of her smile. For the hundredth time, he wished he could make Frances's slings disappear— just as he longed to restore her faith in him. He'd been preparing himself for the chance that the doctor wouldn't free her from her constraints today, sensing Frances would sink even lower into depression if that's the way her appointment went.

"The two new *mamms* are doing well," he assured her. "And from what Minerva's told me, all three babies are perfect—and she's exhausted, after tending to their births for about thirty-six hours straight."

Frances's eyes widened, a sign that she was at least listening to him and sympathizing with Minerva.

Marlin extended his arms. "How about if I help you into the rig and we'll be on our way?" he asked lightly. "I've been praying long and hard that the doctor will let you start your therapy today, knowing you'll feel so much better."

Frances lowered her gaze, paying close attention to the stairs as she descended them. "High time," she muttered. "I can manage fine, *denki*. I'm sorry Amos has inconvenienced you by asking you to take me. I can ask Roman to drive me—"

"I'm happy to take you, Frances," Marlin insisted, searching for words that would make her feel more comfortable. "Even if you don't want me to court you, we can still be friends, ain't so? We've been friends since we came to live at Promise Lodge, after all—even while Floyd was alive."

Frances appeared too focused on stepping into the rig to reply. She'd grown accustomed to keeping her balance even though she was unable to grab hold of things, and although Marlin had hoped for an excuse to steady her, he admired her fortitude. She placed a foot on the step, sprang into the rig, landed on the padded seat—and scooted to the far side of it—without his assistance.

Marlin got in and took up the lines, making the best of a difficult situation. After a couple of futile attempts to start a conversation, he let Frances gaze out the window for the rest of the trip to the clinic in Forest Grove. The *clip-clop, clip-clop* of his horse's hooves punctuated the uncomfortable silence and made the humidity seem more intense. As Marlin blotted his sweaty neck with his bandanna, he was aware of how frustrated Frances must feel because she couldn't wipe the dampness from her brow—but he didn't dare offer to do that for her.

At the clinic, Frances allowed him to open the door for her before she strode toward the admission desk. When he followed her, she frowned. "I can do this myself," she insisted. "After all, I've been seeing the doctor for *weeks* now."

With a sigh, Marlin took a seat in the waiting area. After a nurse in turquoise scrubs escorted Frances down the hall toward the exam rooms, he prayed that he'd be able to help her without further damaging their friendship—if friendship was all he could hope for. He was paging through an old magazine without really seeing it when the nurse came out to speak with him.

"Dr. Flanagan would like you to join us, sir," she said in a low voice. "He wants to be sure someone can assist Frances with her exercises between home visits from the therapist he's arranged for her."

Marlin's heart skipped a beat. Frances wouldn't be happy about his help, but if the doctor wanted him to participate, how could he refuse? As he entered the small room where she sat with a slender man in a shirt and tie, he ignored Frances's scowl. "Look at you!" he said happily. "Out of your slings and—"

"And I'm as weak as a baby bird that can't fly," Frances interrupted bitterly. "I'm still *useless*—just as I've been ever since I fell down the stairs."

Dr. Flanagan shook Marlin's hand, gazing at him purposefully. "Think how much better you'll feel when you get your arms massaged and start moving them again, Mrs. Lehman," he said. "If you do the exercises on these printouts between your therapist's visits, I predict an improvement in your mindset, as well—but if your family and friends don't think you're doing better, I need to know about it," he added with a rise of his eyebrows.

Marlin nodded subtly in response. "Your girls and your friends and I will help you every step of the way, Frances," he said as he accepted the stapled pages. "We've all been concerned about your depression lately."

The doctor nodded. "And how are you related to Frances, Mr.—?"

"Marlin Kurtz," he replied, thinking quickly. "Frances isn't a member of my family, but it's not because we haven't *talked* about getting married."

Smiling, Dr. Flanagan took Frances's hand and gently raised her arm. "My Plain patients usually recover quickly because they're surrounded by family and friends—less chance of isolation, and more incentive to remain involved in their therapy," he said as he slowly maneuvered Frances's arm. "Do I have your permission to show Marlin how to move and massage your arms?"

Frances looked from the doctor to Marlin, miffed at the way they were conspiring to help her. "I don't have much choice, do I?"

Dr. Flanagan placed her hand in her lap, focusing intently on her. "You can choose to start your therapy now, or you can wait for your therapist to come—which might not be until next week," he added in a businesslike tone. "You can also choose to have Marlin show your daughters how to guide you through these exercises when you get home, if you don't want his help. But while he's here, you might as well put him to work, right?"

Frances let out an exasperated sigh. "Oh, *fine*. Let's just get on with it."

Marlin bit back a smile, watching as Dr. Flanagan demonstrated the simple movements that would help Frances regain the strength in her hands and arms. As the doctor coached him, Marlin relished the feel of her soft skin even as he realized how weak her muscles had grown from lack of use over the past few weeks.

"That'll be enough for now," Dr. Flanagan said after Marlin had finished. "Some gentle massage will increase the blood flow and keep your arms from getting sore after your exercise sessions—"

"Mary Kate and Gloria can see to that part," Frances put in quickly. "Folks will *talk* if they know Marlin is at the house giving me a massage."

Marlin tried not to feel disappointed about Frances's attitude toward him. As they left the exam room, he had to walk quickly so he could open the clinic and buggy doors for her. In her haste, Francis stepped up into his rig a little too fast so he placed his hands at her waist to steady her.

"You thought it was just hunky-dory that the doctor asked you to help me, ain't so?" she challenged after she'd positioned herself on the seat.

Marlin took up the lines, careful not to smile too widely. "If it hadn't been me helping you, it would've been Amos, *jah?*"

"Schemers—all three of you!" she muttered. At least she seemed more engaged and energetic than she'd been during their drive into town.

When Marlin got back to the Lehman place, Frances reluctantly allowed him to help her down from the buggy before striding to the house ahead of him. He noticed that she kept her arms folded close to her body, as though they were still in slings. He also saw that when she tried to grasp the stair railing, her hand couldn't grip it very tightly.

But with patience and therapy, she'll recover, he thought as he followed her into the house with the exercise sheets.

*And hopefully with Your help, Lord, she'll regain her sense
of perspective about our relationship, too.*

"Mamm, what'd the doctor say?" Mary Kate asked as
they entered the kitchen. "Looks like you're a free
woman—no slings!"

"I'll be fine—and I'll be a lot better if you've got a glass
of iced tea handy," Frances insisted as she gingerly pulled
her chair out from the table. "Marlin's got my exercise
list, and you're to work with me three or four times a day,
Mary Kate."

Mary Kate smiled her thanks to him before she opened
the refrigerator. "And while we're working your arm muscles, we can decide on the furniture you want to get rid of,
Mamm," she said. "While you were gone, I got a call from
the fellow who's going to load it up and sell it. He'll be here
on Friday."

Marlin sucked air. What could he say to change her
mind—in a way that focused on her needs rather than his
own? "Are you *sure* you want to get rid of everything?" he
asked gently. "I can understand why you might want to live
at the lodge with the single ladies for a while. But what if
the day comes when you wish you still had your family's
keepsakes and—"

"Gloria and I feel this place is too big and quiet," Frances
interrupted. Her expression waxed stoic, even as she swallowed hard. "The money from selling the furniture—and
hopefully the house and property—will support us for a
long while. My mind's made up, Marlin, so don't try to talk
me out of it."

Marlin declined Mary Kate's offer of iced tea and headed
home, baffled by Frances's attitude. He'd been hoping that
over the past few days she would've reconsidered the decision she'd announced at church. She sounded so resigned to
letting go of her possessions, so *final* about living at the

lodge—as though she'd rather give up everything she loved than marry him.

He'd decided to let Harley and Minerva have the Kurtz house when he and Frances married, figuring she'd have fewer confrontations with his disapproving son if they lived in her place. But if a new family moved to Promise Lodge and bought her property before he could convince her of his love, that option would no longer be open to him.

You have a lot of thinking to do in the next few days, he told himself as he drove the rig past the barrel factory. *Frances seems determined to live without you. How are you going to handle that?*

Chapter Twenty-Two

Phoebe gazed at the three babies in their carrier baskets, lined up in a row on the table in the Helmuths' big kitchen. The one on the left wore a yellow crocheted cap and onesie, the center baby wore white, and the one on the right sported pale green clothing—and all of them had carrot-colored fuzz for hair.

"How do you tell them apart?" she asked with a laugh. "Or is that a mother thing, and you know which girl is Corene and which is Carol?"

Barbara laughed, looking proudly at her tiny new daughters—and beside her, Bernice beamed at her son. Phoebe had always had trouble telling the Troyer twins apart when they were growing up, too, but she wasn't going to admit it.

"I asked Minerva to dress Corene in green and to put Carol in white, because we had the most onesies in those colors," Barbara explained. "I figure to keep dressing them that way until I can figure out who's who from their personalities, because right now they truly are identical."

"So if a baby's in yellow or blue, he's mine," Bernice put in with a laugh. "We've color-coded our husbands' clothes for years, so we're used to this system."

"Well, no matter what they're wearing, they're all beautiful," Phoebe murmured enviously. She tried not to imagine

what a baby she and Allen might make would look like,
even as she longed to find out someday. "I wish you all the
best as you get accustomed to motherhood and raise these
wee ones."

"We're more grateful than you know for the casseroles
and pies you brought us," Bernice said as she gazed at the
food on the counter. "Sam and Simon are the most helpful
husbands in the world, but they're not much *gut* in the
kitchen."

"*Jah*, and it might be a week or two before we new
mamms catch up with ourselves or get any real sleep," Barbara admitted with a tired sigh. "Mattie's been helping when
she's not working in her garden plots, and your *mamm*'s
coming tomorrow to do our laundry, bless her. What would
we do without our friends?"

"Count on Irene and the Kuhns and me to bring your
supper for a while—or whatever else you might need,"
Phoebe added. "We're all happy to help."

After she'd visited for a few more minutes, Phoebe left
the big Helmuth house and mentally prepared herself for the
next place she planned to go. After sounds of loud hammering had piqued her curiosity, she'd looked out one of the
lodge's upstairs windows Tuesday afternoon—and what
she saw had made her jaw drop. Allen had parked his tiny
home under the trees about ten yards from the far side of
Rainbow Lake, and he'd built a new wooden dock on the
water's edge!

She didn't ordinarily bake on Wednesdays, but she'd
gotten up early in the morning to make pies and casseroles
for the Helmuths—and two fruit pies as a peace offering
for Allen. If he no longer wanted her company, that was
one thing, but if she'd scared him off with her talk of

claiming the land up the hill from the lake, that was something else altogether.

She had to know where she stood with him. Allen was too proud to admit why he'd made his sudden move, and why he hadn't claimed his pies lately. If he believed he'd received all the treats he had coming as payment for the wooden pie shelves he'd built for her and Irene, Phoebe intended to correct his misconception. She was willing to bake pies for him for as long as it took to convince him they belonged together.

When Phoebe stopped by the bakery to pick up Allen's pies, she said a little prayer. *Lord, remind me that this visit isn't about me—it's about us. Help me understand what Allen might not be able to put into words . . . and help me graciously accept his rejection, if that's what it comes down to.*

As Phoebe placed the two pies in her metal pie carrier, she hoped the gooseberry and the strawberry-rhubarb fillings would entice Allen to talk to her openly. He'd spent the past week and a half avoiding her, under the guise of being immersed in building the two tiny homes he'd sold. She wanted the truth about his feelings, so she wouldn't have to endure any more of the questions, the emptiness, his absence had caused.

Phoebe stepped outside and walked around the Kuhns' cheese factory and the fence that held her *mamm*'s dairy herd. The cows were in the barn for their second milking of the day, so she had an uninterrupted view of Rainbow Lake and the grassy verge surrounding it. She gazed across the sunlit surface of the water, which glittered like a million diamonds, and stopped. To be sure she was seeing clearly, Phoebe shaded her eyes with her hand.

On the far side of the lake, Allen was sitting in a lawn

chair on his new wooden dock, holding a fishing rod. He wasn't working, so he had no excuse not to talk to her.

Bolstering her nerve for whatever might happen, Phoebe strode across the grass—and for good measure, she waved at the young man who'd so effortlessly captured her heart.

Allen caught sight of a white *kapp* and apron in the sunlight. He immediately recognized Phoebe even though she was a distant figure standing by Christine's dairy barns.

He gripped his fishing rod. She was heading his way, reminiscent of an angel as she appeared to float gracefully across the grass. It was only right to return her wave. The sight of her metal carrier made his stomach rumble, even though he knew why she was bringing him pie—and even though there was no escaping the mission that was undoubtedly uppermost in her mind.

But it was all right. Phoebe was bridging the gap between them—as he should've done; he just hadn't known how. Even though he was the man, and he was a few years older than Phoebe, the reality of committing to a relationship was foreign to him because he'd always taken the easy way out with the girls who'd gotten serious about him. He hadn't had a thing of value or permanence to offer those young women, but Dat had changed all that.

Allen smiled, allowing his body to relax in the shaded lawn chair. During the past week he'd come to realize that having land at Promise Lodge had given him roots—something he'd purposely avoided before—yet he felt *free* now. His father's unexpectedly generous gift of land, with no religious strings attached, had made him willing to settle down close to his family. *Never* had he expected that to happen.

His heart began to pound, but it was a good feeling—a sense of being alive and open to whatever might happen with the beautiful young woman who was approaching him. "Hey there, Phoebe," he said. He figured he should be the first to speak, since she had made the first move.

"What a great setup!" Phoebe looked over at his tiny home, nestled in the shade of the big maple trees. "And you've built a new dock—which is making all the ladies at the lodge mighty curious as they look out their windows."

Allen smiled, knowing Phoebe was the curious one. He reeled in his bobber and line so he wouldn't get distracted if he caught a fish. Should he reveal the truth, or keep her waiting? A glance at her pie keeper reminded him that the sooner she knew the facts, the sooner he would have his pie—or she'd walk away from him, if his news didn't set well.

"Ruby and Beulah and Irene are probably glad for something new to talk about," Allen hedged as he stood up. "Let me get you a chair, Phoebe. You're the first guest I've had since I moved to my new place."

Allen could feel the weight of her gaze as he jogged to the little slate-blue house. When he returned with another lawn chair and opened it for her, Phoebe's eyes were wide with speculation.

"Your new place?" she asked in a voice piqued with interest.

Allen smiled at the way she made him do the talking. When she sat down beside him, he resisted the urge to grab her hand. "Considering that Mattie has given her two sons some acreage, and that your *mamm* figured to do the same for you and Laura, Dat has realized that as the other founder of Promise Lodge, he was entitled to do the same for me."

Phoebe was following his words closely, watching them come out of his mouth. "And?"

Allen chuckled. Her pretty face was alight with the knowledge of where this story was going, yet she was showing amazing restraint. "I chose the land that included Rainbow Lake," he said, extending his arms in both directions.

One of her eyebrows arched. "But the lake belongs to everyone," she pointed out warily.

"And everyone can still enjoy it—except now I'm going to keep it stocked with fish and see that the grass around it is mowed. I've become the lake's keeper, and the land around it is mine."

Phoebe turned in her chair, pointing behind them. "But *I* spoke for this land! And you knew that!" she added, aiming an accusing finger at him. "You *knew* I wanted a house on the hill so—so we could watch the sun rise over the water every morning and—"

Allen grabbed her hand, stifling a laugh. "Careful there, or you'll shoot me with this thing."

"Allen, this isn't funny!" Phoebe blurted. "I asked Mamm for this tract of land and she gave it to *me*! And Truman's to build a road up the hill—"

"He'll be here on Saturday to do that," Allen interrupted. When she struggled to free her hand from his grasp, he gently held it tighter. "Honey-girl, you've got it all wrong. My property line follows the row of big trees behind us, and you still have the place on the hill and the land to the west. We're neighbors. Didn't your *mamm* tell you that after she and Dat discussed the boundary?"

The fight suddenly went out of her, yet she was still on edge. "No," she admitted. "I've been busy baking pies, and she's been helping with the Helmuth babies."

Allen brought her hand to his lips and kissed her

knuckles. He was pleased that Phoebe was standing up for what she believed was hers rather than letting him trample all over her plans. "So you have your land, and I have mine," he pointed out softly. "When you build your house on the hill, you can still look out over Rainbow Lake, like you wanted to."

Phoebe's lower lip was quivering, so Allen sensed he'd better steer the conversation in a positive direction again.

"Actually, I was surprised nobody had spoken for the lake," he continued, "but the land surrounding it, and the woods that extend back to the borderline of Promise Lodge property, aren't much use to folks who'd want to raise crops or pasture animals. But I'm a carpenter rather than a farmer, so that's not a big concern to me."

"*Jah*, probably not," Phoebe agreed with a sigh.

Allen prayed he'd say the right words. Her abject disappointment gnawed at him, making him feel guilty for not blurting a declaration of his love for her—but he didn't want to lead her astray with pretty promises made too soon. "Now that I'm building tiny homes, I love the work I'm doing," he said. He longed to look into Phoebe's beautiful blue eyes, but she'd glanced away. "I *belong* at Promise Lodge, in ways I never felt when I was growing up in Coldstream with a preacher for a *dat*—and a bishop whose hatband surely must've been two sizes too tight, as narrow-minded as he was."

Phoebe sighed. "*Jah*, Obadiah Chupp has always run his district with an iron grip," she recalled softly. "The lives we're enjoying now would never have been possible if our parents hadn't broken away and come here."

"And I couldn't have gotten licensed in plumbing and electricity—couldn't have gotten any education beyond our little one-room schoolhouse—if I hadn't left Coldstream and my family," Allen pointed out. "We're all better off now. I'm a different man because I lived English for a while, but I've come back. For *gut*."

Phoebe focused on him, her eyes shining with unshed tears. "So what does that mean for me? For us?" she asked. "*Jah*, you have your land and I have mine, but that doesn't paint a very cozy picture. You've barely spoken to me lately—you've made all these changes without telling me, after I was excited and open and honest about my feelings for you."

Allen sighed. "Guilty as charged," he murmured. "I could say it's a guy thing, because it was easier to duck out than to admit how you . . . *scared* me when you talked about getting land and building a house. But now the playing field's been leveled and we're equals. I have land, too."

Phoebe hung her head. "I was stupid to rush ahead and ask Mamm for land when—"

"You're anything but stupid, honey-girl," Allen countered. He lifted her chin with his finger until she held his gaze. "So think about it from a different angle. Why might I have wanted land that adjoins yours? I could've had any unclaimed tract I wanted, after all."

When Phoebe blinked, a fat teardrop dribbled down each of her cheeks. Allen longed to kiss them from her face, but it wasn't the right time. Not quite.

"You tell me," she murmured. "Seems I've made some wrong assumptions."

Allen leaned closer to her, inhaling her fresh scent and savoring the sight of her flawless face, mere inches from his. "I'm betting we can get it right, if you'll give our feelings time to grow," he murmured. "I'm crazy about you, Phoebe. And I would *love* to live in a house overlooking

Rainbow Lake—with you. But let's invest some time in courting first, to be sure. Okay?"

Phoebe's eyes resembled pale blue saucers as comprehension sank in. "You really will join the Old Order?" she asked softly. "In my daydreams, I tend to skip ahead of all the things that need to happen before we can share a house—"

"You're not the only one with dreams, Phoebe," he put in solemnly. "And now that my business is up and running, and I'm settling on some land—"

"And you have a house!" she pointed out. "I—I'm not sure I'd want to live in a tiny home forever, but it would be a *gut* place to start out."

"A tiny home brings a whole new meaning to the concept of *togetherness*," Allen said with a laugh. "I couldn't stay in one for the long haul, either—but I'm happy to be building them for other folks. I drew up plans for a couple more of them this past week, by the way. That's another reason you haven't seen much of me."

"You've sold two more? Wow, congratulations!"

When Phoebe threw her arms around his neck, ecstatic about his success, Allen saw no reason to hold back any longer. He kissed her softly, elated and relieved that she poured herself into kissing him back. As the kiss continued, he was vaguely aware that anyone at Promise Lodge could see them out here on the dock, but it didn't matter. He had nothing to hide—and no reason to run anymore.

After several heart-pounding moments, Allen finally eased away from her. "Sure glad we got that straightened out," he murmured.

"I love you, Allen," Phoebe whispered. "I want you to know that, even if we don't—and I should've let you say that first, but—"

Allen's heart raced like a runaway horse. Those three little words upped the ante on a relationship, because they couldn't be taken back. "But you're braver than I am, and you wouldn't say it if you didn't mean it," he pointed out softly. "Your courage and your honesty are two of the things I love about *you*, Phoebe. You know what you want, and you go after it. You get right to the point instead of dancing around it. That's a rare and beautiful way to be."

Her eyes widened until he thought he might fall headfirst into her open soul. Allen took a deep breath, confident that from here on out they'd be on the same page, heading toward the same fulfilling future.

"*Denki* for not saying I'll have to give up my pie business after we marry," Phoebe said. "Or is that another faulty assumption I've made?"

Allen smiled. He knew plenty of Old Order men who would insist that their wives be stay-at-home women focused on their husbands and kids. "Well, while it's just you and me living in our tiny home, it'll take you maybe ten minutes to redd it up—and what'll you do with yourself for the rest of the day?" he teased. "I know you love your baking business, just as I know that once we have our house overlooking the lake and some other little *priorities* start arriving, you'll rethink how you spend your time. We both will."

Phoebe's face took on a soft glow. "*Jah*, when I visited the Helmuth wee ones a while ago, I got a major case of baby envy," she murmured.

Allen had no trouble imagining what a loving, competent *mamm* Phoebe would be . . . not to mention how much he would enjoy creating babies with her. He took her hand, reveling in the soft strength of the fingers that slipped between his. As he sat in the shade, with a summer breeze blowing off the shimmering surface of Rainbow Lake, he knew the meaning of true contentment.

"So it's all *gut*?" Phoebe murmured. "We're a courting couple, and we have a home place waiting for us when we're ready for it—and meanwhile, we have businesses that'll support us." With a satisfied sigh, she let her head drop back against the lawn chair. "I think we need to celebrate with a piece of pie."

"You've got all the right ideas, Phoebe," Allen said with a chuckle. "I'll be right back with a couple of forks."

Chapter Twenty-Three

As Frances gazed around the main room of her new apartment on Friday morning, she took a deep breath to steady her racing pulse. Her sofa from the house looked a little worn in the light streaming in through the large windows. Floyd's recliner and her rocking chair seemed almost foreign to her in their new setting, but she reminded herself that she'd get used to these changes—just as she would gladly adjust to spending less time sweeping, dusting, and doing dishes.

Christine and Rosetta smiled as they emerged from her new bedroom. "Your bed's made and you're all set!" Rosetta said, nodding at the arrangement of the front room. "Once you get your clothes hung in the closet and a few things on the walls, this place will feel like home."

"It looks a lot different than it did when I lived here—as well it should," Christine added. "These rooms gave me a place to regroup after we moved away from the farms we'd known all our lives. I hope you'll find the same peace and comfort here, Frances."

Peace and comfort. With all her heart, Frances yearned for those elusive elements of the life she'd shared with Floyd. For the moment, however, she put on a smile and tried to sound cheerful. "*Denki* for your help, ladies. I couldn't have done this without you. And Rosetta, you have no idea how excited Gloria is about her new job—and her blue-sky bedroom with the fluffy clouds painted on the ceiling," she added with a chuckle.

"I'm not a bit surprised she chose the rooms Maria redecorated," Rosetta remarked. "And after reading the first post she's sending to *The Budget*, I think she'll do very well as Promise Lodge's scribe, too. Her description of Phoebe and Irene's new pie business, and Allen's tiny homes, and how we encourage Plain ladies to live in the lodge apartments will probably attract some new residents for us."

Frances was pleased to hear Rosetta's positive comments, especially because she had a large, empty house she was hoping to sell someday soon. As the loud rumble of a truck engine and the crunch of gravel beneath tires came through the window with the morning breeze, she tried not to think about how many beloved pieces of furniture, dishes, and other items she would never see again now that the auctioneer was leaving with them. For a few painful moments, visions of her mother's walnut hutch, quilts her aunts had made, and the beautiful bone china cups and saucers she'd received as birthday presents flashed through her mind.

But it's the best thing for both of us to sell those things—and they're only things, *she reminded herself.* It's a fresh, unencumbered way to live within our means.

When Gloria entered the apartment, Frances focused on her daughter's glowing face.

"I'll feel like I'm living in heaven, waking up in the clouds each morning!" Gloria exclaimed. "Whenever you want to explain your bookkeeping system, Rosetta, I'm ready to take it on."

"That's what I like to hear—a can-do attitude," Rosetta said as she slipped her arm around Gloria's shoulders. "Unless my nose is mistaken, Ruby and Beulah have been baking, so maybe we can all have a little treat to celebrate your new home before we get down to business."

"I miss the aroma of someone else's cooking filling the air," Christine said as they headed into the hallway. "The Kuhn sisters have a real talent for making the lodge feel like home."

Frances let the others walk ahead of her. She paused outside her apartment to study the lobby's huge chandelier made of antlers, and to admire the graceful curves of the double staircase that descended to the main level—so different from the ordinary stairs in the houses where she'd previously lived. When the front door opened and Bishop Monroe entered ahead of Marlin, she had a sense of watching them from a high, hidden vantage point—until Marlin sensed her presence and gazed up at her.

"Are you all right, Frances? Shall I steady you as you come down the stairs?" he asked kindly.

Frances sighed. He really was a compassionate man, but she had to learn to rely on her own strength. "I'm fine, *denki*," she replied as she carefully took hold of the bannister. "I can already tell that my therapy and exercises are improving my grip."

"Glad to hear it," Monroe said in a voice that filled the high-ceilinged lobby. "We got your stuff all loaded up and Ted, the auctioneer, didn't think he'd have any trouble selling it. His sale barn's on the south side of Cloverdale, and he's adding your consignment to the auction he's got scheduled for a week from tomorrow."

Frances gripped the wooden railing. *Come the first weekend in June, our furniture will belong to other families*, she thought. *There's no changing your mind—no getting it back.*

It took all her effort to continue down the stairs without faltering—or crying. When she reached the lobby, Marlin's carefully composed facial expression told her he didn't agree with the way she'd disposed of her household belongings, but he was diplomatic enough not to say anything. "Something smells delicious," she remarked. "Why don't you fellows join us for some of the Kuhns' goodies, after all the carrying and loading you've done this morning?"

"You don't have to ask me twice!" the bishop said with a laugh. "While we worked, we could smell the pies Phoebe and Irene are baking. So even if we're not hungry, we're ready to eat."

Frances couldn't help smiling. The local men never turned down an opportunity to eat whatever Ruby and Beulah had whipped up. "I really appreciate you fellows' going back to clear out my house after you carried my furniture up to my apartment," she said. "I believe it was the right thing to do, but I—I just couldn't watch."

"Understandable," Marlin said as they all entered the dining room. "It would've torn my heart out if I'd gotten rid of our household stuff after I lost Essie. But we all handle our grief differently."

The Kuhn sisters were setting a stack of small plates on one of the tables, along with a big tray of cookies and bars, so Frances focused on them to keep from crying. It had been an emotional morning. She needed some time alone later, to fully deal with her feelings.

"Welcome, Frances and Gloria!" Beulah crowed as she gestured for everyone to sit down. "We're so glad to have you two joining us—and pleased to hear you're going to manage the day-to-day business of the lodge now, Gloria. We'll try to behave ourselves and not cause you any trouble."

Rosetta laughed as she took her seat. "Your first assignment, Gloria, will be keeping a lid on the wild parties we've been known to have here," she declared as Ruby passed the cookie tray to Frances. "When there aren't any men around to keep us in our places, we women lose all sense of decorum and control, you know."

"Really? I sure hope you'll let *me* live here, too!"

At the sound of an unfamiliar voice, everyone looked toward the dining room doorway. When Frances turned in her chair, she saw a tall, stalwart woman of perhaps forty gazing at them. She held an old suitcase in each hand, and her deep blue cape dress, sensible black shoes, and a *kapp* with an organza heart-shaped crown announced that she was a Plain woman who'd probably come from out East rather than from anywhere nearby.

Rosetta approached their guest with her hand extended. "Welcome to Promise Lodge!" she said. "We do indeed welcome women who need a place to live. I'm Rosetta Wickey—and you've arrived just in time for cookies and coffee! Come and sit down with us!"

A look of extreme relief transformed the newcomer's face as she set down her luggage to grasp Rosetta's hand. "I'm Annabelle Beachey—and I'm happy to report that I didn't get run down by that big truck that was heading down your road," she said with a short laugh. "Is somebody already moving out? This place hasn't been around all that long, the way I understand it."

"We've just marked our first-year anniversary," Christine put in as she pulled a chair out for Annabelle. "That truck held some furniture belonging to Frances and Gloria, who have shifted into an apartment because the man of their family has passed away. Their lovely home is for sale, if you're interested."

"Ah. Sorry for your loss, ladies." Annabelle perched on the edge of the chair, quickly focusing on each face around the table. "I'm surprised that you two fellows are tolerating the sort of talk I heard when I came in, about not keeping these women in their places. Have I died and gone to heaven?"

Bishop Monroe's baritone laughter filled the dining room, and Marlin was chuckling along with him. "We run a Plain community that's more progressive than most," he explained. "I'm Bishop Monroe Burkholder. Seated beside Frances Lehman is my cohort, Preacher Marlin Kurtz, and you're sitting by my wife, Christine. We're Old Order Amish, but we welcome residents of any Plain denomination—like Ruby and Beulah Kuhn, who are Mennonites," he added as he gestured at the two ladies in floral-print dresses. "We're delighted to meet you, Annabelle."

"What brings you to Promise Lodge?" Marlin asked. "Most of us came for a fresh start after we suffered some serious setback where we'd been living previously."

Annabelle's smile faltered a little. "I know a thing or two about setbacks," she said in a subdued voice. "My husband of more than twenty years up and decided to leave the Old Order—and me along with it. Phineas declared himself free of all the constraints that our faith and the institution of marriage had shackled him with. I have no idea where he made off to."

She sighed, gathering her courage. "After he left, his brother took over the farm," she continued. "He offered to let me stay, but I didn't want to be an abandoned wife—a pariah—dependent upon his hospitality, so I took my chances and came here. What did I have to lose? I don't have any children, and everything I own is in those two suitcases."

Frances sat back, rather amazed at what this woman had just shared with them. Annabelle was between a big rock and a very hard place, because as long as her errant husband was alive, she couldn't remarry. She was doomed to remain beholden to whoever would take her in—and she would be the topic of a lot of gossip.

"We're sorry to hear that, Annabelle," Bishop Monroe said, shaking his head as he chose a cranberry-date bar and a couple of peanut butter cookies from the tray. "We've got some apartments upstairs that might be just the ticket for starting over and considering your options."

"Gloria and I will take you upstairs when you've eaten your cookies," Rosetta said as she took the seat next to Annabelle. "As it happens, I've just hired Gloria as my apartment manager, so you can help me give her some on-the-job training."

"These look delightful," Annabelle murmured as she chose a sugar cookie bar and a chocolate-chip cookie. She gazed ruefully at Rosetta. "Trouble is, all I've got to pay rent with is the egg money I'd stashed in my button jar—and if I hadn't switched it out of my coffee can, Phineas would've gotten to it before I knew he was leaving. Last thing I saw of him, he was rifling through the pantry looking in all the canisters for my cash."

"Don't you worry about rent money," Beulah insisted as she poured a mug of coffee and set it at Annabelle's place. "We've started a fund to help cover rent and expenses for new gals who need a little help."

"*Jah*, and we can talk about ways to earn your rent, too," Ruby put in with an encouraging smile. "You don't impress me as a freeloader or as somebody who enjoys accepting charity, Annabelle."

"I don't expect a free ride," Annabelle confirmed. "I'm just glad I recalled reading about this place in *The Budget*, so I could tell my driver where to bring me. She's done a lot of driving for our family, and when she heard my predicament, she brought me out here for next to nothing. God's surely been watching out for me."

"Where are you from, Annabelle?" Christine asked. "We've got distant cousins in Pennsylvania who wear heart-shaped *kapps* like yours."

"You've pegged me right," she replied. "I hail from Bird-in-Hand. I suppose there are plenty of places closer to home I could've gone, but your scribe's letters in *The Budget* made this place sound . . . well, so refreshing. So welcoming."

"I'm glad you found us," Rosetta murmured, placing her hand over Annabelle's wrist. "And I'm glad my column conveyed the spirit of open invitation we hope to extend to folks."

A sense of warm contentment settled around the table as everyone savored their cookies and coffee. Frances noted the weary lines on Annabelle's face, and the way her hand trembled as she closed her eyes gratefully over a big bite of her chocolate-chip cookie. She sensed Annabelle hadn't had an easy life with her husband—and perhaps had come to Missouri so he had less chance of tracking her down. She was awfully young to consider living out her life alone, ineligible for remarriage—but Phineas hadn't given her a choice.

Maybe she's better off without him—and Lord, I'm so blessed that I never once thought about my Floyd that way.

Frances decided that her new mission would be to become a good friend to Annabelle, to help her settle in and make a new life at Promise Lodge. After Rosetta and Gloria took their new guest upstairs to choose an apartment, the men went on about their day and Frances helped Ruby, Beulah, and Christine clear the table.

"What a story that poor woman has," Ruby said quietly.

"*Jah*, that underhanded husband of hers—rifling through her pantry for her stash before he abandoned her!" Beulah muttered as she ran hot water into the sink. "After more than twenty years, it seems Annabelle suddenly wasn't worth his time."

"Not to mention that Phineas committed the unforgive-able sin—leaving the Amish faith," Christine put in as she took a tea towel from the drawer. "It was different when Rosetta married Truman, because they consulted with Monroe and she stayed faithful after marrying a Mennonite. It's another thing altogether when a longtime church member jumps the fence."

Because she'd been a bishop's wife, Frances was ac-quainted with this situation. A family that belonged to their church in Sugarcreek, Ohio, had abandoned the Old Order to take over a profitable restaurant that attracted a lot of English tourists—and they'd embraced electricity, cars, and the English lifestyle. Floyd and the preachers had preached for *weeks* about the dangers of turning away from God and becoming motivated by money. The way the Amish saw it, that family had sacrificed their souls and lost all chance at salvation.

"You have to wonder *why* Phineas left," Frances said softly. "Now he's alienated his friends and family—the folks most likely to help him deal with whatever crisis he must've been going through. I can't think he'll get much help amongst the English, and it'll be tough for him to get a job without a driver's license."

"He'd probably been making his escape plans for a while and Annabelle didn't realize it," Beulah muttered. "Nobody with a lick of sense would take off before he had a plan in place."

"Puh!" Ruby exclaimed. "If he was scrounging around for Annabelle's egg money, he must've been desperately short of cash."

"Or else he was just *mean*, hitting up her little fund as a final way to humiliate her," Christine said with a scowl. "If that's the case, I hope he's truly out of her life. Nobody needs a man like that."

After the kitchen was cleaned up, Frances slipped upstairs to her new apartment. She did her hand and arm exercises while gazing out her windows at the trees and bushes that were her new scenery. When she caught sight of a lone figure on the distant hill, however, a lump formed in her throat. Marlin was standing outside his barrel factory, staring off into space as though he didn't know what to do with himself. And when she turned to look in a different direction, she saw the house she and Gloria had left . . . the home Floyd had provided for their family.

At the thought of returning to give the house a final redding up, a sob escaped her. If she worked slowly, Frances was able to handle a broom now—but did she have the strength to face those empty rooms? The memories that lingered there?

Frances burst into tears, muffling her sobs with the green afghan Marlin's Fannie had crocheted for her. *What have I done? Why did I think leaving that house—our home—was such a fine idea?* she fretted.

She'd done it so she'd have money to live on. And she'd done it partly for Gloria. But Gloria had a new job managing the lodge, a colorful apartment, and the weekly responsibility to write Promise Lodge's column for *The Budget*.

And what do you *have now?* Frances's inner voice demanded. *You've sent all the treasures and trappings of your adult life down the road in a stranger's truck. You're left with nothing—and nobody. You're no better off than Annabelle— except you brought this on yourself, and she didn't.*

Frances wiped her face on her sleeve and turned away from the windows. She wasn't ordinarily one to throw pity parties, and her laments weren't entirely true: she had turned Marlin away, but she still had Gloria, Mary Kate, Roman, and little David—not to mention Lester. The Kuhn sisters, along with Rosetta and her sisters, were wonderful friends who truly cared about what happened to her—they wanted her to be healthy and happy again. And Frances sensed that Irene and Annabelle would soon become her good friends, as well.

Even if she composed herself and ate supper downstairs with her new neighbors, however, it was going to be a lonely afternoon—and one of the longest nights of her life.

Chapter Twenty-Four

As she and Gloria sat at the breakfast table Saturday morning enjoying crisp waffles and juicy sausages, Frances tried hard to raise her spirits to the other ladies' level of cheerfulness. Annabelle had recovered from her long trip and seemed to be healing from the pain that had brought her to Promise Lodge. She was listening attentively to the Kuhn sisters and Irene as they recounted their arrivals, as well as to stories about the romances that had moved Mattie, Christine, and Rosetta into homes with their new husbands.

"It's nice to hear about women who've had second chances at happiness," Annabelle said as she drizzled syrup over her second waffle. "I can't hope for such a fairy-tale ending to *my* situation, but I can already tell that living amongst the friendly folks here will be a big improvement over staying where I was."

A curious glance from Beulah made Frances focus on her food. She hoped the well-intentioned *maidel* wouldn't ask why she, too, was no longer anticipating a happily-ever-after— why the flame she and Marlin had kindled had gone out. The squeak of the back screen door and quick footsteps crossing the kitchen floor made everyone look up from her breakfast.

Minerva stopped in the dining room doorway to catch

her breath. Her face was pale and her eyes were rimmed in red. "We—we have some awful news," she said as she approached the table. "When Bernice went to get Caleb from his crib this morning, she—she couldn't wake him. Looks like he died sometime in the wee hours, for no reason that I was able to figure out."

All the ladies gasped, their smiles vanishing. "Oh no! Bernice must be heartbroken," Ruby murmured.

Irene shook her head in disbelief. "But he was just born on—"

"Tuesday," Minerva put in sadly. "Barely four days old, he was."

"How are Barbara and Sam?" Frances asked. "They're probably worried that their little girls will come down with whatever Caleb succumbed to."

"The whole Helmuth household is in a state of shock. Mattie and Amos are headed over there right now to help," the midwife replied. "I suspect it's sudden infant death syndrome, rather than a contagious illness, because when I checked on the babies yesterday afternoon, they were all three well—nursing and napping, as they're supposed to do. For reasons we can't explain, some babies just stop breathing."

"It's a mystery, why God calls such tiny angels home," Beulah said with a sigh. "Our brother and his wife lost one that way years ago. Our best efforts and urgent prayers couldn't heal the emotional wound or take away the pain of that empty crib."

"The best thing we can do is help them prepare for the funeral—clean their house before the visitation and burial," Ruby said gently. "Count on Beulah and me to prepare the meal for after the service, here in the dining room."

"Phoebe and I aren't doing our regular baking today, so we'll make the pies and freeze them until we know the funeral date," said Irene as she rose from the table. "I've heard Barbara say the Helmuths have quite a large family out in Ohio, and it'll take them a while to get here."

"I'll go to the Helmuth place now and see what they'd like me to do," Gloria put in. "They have a big house to clean, and what with tending three new babies, they haven't had much inclination to scrub floors or wipe down kitchen cabinets and such."

"I'll go with you, dear," Frances said, recognizing a welcome chance to be useful.

"If somebody's got a sewing machine and knows a place to buy some nice white fabric, I'd be happy to make the baby's burial clothes," Annabelle put in. "I've done a lot of sewing for the Mennonite Relief Mission near our place in Pennsylvania, so I can practically make little clothes in my sleep."

Frances smiled at the way their newest resident had jumped in to help folks she hadn't even met yet. "Before I moved out of my house, I brought a bin of fabric over—including the large pieces left over from making my Floyd's burial clothes," she said softly.

"I'll fetch that bin from the storeroom for you, Annabelle, and you can use our sewing machine," Beulah offered. "It'll be a real comfort to Bernice and her family that you've offered to make the baby's clothes."

"You know, we also have some young single fellows—and a widower—who could use some new shirts and work pants," Frances told Annabelle as she began stacking the dirty dishes. "Lester and the Helmuth cousins don't have wives to sew for them, so we'll introduce you to them soon."

"And they're all earning *gut* money, so don't sell yourself short when you set your prices with them," Ruby teased.

Despite the sad news they'd just heard, Annabelle smiled

brightly. "Seems the clouds might have a silver lining for me after all," she said. "I appreciate the way you're all looking out for me!"

After Minerva left, they washed the dishes and went off in their various directions. Irene was going to speak to Phoebe about baking pies, while the Kuhns were headed into Forest Grove to stock up on groceries—and Annabelle decided to go with them. As Frances and Gloria started across the grassy lawn toward the Helmuths' double-sized house, they waved at Alma Peterscheim and her daughter, Deborah Schwartz, who were walking toward them.

"Such sad news that we've lost one of our wee ones," Alma murmured when they'd caught up. She slipped an arm around her daughter, whose eyes were wide with disbelief. "I've told Deborah not to let this dampen her excitement over having her own baby, come September."

"*Jah*, we can only focus forward and do our best to have healthy babies—just as Barbara and Bernice did," Frances remarked. "Worrying about what might go wrong only causes stress that doesn't help the *mamm* or her child, either one."

When they arrived at the big Helmuth house that sat across the parking lot from the nursery's greenhouses, a gray hearse was pulling out onto the county highway. Frances sighed at the sad sight, aware that the baby inside it represented Bernice's entire world. The funeral home near Cloverdale would prepare the tiny body for burial and then return it to be dressed and placed in a plain, handmade casket.

When Frances and her companions stepped inside, Bishop Monroe and Marlin were already in the big front room with Mattie and Preacher Amos, as well as Sam and Barbara and Simon and Bernice. The red-eyed grandparents sat on a love seat near the long couch, where Amos's daughters and their husbands sat bunched together as though they couldn't bear to have even air come between them. Mattie and Barbara were holding Carol and Corene to their shoulders, which made Bernice appear all the more bereft without a baby to cradle. The two church leaders spoke in low voices, offering comfort and assistance.

"Have you called your parents yet, Simon?" Bishop Monroe asked gently. "We'll plan the funeral for a date that allows them time to arrive—"

"We haven't been able to face that phone call yet," Barbara blurted with a shake of her head. "Just a few days ago we were calling family members in Ohio to tell them our *gut* news, and now . . ."

"It's a painful day, and it's not our intent to rush you," Marlin said somberly. "At your age, you've not had much practice at making such a tough phone call—"

"If you'd like, Sam and Simon, I can call your folks," Mattie offered as she stood up to walk with her gurgling grandbaby. "Grandparents have a lot in common, and over the years we've figured out how to share sad news."

Barbara grasped her sister's hand and turned toward Simon. "Maybe that would be best, don't you think? If we didn't have to make all those calls, this ordeal would be a bit easier to bear."

Bernice stared at the hardwood floor as though she hadn't heard her twin's suggestion, but Simon brightened a bit. "I'm for that," he said. "I've been trying to find words all day before I go out to the phone shanty, but I'm afraid I'll leave a totally irrational message or I'll not be able to talk at all."

"Consider it done," Amos put in. He let out a long sigh. "It's a blessing that the undertaker can have Caleb back to us by this evening, considering that tomorrow's Sunday and Monday's the Memorial Day holiday."

"That would be a long time for our wee boy to be in a

strange place," Mattie murmured. She lovingly stroked the cheek of the little girl she held.

Amos cleared his throat, more emotional than Frances had ever seen him.

"I'll get to work on the little . . . casket," he said in a halting voice. "Not exactly the sort of gift I'd figured on giving a grandchild, but God had other plans."

Mattie hung her head and the four Helmuths began to cry quietly, clinging to one another. Frances and Gloria stepped behind the couch to place their hands on the young parents' shoulders while Alma slipped her arm around Mattie's waist, smiling at the baby on her shoulder.

"We have a new resident, Annabelle Beachey, and she's offered to make the burial gown," Frances put in softly. "The Kuhns are planning food for after the funeral, and Irene and Phoebe will make the pies. We're all so sorry for your loss, and we're here to help with whatever you need."

Bishop Monroe nodded. "*Gut* friends are a blessing at times like these—especially because a lot of us left our families to come here."

"At Promise Lodge, our friends *are* family now," Alma put in staunchly. "As Minerva spreads the word today, more folks will come to help get your house ready—and Eli will be glad to preach so you won't have to even think about that, Amos."

"Many hands make light work—and they help us bear our burdens, as well," Marlin said with a nod.

When Bishop Monroe and Marlin stood up, signaling the end of the meeting, Amos rose, as well. "I'll get going on my construction project—and I'll ask Roman to dig the grave," he said with a sigh. "Do you have any preference about where it should be? So far, Floyd's the only one buried in our cemetery."

All four of the Helmuths' faces went blank. "Maybe we

should walk to the cemetery and look it over," Sam suggested. "The fresh air will do us all *gut*."

Frances took this as her cue to head for the kitchen and assess the cleaning jobs the women would tackle. When she saw no dirty dishes, she guessed that in the shock of baby Caleb's death, nobody had eaten breakfast. As she peered into the refrigerator, she heard someone behind her—surely not Gloria, who hated to cook. "Let's fix them a meal first thing, Alma," she said.

"I'd be happy to help you with that, Frances. I'm pretty *gut* at scrambled eggs and toast, if that sounds reasonable."

Frances blinked, backing away from the open refrigerator to gaze at Marlin. "I—we women can cook, if you—you probably have other things to do," she stammered.

Marlin shrugged, his expression subdued. "It would be a way to spend some time with you, even if other folks are around," he murmured. When Alma bustled into the kitchen, however, he cleared his throat. "So—how's your new apartment? And Annabelle has offered to sew the burial gown? That's very kind of her."

Nodding, Frances noted how sad and tired Marlin appeared—but it was probably due to Caleb's death rather than because of any feelings he had for her.

"I can't wait to meet our new resident!" Alma put in as she assessed the condition of the room. "We'll have to throw her a welcome party after the funeral's behind us. Are you thinking some breakfast is a *gut* idea, Frances?" she asked. "It doesn't smell as though these poor folks have even made coffee yet this morning."

"*Jah*, I think they'll be better able to face this difficult day if they've had a bite to eat," Frances replied as Alma began filling the percolator with water. She was grateful that her friend was making conversation so she and Marlin didn't have to—even as she realized her attitude could use an adjustment. Marlin had been nothing but kind to her, after all.

"I'm settling in," she said to him, hoping her smile looked more convincing than it felt. "Gloria has gotten her first lesson on apartment management, helping Rosetta with Annabelle's arrival—and she's *delighted* to be waking up in heaven, surrounded by the blue sky and clouds you fellows painted in her bedroom."

The lines on Marlin's face lifted. "Glad to hear it. I suspect you ladies will do better at breakfast prep without me in your way," he added with a nod at Alma, "so I'll head back to my barrel factory. I've got some wood Amos can use for Caleb's casket."

As Marlin departed, Alma stopped spooning coffee into the percolator basket to focus on Frances. "That man looks like he could use a wife," she hinted.

"Maybe someday he'll find one," Frances shot back. And that was all she intended to say on the subject.

Chapter Twenty-Five

Saturday evening was the bleakest Barbara could recall enduring in her life. Shortly after the hearse returned baby Caleb's body, she dressed him in the plain white gown Annabelle had sewn—because Bernice couldn't bear to look at her deceased child, much less touch him. Dat and Mattie had brought the little casket, which resembled a small, flat breadbox made of pine and painted white. Barbara lined it with a white baby blanket one of the lodge ladies had crocheted.

The moment Simon laid his tiny son inside the casket, the air stopped moving. Even with the windows open, the house grew oppressively still and even hotter than it had been during the day. It seemed appropriate for the six of them to bow in prayer, but the moment of remembrance was cut short when Bernice bolted from the front room, wailing uncontrollably as she ran upstairs.

"I'm really worried about her," Barbara murmured. Her sister's crying had wakened the little twins, who'd been sleeping fitfully in their baskets, so she and Mattie scooped them up. "Bernice hasn't been talking to us or eating or even drinking water—and in this hot weather, that's dangerous."

After a long look at his tiny, silent son, Simon sighed loudly. "I'll take a pitcher of water upstairs and sit with her.

Gut night, all. Our day started around three this morning, and I've endured all of it I can bear."

When he'd left, Dat glanced at the clock. "Only seven thirty. It'll be too light and too hot to get to sleep for a while yet—"

"But we should go home and let these poor kids get some rest," Mattie put in firmly. "We've done all we can for Caleb. Bless his little heart, he's the only peaceful one amongst us."

Dat cleared his throat as though he had something he wanted to say, but a loud knock on the front door interrupted their subdued conversation. Sam went to answer it, and a few moments later he came back with Irene.

"Look who's brought us an air conditioner, along with a generator to run it!" he said. "Where shall we put it?"

Barbara felt a surge of gratitude and relief as she reached for Irene's hand. "Oh, but that's a generous offer. You didn't have to do that!"

Irene squeezed her hand. "Phoebe and I had decided to get a window unit for the bakery, but I thought you folks could use it while you wait for your family to arrive—and if it's hot on Wednesday, keep it for when you've got a crowd in here. With all respect for your Amish restrictions, tough times go a lot easier on folks if they're not also miserable from the heat."

"You're a godsend, Irene. We'll be forever grateful," Dat said as he studied the arrangement of windows in the front room. "For now, shall we put the unit in the *dawdi* rooms you built for when your parents visit, Sam? It's a much smaller space, so it'll be easier to cool."

"*Jah*, and let's put Caleb in there," Barbara suggested. "Maybe I can convince Bernice and Simon to sleep in that room tonight so they'll rest better."

"Maybe you four and the twins should all sleep in there

tonight," Mattie suggested as she blotted her forehead with her sleeve. "And maybe you wish I'd stop giving you so much advice," she added with a tired smile.

About fifteen minutes later, the air conditioner was filling the *dawdi* room with its quiet hum and the blessed relief of cooler air. Sam gently placed the casket on top of the dresser. "I'll ask Simon to bring some bedding," he said wearily. "You girls can have the bed and we'll bunk on the floor. I'll bring your rocking chair, too."

Barbara nodded gratefully. After her *dat* and Mattie left, she glanced around the large, simple room with its double bed, dresser, a small sofa, and a recliner. A bathroom was built off to the side, and the doorways were wide enough to accommodate her mother-in-law's wheelchair. Although she'd missed seeing Sam and Simon's parents every day, she dreaded their arrival and the fresh welling up of grief it would mean.

When Bernice opened the *dawdi* room door, Barbara immediately noticed her twin's reluctance to come into the cooler room. She also sensed that Bernice and Simon had had some cross words before he'd convinced her to come downstairs for the night. "We'll all get better rest in here," Barbara murmured as she wrapped her arms around her sister's trembling shoulders.

But Bernice was having none of her comfort. "Why did God take my son but let your twins live?" she wailed as she pushed Barbara away. She burst into tears again. "What did Simon and I do to offend Him? It—it's not fair!"

Barbara's soul shriveled as she struggled to find an appropriate response. Her sister's shove had stung even more than her heartrending question. "We'll never know the answer to that," she replied as she, too, began to cry again. "Caleb seemed every bit as healthy as our girls—Minerva said so, too. And you fed him and handled him the same way I did Carol and Corene—"

"It's like your *dat* said," Simon put in wearily, as though he'd covered this ground with Bernice several times already. "God has His reasons for taking the wee ones back—often because they've got some health problems we won't be able to deal with. He doesn't want Caleb—or us—to suffer a greater burden than we can bear."

"We'll all feel better if we get some rest," Sam suggested with a sigh. "Even if we can't sleep, some time in quiet prayer will be *gut* for our souls."

"I can't pray!" Bernice blurted out. "I have nothing to say to a God who robbed me of all I had to live for."

A fresh wave of alarm surged through Barbara as her sister stalked out, slamming the door. As the startled twins began to cry, Simon followed his wife from the room.

Barbara lifted Corene from her basket and went to the rocking chair to feed her. "What're we going to do about Bernice?" she whispered to Sam as he soothed little Carol. "It's not like her to speak so bitterly about anyone, much less about God."

"Maybe she needs time to release her anger. She lost her son only this morning," Sam pointed out. He gazed tenderly at the tiny girl he held. "In Bernice's shoes, if I'd lost my precious child, I'd be out of my mind, too—probably not aware of what I was saying or how desperate my behavior appeared to the folks around me."

Or how dangerous, Barbara thought. As the milk surged from her breast to nurture Corene, she realized Sam was right—just as she knew she was the person most likely to penetrate her twin's deep depression. A few minutes later she savored the satisfaction of feeding Carol as she watched her husband lovingly burp Corene against his shoulder. If only she could share her joy with Bernice—the deep peace she'd found while gazing into the two tiny faces God had entrusted to her care . . .

When both twins were dozing in their baskets and Sam was nodding off over a magazine, Barbara slipped out of the *dawdi* room. In the oppressive heat of the front room, her sister stood staring out the window at the darkness, fanning herself with a folded newspaper. Simon lolled in the recliner with his shirt open and his mouth hanging slack. Barbara approached her sister slowly, praying for the right words to go along with her best intentions.

"Bernice," she whispered, placing a cautious hand on her twin's shoulder. "I might not feel your loss as keenly as you do, but I'm just as puzzled about why my babies have lived while your Caleb has not."

Bernice sniffled as she stared bleakly out the window.

Barbara inhaled slowly, hoping her twin would understand what she was about to do. "You and I have shared everything since before we were born, so what if—well, I want you to have one of my babies, Bernice," she pleaded. "*Please* choose one of the girls and raise her as your own—"

"Why would I want to do that?" Bernice demanded. "It wouldn't be the same, and we both know it."

Barbara closed her eyes against a fresh welling up of pain, of despair over her sister's bitterness. "I had to offer. And if you change your mind—"

"I won't. Just forget it, all right?"

Barbara winced. "If you come to realize that either Carol or Corene might be a comfort to you, let me know," she whispered. "Meanwhile, you'll feel a lot better if you and Simon spend the night with us in the *dawdi* room where it's cooler. *Please* don't let your grief become a wedge that separates us, Bernice. To me, that would be a tragedy even more devastating than losing baby Caleb."

Her sister fanned herself more forcefully, shutting Barbara out with her silence.

Lord, I don't know what else to do, Barbara fretted as she returned to the *dawdi* room. *Keep Bernice in Your care until we can find a way to help her.*

Chapter Twenty-Six

As Frances sat in the Helmuths' large front room on Wednesday morning, surrounded by mourners at Caleb's funeral, she saw Marlin in a new light. She'd known him to be a fine man and a patient, loving father, but as he preached the second, longer funeral sermon, he expressed his thoughts with such tender eloquence that everyone in the room listened raptly to his words of encouragement.

"Although I've preached the Old Order faith for nearly twenty years, as I combed the Scriptures for inspiration earlier today, I perceived a paradox," Marlin said as he gazed out over the crowd. "We're familiar with the verse in Matthew's nineteenth chapter where Jesus says 'Suffer the little children'—which means *allow* them—'and forbid them not, to come unto me: for of such is the kingdom of heaven." And when one of our wee ones dies, we immediately say it's the will of God that we suffer such a horrendous loss. Such an idea is part and parcel of our Amish faith."

Marlin clasped his hands in front of him. As he looked at Caleb's tiny body, swaddled in a crocheted blanket in the open white casket that was in the center of the room, he considered his next words. "The verse we are *not* so well acquainted with comes before that, in the eighteenth chapter of Matthew, and it tells us that 'it is not the will of your

Father which is in heaven, that one of these little ones should perish,'" he continued earnestly. "So as I envision Caleb in heaven with the angels, lifted up and cared for in the presence of God Himself, I can't believe that God wanted Caleb to die any more than we did. I can't imagine God snatching a baby away as part of a mysterious, painful plan He expects His people to endure. Instead, I now prefer to believe that God is suffering right along with us today."

Frances straightened on the pew bench, her brow furrowed in thought. Indeed, whenever a child died, folks automatically said it was God's will—perhaps because they didn't know any other acceptable explanation, and because they'd been taught this belief all their lives. The people seated around Frances seemed as startled by Marlin's assertion as she was, yet they were hanging on his words, yearning for an explanation that would soothe their troubled spirits.

"After all, the Bible also tells us that God is love," Marlin continued gently. "So I choose not to blame God—not to see our Heavenly Father as an active, willing participant in Caleb's death or in anyone else's. I believe He grieves right alongside Simon and Bernice and their families—and all of us here at Promise Lodge."

Frances glanced at the two men who sat on the preacher's bench, and at Preacher Amos, who sat on the men's side of the room, as well. Bishop Monroe's brown eyes were wide with the possibility that Marlin had hit upon a worthwhile interpretation of the Scriptures, while Preachers Eli and Amos contemplated Marlin's suggestion with expressions of staunch disbelief and disapproval at first . . . until a ray of hope lit Amos's sorrow-lined face.

"I have no answer to our questions about why Caleb didn't live longer than four days," Marlin continued in a voice that thrummed with faith, "but I choose to envision him in the arms of Jesus our Savior with God holding them both in His everlasting embrace. This way, I can believe that Caleb has gone on to his reward, free from the trials and tribulations of this earthly existence. That thought brings me peace and helps me move past my previous doubts about God's intentions for his littlest angels."

Frances dabbed at her eyes, moved to tears by Marlin's beautiful imagery of Caleb being cradled in Jesus's arms as God surrounded both of them with His powerful love. Some of the men across the Helmuths' front room appeared to struggle with a suggestion that countered what they'd been taught all their lives, yet the women were glancing at one another with wide, expectant eyes. Could it be true, what Marlin was preaching? Had the hard and fast Amish doctrines about God's will, passed down through generations, given them the wrong idea about Him?

"I'm not saying that everything we've always been taught about God's will is incorrect, because the preachers and bishops we've listened to have been inspired by God, just as I am," Marlin insisted as he read the faces in the congregation. "I'm just suggesting a shift in our vision. Today God has asked me to comfort His people."

Marlin smiled gently at the congregation, and when his gaze lingered on Frances for a moment, she felt as though she might float away despite the heaviness in her heart.

"If we can believe that Caleb will forever bask in the glorious sunshine of the Lord," Marlin concluded, "maybe we can claim some of that heavenly sunshine for ourselves as we anticipate the day that we, too, shall behold God's glory."

Frances's mouth dropped open. As a bishop's wife, she'd listened to many sermons on the futility of speculating about which way a soul went when it departed its earthly body. Floyd had insisted that by the end of a person's life,

God had already decided if that man or woman was destined for heaven or hell, so Amish folks didn't talk much about where their departed friends and family members would spend eternity.

But surely a blameless baby goes straight to the arms of Jesus, just the way Marlin described it, Frances thought as he took his seat on the preachers' bench.

"A shift in our vision," Bishop Monroe reiterated as he stood to bring the service to a close. His handsome face glowed with an inner radiance as he gazed at little Caleb's body and then at all the folks who listened to him. "It seems exceedingly appropriate here at Promise Lodge to open ourselves to a shift in our vision when our Lord opens our hearts to such a possibility, doesn't it?"

The bishop stood tall, raising his right hand to pronounce the benediction. "May God hold Caleb in His love forever, and may we feel our Lord's comfort and a peace that passes all understanding as we move beyond our loss. Amen."

A soft collective sigh filled the room as everyone absorbed what the bishop had said, and how he'd reaffirmed the rightness of Marlin's ideas. As Frances filed past Caleb's casket for the final time, it seemed her vision was already shifting. The last funeral she'd attended had been Floyd's. In her darker moments, she'd wondered if her husband's crying out to angels to catch Amos as he fell from the shed roof— or his refusal to follow doctor's orders—had doomed him, in God's eyes.

But what if he's now standing tall and healthy in heaven, healed by the touch of the Master's hand? Can't you just see him beaming at Jesus as God wraps His all-encompassing arms around the two of them?

Frances sucked in her breath. It was a dazzling idea, and it made her pulse beat faster. The hint of doubt about

Floyd's eternal status vanished as she continued to consider her new vision of him, while she followed the flow of mourners out into the yard. In the heat of late morning, folks clustered in the shade beneath the big trees, awaiting the appearance of the Helmuths and Caleb's closed casket.

When someone grasped Frances's hand, she blinked. Annabelle was standing beside her in the crowd, unabashedly wiping tears from her face.

"God has surely led me to Promise Lodge," Annabelle said in a quavering voice. "What a powerful message—what a vision of hope Preacher Marlin gave us! Where I come from, the preachers dish up the usual phrases about ashes to ashes and how the Lord giveth and taketh away, and—well," she added as she smiled through her tears, "I feel revived. Revitalized."

"Preacher Marlin's following our bishop's lead, focusing on all things bright and beautiful rather than dwelling in the valley of the shadow," Frances confirmed. "My late husband, Floyd, was our previous bishop—"

"Oh, I'm sorry if I called up your grief," Annabelle interrupted ruefully.

Frances looked into Annabelle's deep green eyes, sensing her new neighbor was going to become a good friend as time went by. "No, it's not that way," she murmured. "Floyd was a conservative bishop who didn't venture away from traditional teachings. Although I have no trouble imagining the outraged expression on his face if he'd been here listening to Marlin's sermon today, I . . . I think he would've seen the value of shifting his vision, after he'd thought about it awhile.

"Then again," Frances added lightly, "I've been *mistaken* a time or two about what Floyd might've said or done."

Annabelle's face creased with a smile. "*Jah*, any woman

who assumes she knows everything about her husband is setting herself up for a rude awakening—or at least some surprises."

Frances wondered again what had compelled Annabelle's husband to leave her and the Old Order, but it wasn't the proper time to discuss such a topic. The crowd around them became respectfully quiet as Simon and Sam emerged from the house carrying the little casket between them. Barbara and Bernice followed behind them, their wet faces pale beneath their black *kapps*. Preacher Amos and Mattie stepped into the procession behind Enos Helmuth, who pushed his wife, Dorcas, in her wheelchair. All told, Frances had counted nearly thirty Helmuth relatives from Ohio. They'd hired a driver and a bus to make the trip, and they were staying either in the cabins behind the lodge or in the homes of Promise Lodge folks.

Everyone walked silently across the lawn and the road, entering the neatly mowed cemetery that was surrounded by a black wrought-iron fence that Mattie's son, Noah, and Preacher Eli had constructed. After Bishop Monroe said a few words, the casket was lowered into the small grave Roman had dug. As men in the family took turns shoveling dirt back into the grave, Marlin read the words of a familiar hymn—because singing wasn't considered proper at a funeral.

When the grave was filled, Bernice began to sob quietly as Barbara, Sam, and Simon gathered around her. With a parting glance at Floyd's simple white grave marker on the other side of the cemetery, Frances started toward the lodge along with the other women who were helping with the meal.

Something made her stop and look up. Frances found herself gazing at the two-story white house she and Gloria had recently vacated . . . the home Floyd had built for their family when God had led them to Promise, Missouri.

Life is so short and unpredictable, Frances realized with a sigh. *Maybe it was my grief that made me sell everything— and maybe that wasn't such a gut idea.*

She blinked back sudden tears, hoping the women around her wouldn't ask what had upset her. Frances hated to admit it, but a week in her small, simple apartment had proven to her that the absence of housekeeping chores wasn't the blessing it seemed to be for Irene and the Kuhns—although Gloria appeared happier than she'd been since before her *dat* had passed.

Frances busied herself with cutting and plating the pies Phoebe and Irene had baked, pleased that she was wielding the knife and metal spatula more steadily now that her hands were getting stronger. As folks went through the buffet line, helping themselves to the Kuhns' baked chicken, potato salad, cucumbers and onions, and four-bean salad, she heard Lester's voice above the rest.

"Marlin, your sermon gave me a whole new outlook," her brother-in-law said. "Instead of asking God again why He allowed my wife and son to die in that horrendous buggy crash, I could see them standing with Jesus while you were preaching! And they were healthy and whole! I—I think I can move on now, thanks to you."

Frances's knife stopped halfway across a strawberry pie. When she found Lester's face in the crowd, she was amazed at his transformation. He was smiling, and he appeared more peaceful than she'd seen him in weeks. Marlin was modestly accepting Lester's praise, claiming that the words had been God's rather than his own—but other folks chimed in with similar remarks.

"Preacher, that was a truly inspiring message," one of the folks from Ohio insisted.

"I'm reconsidering my Willis's passing now, too," Christine put in. "And I don't think God had a thing to do with our barn burning down that night, nor did He allow Isaac Chupp to set it afire as part of His will. It was Isaac's meanness at work, not God."

Frances's eyebrows rose. Who could've anticipated the power of Marlin's words? Who could've foreseen the comfort folks felt when they'd shifted their vision?

Maybe you need to shift your vision, too. Maybe selling everything and moving to the lodge aren't the only mistakes you've made in your grief.

Blinking rapidly, Frances focused again on the pies she was cutting. It wouldn't be long before the folks coming through the food line would set their loaded dinner plates on the tables and select their desserts—and she didn't want to call attention to her flustered state of mind by sniffling or swiping at tears.

"Look at these pies! How am I supposed to choose?" one of the Ohio fellows joked.

"I'll take one slice now and pray there'll be extras left after everyone's gotten a piece," the man behind him said.

Frances smiled, focused on her cutting so she could keep up with the pie slices that were disappearing from the dessert table. When most folks were seated and eating, she decided to cut the final four pies on the table behind her before she filled a dinner plate.

"How've you been, Frances? It's *gut* to see that your hands and arm muscles are recovering."

Frances paused with her knife poised above a blackberry pie. There was no avoiding Marlin as he stood on the other side of the table, awaiting her answer. He looked so handsome in his black vest and white shirt, with his freshly trimmed hair and beard, that she had a hard time not gawking at him the way a schoolgirl mooned over the first cute boy who kissed her. Somehow she reined in the memory of Marlin's kiss—which had been much more soul-searing and satisfying than any mere boy's could've been.

"You know how sometimes your thoughts buzz around like bees?" she asked softly. "I've just realized that I made a big mistake, selling off my furniture—but at this point, what's done is done. The auction's set for Saturday."

Marlin considered her response as he looked over the selection of pie slices. "You don't like living at the lodge?" he asked. "There've been times when I've wished *I* could move into a couple of rooms upstairs. Life would be simpler without family members objecting to decisions, thinking they know better than you do—don't you agree?"

Frances blinked. Did Marlin want to get away from Harley so badly that he'd move into an apartment? Or was he teasing her—asking about Gloria, perhaps?

"Your sermon today made me rethink a few things," she admitted. "I realize now that it was my grief and depression that made me sell everything—just as you and Amos tried to tell me. In my fear, I thought it was the prudent thing to do, to support myself and Gloria. Now . . . I see things differently."

Frances inhaled deeply, hoping the extra oxygen would clarify her thoughts. "Maybe life's too short to live within the limits I've set," she said softly. "I was wrong to turn you away and to treat you so unfairly after you'd been nothing but *gut* to me, Marlin. I—I'm truly sorry."

Marlin gripped the pie plate he'd picked up. He looked around to be sure no one else was within earshot. "What does this mean, Frances?" he whispered. "If you want me to court you again, well—I'll have to think about it."

As Marlin returned to his table, where he sat surrounded by his kids, Minerva, and some of the Helmuth kin from out East, the bottom dropped out of Frances's heart. In her attempt to prove she could support herself, had she burned her bridges? Had her plan for happiness backfired because she'd tried to be too independent?

Chapter Twenty-Seven

On Friday morning Barbara realized she didn't have enough hands. She was trying to nurse a very fussy Corene while Carol wailed in her bassinet next to the rocker, and she was becoming more frustrated by the minute. Bernice had stayed in bed. Sam and Simon had returned to work, feeling they needed to be at their busy nursery in the peak of growing and planting season.

It was her first time trying to handle both babies all by herself.

"Mamm, how did you manage when Bernice and I came along?" Barbara prayed aloud as she kept rocking. "Send me some help! I can't go fetch Minerva right now—and I'm really worried about Bernice. She's so depressed, and I don't know how to help her. I've got two noisy, hungry mouths to feed and these crying babies are driving me crazy!"

But Mamm had passed years ago. Imagining her mother with Jesus, as Preacher Marlin had described, had helped Barbara get through Caleb's funeral, but it wouldn't bring her the assistance she so desperately needed on this hot, muggy morning. A few feet away, the vacant rocking chair beside the empty bassinet with the light blue blankets reminded her just how alone—and lonely—she felt without her twin's constant company.

After Barbara tried a third time to feed crying Corene, she switched the babies. Maybe Carol would settle down—and thereby quiet her sister—while she filled herself with milk. "Come on, sweetie, you're a *gut* little eater," she pleaded with the tiny, red-faced girl as she settled into the rocker again.

Instead of nursing, however, Carol turned her head and began to cry even louder. The poor little thing was damp with the heat and her exertions—and even though Barbara and the two husbands had agreed that Irene should have her air conditioner back, she longed for the luxury of a cool, quiet room again. The nursery, ordinarily so cheerful with its yellow walls and sunshine coming through the windows, echoed with the twins' escalating wails.

Barbara tried to reason things out. Should she move the girls to the kitchen? The rooms downstairs were only slightly cooler—and the thought of fetching the two carrier baskets from the mudroom, returning to the nursery, and shifting the girls to the lower level suddenly seemed over-whelming. Exhausted as she was, she didn't dare carry a wailing baby in each arm as she navigated the stairs.

Out of sheer frustration, Barbara started to cry along with Carol and Corene. After giving birth, and then dealing with Caleb's death and the influx and departure of guests this week, she felt so drained that all she could do was suc-cumb to her doubts.

What if they're sick? Should I leave the room and let them cry themselves to sleep? Maybe instead of my milk they really want water. What if they're refusing my milk because it doesn't taste right? What if—

Advice from every mother Barbara knew was spinning in her mind, to the point she realized she was clutching Carol too tightly in a rocking chair that was moving so fast that *anyone* would be upset. She stopped rocking, and stopped trying to coax Carol's mouth to her breast. Totally discouraged, Barbara hung her head and sobbed.

A few moments later she sensed someone standing in the doorway. When Barbara glanced up with tear-filled eyes, she saw Bernice taking in the chaos that filled the nursery. Had the babies wakened her? Was she going to complain that she couldn't sleep because of their noise?

Barbara didn't have the energy to ask. She shifted Carol higher on her shoulder and slowly began to rock again, unsure of what to say to her bereaved sister. The past six days had felt like six weeks because Bernice had broken her long, painful silences only to remark about how unfair it was that her son had died, and to say that Barbara's two healthy children would torment her for the rest of her life.

Bernice had apparently forgotten that Barbara had offered her a child. She was living in her own private hell, refusing to let anyone else share her misery or ease her suffering. Poor Simon was at the end of his emotional rope. He'd talked about taking Bernice to see a doctor or a grief counselor, but his wife had refused to go.

Barbara sniffled loudly. The wailing of her two babies seemed like a very small problem, considering the burden her twin sister was bearing.

After several moments, Bernice stepped hesitantly into the nursery. Her red-rimmed eyes swept past Barbara to the bassinet a few feet away, where Corene's cries had escalated to screaming. Although it was nearly nine, Bernice still wore her rumpled cotton nightgown. Her long brown braid was mussed and askew, as though she'd spent a lot of time in bed without getting any rest.

Bernice made a wide, slow circle behind Barbara's rocking chair. As she approached Corene's bassinet, the tautness of her body suggested that she might bolt from the room if the least little thing distracted her.

Barbara swallowed hard, not daring to speak or to stop rocking. *Please God, help me—and my sister—do the right things*, she prayed.

After what felt like an eternity, Bernice stopped beside the bassinet. With a little sob she lifted the baby in the pale green onesie to her shoulder, swaying from side to side as though she was in a trance.

Barbara held her breath, wishing she could see her sister's face and better gauge her emotions. What if Bernice suddenly changed her mind and dropped the baby back into her bassinet? Or what if she ran from the room? How could Barbara follow her to be sure her sister and her daughter remained safe? She hated not being able to trust her sister with Corene, but Bernice's depression had become very worrying.

Amazingly, Corene was settling down and her cries had become short hiccupping sounds. Very slowly, Bernice ambled around the other side of the bassinet, alternately walking and swaying as she made her way toward the empty rocking chair, carefully supporting the baby's head with her hand.

Is Bernice humming? Barbara listened closely, trying to hear the soft melody beneath Carol's continuing cries. She watched closely as her sister lowered herself into the rocker. Bernice was gazing at Corene's face as though her life depended upon the need, the hunger—the trust—she saw in the baby's eyes.

Barbara sat very still as her twin sister loosened the front of her nightgown. When Corene latched onto her breast and began to nurse, Bernice's eyes closed. With a soft moan she let her head loll back against the rocker.

Tears streamed down Barbara's face—although she was now crying in relief and joy and gratitude to God. Her sister's body relaxed and her face took on a beatific expression as she rocked, cradling the baby close. She reminded Barbara of paintings she'd seen of Mary with baby Jesus, her face alight with an inner radiance.

When Barbara glanced down, she realized that Carol's cries had become whimpers. Once again she positioned the baby's mouth near her breast, sighing thankfully when she felt milk surging from her body into Carol's mouth. The steady creak of the two rocking chairs filled the nursery with blissful tranquility. Barbara let out the breath she didn't realize she'd been holding.

"*Denki* for coming to my rescue, Bernice," she said softly. "What would I do without you?"

Bernice let out a tremulous sigh. "My breasts are full, my arms are empty, and my heart aches for a tiny redheaded child," she replied softly. She shifted Corene's position, stroking her cheek and her carrot-colored hair as the baby girl continued to nurse. "Maybe you and God have been trying to tell me something, Barbara. Maybe I'm meant to be a *mamm* after all."

"I've always believed that," Barbara insisted. The sight of her sister feeding Corene was powerful medicine for her soul. "That little girl you're holding couldn't ask for a better *mamm*, or a more devoted set of parents."

For a long moment Bernice held Barbara's gaze. As they rocked, Barbara realized that their identical chairs were moving in exactly the same tempo—and why wouldn't they? She and her twin had always lived synchronized lives, and now that their rhythm had been restored, she sensed that healing could begin.

"You're the biggest blessing of my entire life, Barbara,"

Bernice whispered. "You—and this wee babe you've given me—have just saved me from dying a slow, lonely death inside."

Barbara reached over to clasp her sister's outstretched hand. "You'd do the same for me. You know you would."

Chapter Twenty-Eight

Frances sat on the lodge's porch swing Saturday afternoon, determined to stay busy by crocheting an afghan. *This is how it's going to be from here on*, she told herself as she worked the gray-green yarn in and out of the previous row's stitches. *These women eat dinner and redd up the dishes in short order, so now the whole afternoon looms before you.*

She was sorry she hadn't accepted Beulah's invitation to go to Forest Grove with the other gals—but what did she need to shop for? And even if she saw something she wanted, why would she want to spend the money? Irene and Phoebe were delivering their pies, so Annabelle and the Kuhns had tagged along, eager to find fabric to secretly make a quilt—certain that Allen and Phoebe would announce their engagement any day. Gloria was in her apartment working on her column for *The Budget*.

So Frances sat alone.

With a sigh, she told herself to count her blessings. An early morning thunderstorm had ushered in a cool front, so the temperature was much more pleasant than they'd had for several days. Hummingbirds buzzed around the feeders and the orange flowers on the trumpet vines, seemingly glad for Frances's company. And she had to admit that she enjoyed eating meals she didn't have to cook all by herself. As she waved at Laura and Deborah, who were carrying baskets of vegetables and baked goods out to Mattie's roadside produce stand, Frances also realized she was blessed to live among such industrious, friendly neighbors.

A few minutes later, the sound of buggy wheels made her look up from her crocheting. As Marlin drove in from the road, he lifted his black straw hat in greeting and Frances waved back. He kept heading toward home, however. After he'd left their conversation about courtship dangling by a loose thread at the funeral meal, she wondered where she stood with him.

Maybe he felt she'd been trying for his sympathy when she'd admitted her regrets about the house and her furniture. Maybe he figured she'd gotten exactly what she'd asked for, after ignoring his advice.

Frances focused on her afghan again, determined to find positive topics to think about as she added another row of stitches.

For all you know, somebody's bidding on your furniture at the auction right this minute, she realized. *Maybe sometime this week you'll have a check and you can put that unfortunate decision behind you. At least you'll have money to pay your rent—and next time your friends ask, you can go into town with them.*

Frances blinked fiercely, fighting tears. There was no use in crying over spilled milk or *stuff* she no longer had. Hadn't Jesus preached that it was better to store up treasures in heaven than to accumulate worldly possessions?

She finished off the row she'd crocheted and searched her bag for another color of yarn; something bright and cheerful to lift her spirits. When she found a partial skein of deep, bright gold, it reminded her of the irises that were blooming in a long row beside Christine's dairy barn. As she attached the fresh color, Frances challenged herself to finish the afghan before supper, so she'd have the satisfaction of a completed project to show for her time.

A little while later the sound of tires crunching on gravel made her look up. A big white pickup was pulling under the curved metal sign at the entry to Promise Lodge, its motor rumbling as though it was much more suited to speeding along a highway than rolling slowly along the one-lane road that was bordered by freshly cut lawn and Mattie's vegetable plots. When the truck stopped near the lodge, a burly English fellow got out and approached the porch.

"I'm looking for Frances Lehman," he called out. "Do you know where I might find her?"

Frances let her afghan drop onto the swing as she stood up. "That's me," she replied hesitantly. "How can I help you?"

The man tugged a white envelope from his shirt pocket. "Figured I'd bring your check by while I was in this neck of the woods rather than dropping it in the mail," he explained. "I'm Ted Meeks, the auctioneer. You were getting settled in your apartment the day your bishop and a minister helped me load your furniture into my van. Everything going all right?"

"*Jah*—just fine," Frances added, hoping she sounded convincing. It gave her an odd feeling to accept the envelope he handed her, knowing it held the money she so badly needed.

Or maybe you're just nervous because he's big and tall and English, with a booming voice, she realized. Then another thought occurred to her. "So the auction's over already? I—I thought it might take a lot longer."

Ted smiled. "We had bidders who wanted big lots—whole rooms of matched furniture—at today's sale, so even though we combined loads from three families, it went pretty fast. Some sales are like that. Right folks wanting exactly what we had to offer, and willing to pay top dollar for it."

Frances nodded absently. Ted sounded upbeat, as though the auction had gone well. Did the shine in his eyes suggest that he knew more than he was letting on—or did his baby blues always twinkle?

It was silly, yet she was itching to know what sort of folks had bought her mother's hutch and her bone china cups. But while an auctioneer was selling so many pieces of people's lives, upping and upping the bids as he chanted so fast, he had little idea who was holding up the numbered cards—and probably had no recollection of what any one bedroom set or cabinet had sold for, either. So why should she question him?

"Nice of you to bring this by. Thank you," Frances murmured.

Ted nodded, turning as though he had somewhere else he needed to be. "Appreciate your business, Mrs. Lehman. Have a nice afternoon," he called over his shoulder. After he hopped into his truck, he backed it rapidly down the gravel road rather than turning around in the yard, as most folks did.

As she held the envelope in her hands, Frances resisted the urge to rip it open and read the amount of the check. She sat down in the swing to steady her nerves. Although she'd kept the books for Floyd's business, her husband had managed their finances, so she was holding the most money she'd ever handled in her life—probably enough to see her through the rest of her days, if she budgeted carefully. After the way Marlin had left her hanging at the pie table, Frances had resigned herself to the possibility that she might remain a widow for a long while.

When she couldn't stand the suspense any longer, she carefully opened the envelope along one of its short ends. Why was it so fat, stuffed so full? As Frances pulled out a sheaf of folded papers, she saw that it was an inventory of all the goods she'd surrendered, with every piece of furniture briefly described and every pillowcase and dishcloth accounted for.

No sense in reading this list, she thought as she skimmed the first page. *I'm well aware that everything I loved is long gone.*

Frances gasped, grabbing for the check as it fluttered loose from the inventory sheets. When she saw the amount typed on it, she could only stare.

Six thousand two hundred dollars.

At first it seemed like a lot of money, yet the longer Frances looked at the numbers, the more she felt like crying. The auction company had deducted its percentage, of course—and she hadn't had a specific amount in mind when she'd sent her furniture to be sold—but even so . . .

This is what Ted considers top dollar? Surely an entire houseful of furniture and linens and dishes and—surely I should've received five or six times this amount for what I acquired during more than twenty-five years of marriage, not to mention the memories attached to those pieces!

Frances nipped her lip, unable to look at anything except those black-and-white figures. She was aware that the bedspreads and the chairs were a bit worn, and that some of her table linens had been wedding presents . . . but Floyd had sometimes earned more than this in a busy summer month, back when he'd been running the siding and window business with Lester.

Less than a month of Floyd's income. What'll you do when it runs out—a lot sooner than you figured on?

Frances slumped in the swing. She wasn't worried that Rosetta—or Gloria, the new apartment manager—would kick her out of the lodge because she couldn't pay her rent, but her money problems were far from over. If she didn't sell that big white house on the hill, she'd be strapped for money in a few years.

Her high-flying ideas about proving herself competent and independent suddenly seemed as flighty and unrealistic as something Gloria might've dreamed up. With a sigh, Frances tucked the inventory list and the check back into the envelope, which she slipped into her apron pocket. She needed to compose her emotions—figure out what she'd say when Gloria asked how the auction had come out.

"Ah, Frances! You've found the perfect place for enjoying our cool spell. Mind if I join you?"

Frances squeezed her eyes shut. She'd been so caught up in her thoughts, she hadn't heard Marlin walk across the lawn—and he was the last person she wanted to see at this difficult moment. But how could she turn him away?

"Sure. Why not?" she replied in a quavering voice.

The wooden stairs and porch floor creaked beneath his weight, and after Marlin sat down he began to swing them gently with his foot. Ordinarily, Frances found the forward-and-backward movement of a porch swing soothing, but she was too upset to enjoy *anything* at this moment. At least her afghan was bunched between them, acting as a chaperone. This was *not* the time to snuggle close to the man she'd tried to prove she didn't need, because it wouldn't be long before she'd remind him again exactly how foolish she'd been.

"What's wrong, sweetheart?" Marlin murmured. "You look like you've received some bad news."

Frances pulled her hankie from her apron pocket and blew her nose loudly. It seemed pointless to delay the inevitable, so she laid it all out. "I just got my check from Ted the auctioneer," she said hoarsely. "It—it was very *humbling* to find out how little all my cherished belongings were worth."

Marlin let out a sympathetic sigh. "I've heard that more

than once from folks after they've held estate sales. I'm sorry you're disappointed, Frances."

She glanced sideways at him. He sounded sincere enough, yet there was a shine in his eyes she didn't know how to interpret. "*Denki* again for helping me move all that stuff out of the house," she said in a low voice, "even if it's turned out to be yet another dumb mistake I've made lately. You tried to tell me that selling out wasn't a *gut* idea, and now I'm really sorry I didn't listen."

When Marlin focused on her, his bottomless brown eyes glimmered like sweet, warm molasses. "We all take our turns at doing things we later come to regret," he remarked softly.

"But I've taken more than a turn!" Frances blurted. "Not only have I lost the simple things that were near and dear to me, but I told you I wanted no part of your help—or your company. How stupid was that?"

His eyebrows rose. "You are many things, Frances, but you are not stupid," he insisted. "I've thought about our conversation after Caleb's funeral, and you were right. You made some big, life-altering decisions in a moment of grief—as all of us do—and now you wish you could turn back the clock."

"I'm sorry," she mumbled miserably. She gazed at her hands in her lap. Marlin was being patient and kind, but Frances wished he would leave so she could roll up into a ball and hide for a while.

"You said that on Wednesday, too. I accept your apology, Frances. And I owe you one."

She eyed him closely. "For what?" Marlin seemed suspiciously calm—downright contented and surprisingly pleased to be here with her, considering what poor company she was.

He scooted closer, reaching for her hand. The afghan was still between them, but the warmth of his skin and the gentle strength in his fingers sent dangerous tingles up her arm. "I'm sorry about the way I left our last conversation dangling—as if I could actually *not* want to be with you," he said with an exasperated shake of his head. "Now *that* was stupid."

Frances's heart began to pound, even though she knew better than to hope Marlin wanted to start seeing her again. "No one could ever call *you* stupid," she insisted. "Not after the way your sermon painted such an inspiring picture of Caleb being safe in the arms of Jesus. You dared to speak outside the Old Order box about God's love and His will, and you changed peoples' *lives*, Marlin."

"And you've changed *my* life, Frances," he insisted without missing a beat. "I want to court you again, with the intention of marrying you, as soon as you're ready."

Frances sucked air. Her mind reeled in disbelief. "You can't mean that! You're just feeling sorry for me because I sold off all of my—"

"I love you, Frances," Marlin interrupted her, slipping his arm around her shoulders. "The least you can do is listen to the man who's ready to go down on his knees, if that's what it takes to get your attention. Will you marry me someday? Please?"

Frances wanted to laugh and cry and dance all at once, yet her mouth got ahead of her. "Why should I believe that?" she challenged. "I mean, I love you, too, Marlin, but you surely have no idea what you're letting yourself in for if—"

He silenced her with a lingering kiss.

She wanted to pull away, to keep protesting about how she wasn't good enough for such a wonderful man, but . . . well, Marlin was a very convincing kisser. Frances finally gave in to the tender sincerity of his lips. It felt so good to consider, if only for a moment, that she might not have to spend the rest of her life alone—and broke.

When Frances finally eased away, she sighed softly. "I needed that," she admitted.

"I did, too."

She cleared her throat in an attempt to clarify the dazzling, hopeful thoughts that were spinning in her head. "I—I guess, if we marry, I'll be moving into your place with Minerva and Harley and the kids, *jah*?" she said. "I can't think you'd want to move into my empty house—or to spend all the money it would take to furnish it again."

A boyish grin flickered over his lips as he glanced away. "What if you could have all your belongings back?"

Frances frowned. Had she heard him correctly? Why would he ask such a useless question?

After several moments when she didn't reply, Marlin gazed directly into her eyes. "What if you could have everything back just the way it was?" he repeated softly. "What if I went to the auction this morning and bought it all—lock, stock, and barrel—so nobody else could have it? Would that make you happy, sweetheart?"

The screen door banged as Gloria raced out onto the porch with them. "Oh my word, Marlin—did you *really* buy all of our stuff back?" she asked ecstatically. "Isn't that the most romantic thing you've ever heard, Mamm?"

Gloria squeezed onto the swing beside Marlin and hugged him hard. "I didn't want to say anything—knowing how Mamm was trying to keep us afloat," she gushed, "but— much as I like my new apartment—I was really sad to think I'd never see our furniture and dishes again. It felt like we didn't have a real *home* anymore."

Tears prickled in Frances's eyes, even as her mouth fell

open in amazement. Who could've foreseen Gloria's display of enthusiasm—affection—toward Marlin, after she'd so vehemently rejected him early on? And hadn't she hit the nail on the head? Selling off their belongings had indeed felt horrible, as though Frances had wanted to be rid of everything that represented her life with Floyd and their girls. Everything that mattered.

Gloria smiled sheepishly as she rose from the swing. "I—I guess I shouldn't have been listening at the window," she admitted, "but *denki* again, Marlin. You've given us the best gift ever! I'll go back inside now, so I can't hear what you two are talking about."

As the door closed quietly behind her daughter, Frances began to laugh. "You never know what that girl's going to do next," she said. She gazed at Marlin, grasping his hand between hers. "But Gloria got it exactly right this time. I'm just flabbergasted that you went to all the trouble of—and paid all that money for—the belongings I figured I'd never see again."

Marlin studied her expression closely. "You're sure about that? A few moments ago you were disappointed about the amount of Ted's check."

"But that's before I knew *you* had bought everything." Frances pulled the envelope from her apron pocket and handed it to him. "Take this back. I wouldn't dream of keeping all this money you spent on—on *me*. To make me happy," she added softly. "Sometimes I think you know me better than I know myself, Marlin. *Denki* a million times over for what you've done for me."

Marlin pressed his forehead to hers. "You're welcome, dear. It's *gut* to see you smiling again."

After a moment, he chuckled. "Had I admitted to myself sooner that I didn't want to spend the rest of my life without you, I could've had Ted put your stuff straight into storage," he said with a shake of his head. "But by the time I got the idea, his crew had already displayed your belongings amongst the household goods from a couple of other families, and the sale bills had already been published. So it served me right, having to outbid all the other folks at the auction."

Frances smiled. "That explains why Ted had a twinkle in his eye when he delivered the check. But he didn't say a word about whose money it was."

"I asked him not to. I didn't want you to think I was trying to buy your love."

Once again it seemed that Marlin had just the right way with words. And Gloria had gotten it right, too: he'd done the most romantic thing she'd ever heard of in her life. Frances inhaled deeply, allowing Marlin's scent and presence to settle her emotions.

She wasn't doomed to spend the rest of her life in an apartment, after all. She had every reason to feel extremely grateful—downright giddy—because the handsome man beside her had known how much her simple possessions had meant to her, and he'd reclaimed them despite what it had cost him. It wasn't fair to compare the two men, but she couldn't imagine Floyd Lehman going to so much trouble or expense to correct a big mistake she'd made.

"I do love you, Marlin," Frances whispered, realizing how very blessed he made her feel. "And someday soon, I would be delighted to become your wife."

A gratifying sigh escaped him. "I'm awfully glad we got things settled between us. Glad you've changed your mind about marrying me, Frances."

She leaned into him, resting her head on his shoulder. "Seems I've had a shift in vision," she said as the swing creaked with a comforting back-and-forth motion. "My glass was nearly empty and now my cup's running over. It's a wonderful new beginning you've given us, Marlin."

"A shift in vision," he repeated softly. Marlin pulled her close, and then he winked at her. "Couldn't have said that better myself."

From the Promise Lodge Kitchen

Even though Rosetta's no longer in the lodge kitchen, Ruby and Beulah are still cooking up a storm—and Irene and Frances have their favorite recipes, as well! In this recipe section, you'll find down-home foods that Amish women feed their families along with recipes I make in my own kitchen—because you know what? Amish cooking isn't elaborate, and there are no set ingredients or products that make any recipe strictly Amish. Plain cooks make an astounding number of meals from whatever's in their pantry, their gardens, and their freezers. They also use convenience foods like Velveeta cheese, cake mixes, and canned products to feed their large families for less money and investment of their time.

These recipes are also posted on my website,
www.CharlotteHubbard.com.
If you don't find a recipe you want,
please email me via my website to request it—
or to let me know how you liked it!

~Charlotte

Sugar Cookie Bars

These may be just "plain ole sugar cookie" bars without any chocolate or add-ins, but they are amazingly addictive! You can tint the frosting and decorate them with jimmies in colors to suit any occasion.

Bars

- ¾ cup unsalted butter, softened*
- ¾ cup sugar
- 1 egg
- 1 T. vanilla extract
- ½ tsp. almond extract
- ½ tsp. baking soda
- ½ tsp. cream of tartar
- ½ tsp. salt
- 2 cups all-purpose flour

Frosting

- ½ cup unsalted butter, softened
- 1 T. vanilla extract
- 1–3 T. milk or heavy cream
- 2 cups powdered sugar
- Dash of salt
- Sprinkles and/or food coloring if desired

Preheat the oven to 350°. Line a 9" x 13" pan with foil and spray with nonstick spray.

In a large bowl, cream the butter and sugar. Beat in the egg and both extracts. Mix in 1 cup of the flour along with the baking soda, cream of tartar and salt, and then add the remaining flour. Press dough into the prepared pan and bake about 15 minutes—just until the sides are turning golden and the center looks a little underdone. Cool completely in the pan.

For the frosting, beat the butter in a medium bowl to soften it further, and then add the vanilla and 1 T. of the milk/cream. Slowly add the powdered sugar and salt, and any food coloring you want to use. Add more milk if needed to reach a spreading consistency. Frost bars and decorate with sprinkles, if desired. Lift the foil to bring the bars out of the pan and cut on a cutting board. Makes 2–3 dozen. Freezes well.

*Kitchen Hint: You may substitute the same amount of oil for the butter. It changes the texture, making a slightly denser bar.

Yogurt Bread

This easy bread resembles biscuits in a coffee cake format—moist, tender, and slightly sweet with whatever flavor of yogurt you choose. I like lemon or pineapple best!

　　1¾ cups flour
　　½ cup dried cranberries (or raisins)
　　1½ tsp. baking powder
　　¼ tsp. baking soda
　　1 6-oz. container of fruit yogurt
　　2 T. oil
　　½ cup milk

Preheat the oven to 375° and spray or grease a 9-inch glass pie pan. In a medium bowl, mix the flour, cranberries, baking powder, and baking soda. Make a well in the center of the dry ingredients and pour in the yogurt, oil, and milk. Stir just until all dry ingredients are blended in, and spread the dough in the prepared pan using the back of the spoon. Bake 20 minutes or just until a toothpick comes out of the center clean. Cool about 10 minutes before cutting into wedges, and lift out with a pancake spatula. Makes 8 wedges.

Sloppy Joes

This versatile meat mixture is a real crowd-pleaser. You can make it ahead, and you can freeze it in small batches to reheat later. Makes great sandwiches, but it's also yummy served on baked potatoes and topped with cheese, or as a topper for nachos or homemade pizza!

    2 lbs. lean ground beef
    1 lb. pork or turkey sausage
    1 large onion, diced
    1½ cups diced celery
    Salt and pepper
    2 T. garlic powder
    14-oz. bottle of catsup
    1 cup barbeque sauce

Place the ground beef, sausage, onion, and celery in a Dutch oven or large, deep skillet. Salt and pepper liberally and cook until the meat is done and the vegetables are soft, stirring often to break the meat into smaller chunks. Remove from heat and spoon the mixture onto paper towel–lined plates to drain; dispose of grease in the pan. Run the mixture briefly through a food processor or grinder and return to the pan. Add the garlic powder, catsup, and barbeque sauce and cook over medium heat for 15–20 minutes, stirring often. Makes about 6 cups—enough to fill 12 sandwich buns.

Creamed Chicken

This is the ultimate comfort supper! Amish cooks would most likely start with a whole chicken cut into pieces, but for convenience I buy packages of boned, skinless chicken thighs (you can use breasts, but thighs/dark meat give the mixture a richer flavor). Serve this over biscuits, toast, baked potatoes, mashed potatoes—or corn bread!

2–3 T. oil or butter
1½ pounds boneless, skinless chicken thighs
Salt and pepper
Garlic powder
2 cups chicken stock
1 carrot, diced
1 stalk celery, diced
1 medium onion, diced
3 T. flour
3 T. butter
1 T. chopped dill weed
2 cans condensed cream of chicken or cheese soup
1 cup frozen peas

In a large skillet, heat the oil or butter over medium high heat. Arrange the chicken pieces and season liberally with salt, pepper, and garlic powder. Cook a few minutes until browned, flip the pieces, and brown on the other side. Lower the heat, add 1 cup of the chicken stock, and simmer about 15 minutes or until chicken is cooked through and tender. Remove the chicken to a plate and add the carrot, celery, and onion to the liquid in the skillet. Simmer.

When the chicken's cool enough to handle, cut it into bite-size chunks. When the vegetables are tender, remove them from the skillet. Measure the remaining liquid and add enough additional chicken stock to make 1½ cups. Melt the butter in the skillet, remove from heat, and stir in the flour to make a paste. Add the liquid and stir constantly over medium heat until thickened, then stir in the dill weed, creamed soups, and the peas. When the sauce is blended, add the chicken and vegetables and cook over low heat until mixture is hot and bubbly, stirring often. Makes 6–8 servings.

Cornmeal Bulk Mix

If you have a container of this mix in your pantry, you'll never again settle for the boxed corn bread mixes in the store! You can go either sweet or savory with this versatile blend, and if you have recipes that call for commercial mixes (such as Jiffy or Bisquick) you can substitute the same amount of this mix to make muffins, pancakes, corn bread, etc. A couple of my favorite corn bread recipes follow this one!

    4 cups yellow cornmeal
    4 cups all-purpose flour
    ⅔ cup sugar
    3½ T. baking powder
    2 tsp. salt

Combine the ingredients with a big spoon and store in a large container with a tight-fitting lid. Makes 9 cups. Will keep at room temperature for 3 months.

Kitchen Hint: I store my mix in a plastic ice cream container, labeled and dated.

Sweet Banana Corn Bread

This makes enough batter for an 8" x 8" pan or about 10 large muffins. Moist and tender! Yummy! Double the recipe to make a 9" x 13" pan.

    2½ cups of Cornmeal Bulk Mix
    ⅓ cup sugar
    2 tsp. baking powder
    2 tsp. cinnamon
    2 T. vanilla
    ¾ cup mashed banana
    ½ cup milk
    ½ cup oil
    2 eggs

Spray or butter an 8" x 8" pan or a 12-cup muffin tin. Preheat oven to 350°. In a large mixing bowl, combine the Cornmeal Bulk Mix, sugar, baking powder, and cinnamon, making a well in the center. In a large glass measuring cup or deep bowl, whisk the vanilla, mashed banana, milk, oil, and eggs until well blended. Pour the liquid mixture into the well of dry ingredients, stirring only until the batter is blended. Pour the batter into the prepared pan. Bake an 8" x 8" pan for about 20 minutes, or until a toothpick comes out clean from the center. Bake muffins 12–15 minutes, or until tops are domed and firm. Don't overbake! Serve warm, or cool on a wire rack. After about 5 minutes, lift the muffins out of the tin.

Kitchen Hint: For a 9" x 13" pan of corn bread, double the recipe. Freezes well (use wax paper between layers).

Dilly Cheese Corn Bread

Adding dill relish to this savory corn bread takes it to a whole different level! Great with chili—or split a square of it and spoon Creamed Chicken on top for a filling meal.

    2½ cups Cornmeal Bulk Mix
    1 tsp. salt
    ½ tsp. black pepper
    1 T. dried minced onion
    1 T. dill weed
    ½ cup grated Parmesan cheese
    ½ cup buttermilk or plain yogurt
    ½ cup cottage cheese
    2 eggs
    ½ cup oil
    1 cup drained dill relish
    1 T. juice from the relish

Spray or butter an 8" x 8" pan. Preheat oven to 350°. In a large bowl, combine corn bread mix, spices, and Parmesan cheese until well blended, leaving a well in the center. In a deep bowl, combine the buttermilk or yogurt, cottage cheese, eggs, oil, the drained relish (see Hint) and the pickle juice—this mixture will be lumpy. Pour the liquids into the well of dry ingredients and stir until the batter is lumpy but all dry ingredients are incorporated. Pour into prepared pan and bake for about 20 minutes, or until the edges are lightly browned and a toothpick comes out clean from the center.

__Kitchen Hint__: To drain the relish, press it against a mesh sieve until most of the juice is out, reserving 1 T. of the juice.

__Kitchen Hint__: For more cheese, add about ¾ cup of shredded cheese of your choice, about 5 minutes before the corn bread is done baking.

Jelly Doughnut Cake

This cake makes an easy dessert—you can use any jam or preserves you have on hand—but there's no rule saying you can't also eat it for breakfast!

    ¾ cup milk
    1 cup unsalted butter, melted, divided
    2 large eggs
    1 T. vanilla extract
    2½ cups flour
    1¼ cups sugar
    1½ tsp. baking powder
    1 tsp. salt
    2 tsp. cinnamon
    ¾ cup jam or preserves

Preheat oven to 350°. Spray a tube pan with cooking spray, then place the pan on a sheet of wax paper and draw around it. Cut out the paper "doughnut" and place in the bottom of the pan; spray the paper. In a large bowl, mix the milk, ¾ cup of the melted butter, the eggs, and the vanilla. In a separate bowl, combine the flour, sugar, baking powder, salt, and cinnamon and then gradually add these dry ingredients to the milk mixture until just combined.

Spoon half of the batter into the prepared pan. With the back of a spoon, press a shallow well into the batter so it goes partway up the sides and center of the pan. Spoon the jam into the well, then spread the remaining batter on top. Bake about 40 minutes, or until a pick inserted in the center comes out clean. Cool in the pan for 15 minutes. Run a sharp knife around the outer and center edges of the cake to loosen it before turning it out of the pan onto a plate. Invert the cake on another plate so the rounded side is up and let it cool completely. Brush the top and sides with the remainder of the melted butter. Sprinkle liberally with a mixture of ¼ cup sugar blended with 2 tsp. cinnamon, pressing some of the sugar mixture onto the sides. 8–10 servings.

Kitchen Hint: _Feeling indulgent? Make a glaze of ½ cup powdered sugar, 1 tsp. vanilla, dash of salt, and 2 T. milk—or enough to make it pourable. Drizzle over top of cake so it runs down the sides._

Read on for an excerpt from
Charlotte Hubbard's next Amish romance,

Light Shines on Promise Lodge

As Annabelle Beachey gazed at the happy couple standing before Bishop Monroe Burkholder, ready to exchange their wedding vows, she fought back tears. During the four months she'd spent in an apartment at Promise Lodge, she'd become good friends with the bride, Frances Lehman, and she'd acquired a lot of respect for the groom, Preacher Marlin Kurtz. The love light on their faces shone as a testament to the devotion that had grown between them during their summertime and September courtship—a brilliant example of how God worked out His purpose through the lives of those who kept His faith.

Annabelle sighed with the rightness of it all. The women around her were dabbing at their eyes as Preacher Marlin repeated his vows after the bishop in an endearingly confident voice, gazing at Frances as though she were the only woman in the world. Folks here were still in awe of Marlin's buying back all the furnishings Frances had consigned to an auction in May, thinking she had to sell everything to get by because her first husband hadn't left her with much.

My husband didn't leave me with much, either, Annabelle thought ruefully. *He just left me.*

Annabelle sat straighter on the wooden pew bench, trying not to let her troubles overshadow the joy of the wedding. God had surely guided her to Promise Lodge last May, where the friends gathered in this room had taken her in—had provided her an apartment and their unconditional encouragement after they'd heard about the way Phineas had abandoned her and the Old Order faith.

"I, Marlin, take you, Frances, to be my lawfully wedded wife," the handsome preacher repeated after Bishop Monroe. He went through the familiar litany of sickness and health, richer or poorer, and ended with the ringing declaration, "Till death do us part."

Annabelle pressed her lips together to keep them from trembling. She and Phineas had taken the same vows more than twenty years ago. It had wounded her deeply when her husband had said—without any warning or apparent remorse—that he'd grown tired of the constraints of marriage and the Amish faith, which weighed him down like a heavy yoke. It seemed Phineas had intended to leave without even telling her—except she'd caught him rifling through the pantry looking for her egg money.

She had no idea where he'd gone. And because Amish couples weren't allowed to divorce, her only chance at finding another man to love would come after Phineas passed away. How would she know when that happened? And meanwhile, how was she supposed to get by? Living as her brother-in-law's dependent, beholden to him for every morsel she ate, hadn't seemed like much of an option, so she'd taken a huge chance and found her way from Pennsylvania to Promise Lodge. She'd read in *The Budget* about this progressive Plain settlement in Missouri, where single women could live in comfortable apartments and make a fresh start among families who also desired brighter futures.

Best decision you ever made, too, Annabelle reminded herself. She'd found her niche here along with a small income, sewing clothes for Frances's widowed brother-in-law and three young men who hadn't yet married. Living among Plain women who managed a cheese factory, a dairy, a produce stand, a pie business, and the lodge apartments had given her the perfect incentive for figuring out how to support herself, and she planned to expand her sewing business by advertising it in town.

And once this painfully romantic wedding is behind you, Annabelle thought, *you can get on with the contentment and purpose you've settled into here.*

She put a smile on her face, determined not to let on about her personal problems while everyone around her was so caught up in sharing the joy that Marlin and Frances exuded.

"Friends," Bishop Monroe proclaimed with a wide smile, "it's my honor and privilege to present Mr. and Mrs. Marlin Kurtz."

As applause filled the lodge's big meeting room, Annabelle rose eagerly with the women around her. The best cure for her blues was making herself useful, helping Beulah and Ruby Kuhn set out the wedding feast they'd prepared. The *maidel* Mennonite sisters, who'd come to Promise Lodge last year about this time, were the queens of the kitchen when it came to cooking for large gatherings on special occasions—and as Annabelle passed quickly through the dining room, she couldn't help inhaling deeply to soothe her frazzled soul.

"Your baked ham and brisket smell so *gut,* it was all I could do to keep my seat during the wedding," she teased as she entered the kitchen behind the sisters. "I was trying to think up an excuse to slip back here to sample some of it— to be sure it was fit for serving to our guests, of course."

Ruby and Beulah laughed as they made their way toward the ovens. Their bright floral-print dresses fluttered with their quick, efficient movements as Beulah slipped her hands into mitts while Ruby lowered the oven doors. The hair tucked up under their small, round Mennonite *kapps* was silvery, but nobody could call them *old*.

"I was pleased that Marlin asked for ham," Beulah remarked, deftly lifting the blue graniteware roasters onto the nearest butcher-block countertops. "It's a tasty way to feed a lot of folks with a minimum of fuss—"

"And the pineapple rings and maraschino cherries make it look like party food from the get-go," Ruby put in without missing a beat. "Chicken and stuffing might be the traditional wedding dish, but it looks pretty bland. And who says you have to have that for your second wedding just because you served it the first time?"

"Tickles me pink that Frances and Marlin have finally tied the knot—even if Frances cut the usual mourning period a little short," Beulah said. "Seems to me that pining for her Floyd on and on might be a slap in the face to God anyway, if we believe Floyd has gone to his reward with Jesus. We should be joyful about that, even as we realize how much Frances missed him."

Annabelle considered this new slant on mourning as she sliced the ham and placed it into a metal steam table pan. Did she have it all wrong, feeling sorry for herself because Phineas had abandoned her? After all, she'd done nothing to provoke his departure—his escape—so surely God didn't hold her accountable for her husband's misdeeds. Maybe He'd offered her a chance at a whole new life by allowing Phineas to go his own way, even if her options for remarriage and happiness with another man were severely limited.

God's ways are not our ways, and they're often mysterious to us, she reminded herself. *I've felt humiliated and depressed about being left behind, but maybe I should look at it from another angle. None of these other women have allowed their troubles to take them down.*

Annabelle felt as though a wet, heavy cloak of sadness was being lifted from her shoulders. As she began slicing a second large ham, a genuine smile lit up her face. She had friends back in Bird-in-Hand who would secretly love the freedom of living without the overbearing men they'd married.

Freedom. Mattie, Christine, and Rosetta Bender, the original founders of Promise Lodge, had pooled their resources to buy an abandoned church camp so they'd be free from an oppressive bishop—and they'd been able to do that because they were widowed or unmarried at the time. All three of them had gotten married this past year, to wonderful men who allowed them to make their own choices, so maybe there'd be another chance for Annabelle to find that same sort of happiness someday. At Promise Lodge, the bright blue sky was the limit.

Connect with Us

Visit us online at
KensingtonBooks.com
to read more from your favorite authors, see books
by series, view reading group guides, and more.

Join us on social media

for sneak peeks, chances to win books and prize packs,
and to share your thoughts with other readers.

facebook.com/kensingtonpublishing
twitter.com/kensingtonbooks

Tell us what you think!

To share your thoughts, submit a review,
or sign up for our eNewsletters, please visit:
KensingtonBooks.com/TellUs.